Table of Contents

CHAPTER ONE 1

CHAPTER TWO 7

CHAPTER THREE 19

CHAPTER FOUR 29

CHAPTER FIVE 35

CHAPTER SIX 49

CHAPTER SEVEN 55

CHAPTER EIGHT 67

CHAPTER NINE 77

CHAPTER TEN 85

CHAPTER ELEVEN 93

CHAPTER TWELVE 107

CHAPTER THIRTEEN 113

CHAPTER FOURTEEN 123

CHAPTER FIFTEEN 127

CHAPTER SIXTEEN 141

CHAPTER SEVENTEEN 151

CHAPTER EIGHTEEN 161

CHAPTER NINETEEN 169

CHAPTER TWENTY 181

CHAPTER TWENTY-ONE 193

The Roaming

W.J. Hegarty

Cover Art by Edward Moran

Printed in the United States of America

First Printing, 2019

ISBN-13: 9781693659829

For updates on The Roaming, social media links and exclusive content
visit wjhegarty.com

CHAPTER ONE

Tipping Point

Morning's first light struggled to break through the rain and smoke. The previous night's madness hung in the air of Philadelphia. Isolated pockets of fire still burned. First-responders were forced to spread so thin that the entire city had become one massive triage. Fire chiefs had no choice but to pick which blazes to fight and what fires they would leave to burn. A UH-60 Black Hawk surveyed the damage on its way to the staging ground. From the air, the city looked like a war zone. Thousands either didn't evacuate or couldn't.

Pockets of civil unrest had erupted three nights in a row in response to a growing crisis threatening the Eastern Seaboard of the United States. Gangs and neighborhood watches protecting their own with deadly force had staked claim to some areas. A block here, two or three there. Other large sections of the city had burned to the ground. After the looting had run its course, they put the buildings to flame. Why stop there? Government buildings were next, followed by properties and businesses frequented by those deemed rich or influential. For some it was sport; for most it resulted from frustration. None of it helped. All the chaos accomplished was pushing the already too-thin first-responders past the breaking point. Many of them walked off the job. In a city on the brink, who would care for their families otherwise?

1

The helo touched down in Lincoln Financial Field's parking lot. Discarded papers and debris from a city on the verge of collapse blew in the rotor wash despite a heavy downpour. The National Guard had cordoned off the area. By then, they were holding back a growing crowd of panicked citizens at gunpoint. Hundreds of armed soldiers stood guard around the perimeter. A flimsy barbed wire–topped fence was all that stood between them and tens of thousands of screaming Philadelphians, all seeking answers that these soldiers didn't possess. One hundred yards south of the landing zone, a few protesters broke through the barricade in a mad dash for the helicopter. Pepper spray and Tasers were enough to stop most of them, although a few gun butts assuaged any similar thoughts of an attempted insurgency.

Captain Miller followed his commanding officer, Colonel Takashi, from the transport to the staging area where Brigadier General Sharpe greeted them. The concern on the man's face was unmistakable; whatever was unfolding here must have been serious enough to unhinge a grizzled old soldier like Sharpe. He was a legend to most young Army recruits climbing the ranks in Miller's generation. With a career dating back to before Gulf War I, the man had seen more than his fair share of combat. To stand in this man's presence filled Miller with a sense of pride. Sharpe had requested that Takashi and other unit commanders stationed up and down the Eastern Seaboard help with a classified assignment brewing in Philadelphia.

Takashi stood as no slouch in the seasoned veteran department, either. He cut his teeth under Sharpe's command, fighting Saddam's Republican Guard in the Kuwaiti oil fields in '91. In subsequent years he climbed the ladder to captain on his way to colonel.

Sharpe led the men to a tent on the far side of the parking lot and then to a makeshift staging area. The rain saturated the captain's short-cropped hay-colored hair. He dried it as best as he could as they entered the tent. Miller kept himself well-groomed and clean-shaven, even amidst the growing turmoil. He wore a khaki and green combat shirt over fatigues, in stark contrast to the group of high-ranking officers huddled around a table and already discussing options. This number of warhorses together discussing strategy ensured that something big was going down. All involved were keeping it very hush-hush. Not a word of chatter regarding this meeting *or* those in attendance reached Miller's ear before landing. In the center of the tent, they sprawled a large map of Philadelphia out on the table, marked up with what Miller assumed to be large pockets of civil unrest. The map had select areas highlighted in various colors; their location at the stadium was circled in red. All Miller knew was that riots had broken out in several major cities, cause unknown, or at least they weren't telling him.

Sharpe took his place at the table. He exchanged greetings with his fellow officers before they returned to the topic at hand. Major General Faireborn and Lieutenant General Hauser stood alongside Sharpe. The other two officers Miller wasn't familiar with. At least two men in this tent were legitimate living legends. Plain by the number of stars in the room, Miller was privy to a gathering few witnessed. Takashi led Miller to a far corner of the tent, out of earshot of the classified discussion taking place around the map. Two green soldiers jumped to attention before Takashi was halfway across the room. Israeli, by the looks of it.

What was the IDF doing here? Miller thought.

The young Israelis stood at attention, hands at their sides, chins in the air. Both were decked out in Israel's standard olive-green field dress, their berets folded under each's left epaulet. Their black leather boots had such a shine Miller wasn't sure if the pair of them hadn't just enlisted this morning. The male was long and lanky, and the female was petite and had black hair pulled tight in a bun.

Takashi introduced them. "Captain Miller, I would like you to meet Seren Lev Yadin and Segen Rishon Soraya Shahar of the Israel Defense Forces." Takashi's pronunciation of their Israeli titles in Hebrew was impeccable. He continued. "These soldiers were here on a troop exchange program en route to Carlisle Barracks, where they would have been studying at USAWC. We have some of *our* youngest and brightest in Israel doing the same. Training was to begin next week, before this crisis with the rioting began. Unfortunately for everyone involved, their stay here should never have been under such volatile conditions. We never meant for them to be in harm's way. Regrettably, this is where we find ourselves."

A dripping-wet private hustled up to Takashi from out of the rain, panting and out of breath. "Colonel, you have a call from General Abernathy waiting for you in the comms tent. It's urgent, sir."

"Lead the way, Private. I'll return in a moment, Captain. In the meantime, introduce yourself to the tourists. *We're* stuck with them for the duration of this mess."

"Yes, sir." Miller saluted before turning to the Israelis. "It's a pleasure to meet you both." Miller offered a salute for the bright-eyed soldiers.

Soraya leaped at the chance to introduce herself to the handsome American officer. Despite current circumstances, she remained upbeat and still hoped to learn much while abroad. Thunder roared, threatening to drown out their greeting. "It is an honor to serve under you, sir. I am looking forward to learning all that I can from the United States military while I am here."

"Likewise, and I hope to learn from you, Soraya," Miller replied with a smile that seemed to catch the young Israeli off guard.

She blushed before returning to attention. Miller could swear he heard a hushed giggle, but with the rain beating down on the tent, it could have been anything.

Lev wasn't at all impressed with his younger female counterpart, which was clear as he rushed forward to salute Miller, nearly bowling her over on his way.

Soraya's demeanor changed in an instant. Her smile faded, replaced with a cold stare that gave even Miller chills.

"Seren Lev Yadin reporting for duty, sir." The second Israeli came off too enthusiastic with his introduction.

"At ease, Lev, it's good to meet you, too."

"Sir, if I may," Lev continued. "I graduated top of my class at Rabin Pre-Military Academy and researched all aspects of quelling a civilian uprising. I may be of invaluable help in the coming days. My professors all agreed that I would make rank in record time and—"

Miller interrupted the young soldier mid-sentence. "That's quite the impressive résumé, Lev."

"Thank you, sir. If you like, we can discuss the military achievements of our nations and how Israel and the United States of America came to be such close allies. I have some insights on the history of both of our countries I think you would find fascinating."

"That won't be necessary. Another time, perhaps, but thank you." Miller couldn't get away from this guy fast enough. Lev seemed like a nice enough kid, though Miller had more important things to worry about. He'd love to pick their brains, share tactics and experiences, maybe even learn a little about their homeland, but these were questions for another time. His mind was elsewhere. What the hell was getting this many bigwigs fired up? Why would a case of simple civil unrest require a show of force of this magnitude here at home? Too many unanswered questions. Miller didn't have time to babysit.

Where the hell is the colonel? Miller was about to excuse himself when Colonel Takashi reentered the tent with purpose, marching for the Israelis. "That will be all for now. Dismissed."

The young Israelis saluted before hurrying out of the tent. Lev disappeared around the corner while Soraya stood at attention just outside the enclosure in the rain. Takashi shrugged it off. He was no stranger to young enlisted shadowing their commanding officers and hoping a little experience rubbed off. Takashi gestured for Miller to join him at the table with Sharpe and the other officers, all of their faces racked with concern.

W.J. Hegarty

CHAPTER TWO

The Pine Barrens

Red-orange rays danced through breaks in the foliage as a black ' 68 Dodge Charger raced through the dense New Jersey Pine Barrens. Damon glanced at the clock affixed to the dashboard. "We should never have stopped for lunch. Only an hour after breakfast, too. What the fuck were we thinking?"

Boredom spurred from the long drive made bad decisions come easy. His car's headlights cut through the encroaching darkness, casting long shadows on the unfamiliar terrain. They pressed on ever deeper into unfamiliar territory, miles ago having left any semblance of a paved surface. Mud caked the wheel wells, and low-hanging branches scraped against a pristine paint job. These roads remained unkempt for a reason; no one except locals or those not wanting to be found traveled this far from the beaten path. Every tree branch that hit the car or deep pothole disguised as a puddle increased Damon's growing frustration.

"I'm entrusting this very important errand to you, son." Damon mocked his father's description of, in Damon's opinion, a bullshit job better saved for the help.

His father, Demetrius, was a second-generation Greek immigrant who emulated the Italian mafia of the twenties and thirties as a child. Embarrassed by his parents' struggling corner deli, he felt trapped. A glorified bag boy would not be *his* future. The glamorous lives of Al Capone and Prohibition-era gangsters, the golden age of organized crime, as he referred to it—that was what impressed him.

Demetrius would have that lifestyle for himself, and in the fall of 1972, not yet twenty years old, he began a bloody rise to power. Through extortion, black market dealings, and a swift, violent response to the competition, Demetrius claimed his own piece of Baltimore's violent Westside. Now in his twilight, he tried to instill a certain ethic into his son, Damon, with little if any success.

Despite Demetrius's tutelage, Damon's apathy and laziness persisted. He remained content to suckle off the teat of his father's decades-long struggle to remain relevant in this new, fast-paced, and extremely violent city. Humbling tasks, such as this delivery to bum-fuck, as his son so eloquently phrased it, would only help toughen the boy, he hoped.

Damon was spoiled, to be sure. It was clear in the way he managed his underlings, what few his father had given him due to his lack of faith in the boy. He was infamous for holding back money from his crew after a job. Never mind skimming off the top and outright throwing his underlings under the bus if a situation warranted blame for a detail *he* screwed up. Everyone below him was well aware, but what were they supposed to do about it? After all, they were hired thugs and easily replaceable. More than that, Damon had a quick temper and would not hesitate to beat you to within an inch of your life if the mood struck him. Work under him for more than a few days, and chances were, you'd witness that temper firsthand.

Along for the journey, Damon's childhood friend Markus accompanied him in this endeavor, their first trip this deep into such unfamiliar territory and so very far from home. A late start with more breaks than necessary complicated their impromptu road trip. Navigating the forest at night wasn't part of the itinerary.

Damon continuously changed radio stations, never staying on any one selection for more than a few seconds. "What the fuck? No music still? Man, what is going on today?"

"Yeah, they've been doing nothing but talking for two days now. Like this trip doesn't suck bad enough already. Fuck it, man, put your iPhone back on."

Damon turned on the device. Familiar music momentarily helped ease the boredom of such a long road trip, but not for very long.

"Are we there yet?" Markus said half-jokingly.

"Funny, how the fuck should I know? You're not the only one who's never been to this shithole."

"Yeah, I still wouldn't if you'd do what you're told every once in a while," Markus responded in an *I-told-you-so* manner.

"Ah, fuck that old bastard. He's just bitter 'cause I couldn't give a shit about this thing, as he likes to put it." Damon's imitation of his father's thick Greek accent left much to be desired.

"This thing, whatever, man. Did you tell Esteban we're not going to make his little soiree?" Markus asked, barely hiding a ridiculing tone.

"Yeah, that's fucking funny. On top of this bullshit, now I have to miss out on all that fine senorita ass." Damon smacked the wheel and gave the car a little more gas than he probably should have.

"I'm telling you, man, I wouldn't even stress over it. Cinco de Mayo's overrated, anyway."

Damon ignored his friend's attempt at levity. Stepping on the accelerator again was his only response.

As the miles wore on, Markus turned the radio back on in hopes that a new area would offer something different to listen to. Try as he might, every station he tuned into was repeating the same news broadcast:

"Additional military personnel have been called in to assist National Guard units at the Philadelphia quarantine zone. In an unprecedented move, the president has suspended the Posse Comitatus Act, which strictly forbids the use of United States military personnel on American soil. Armed soldiers patrol the streets of Philadelphia as we are closing out day three of what is being called—"

The broadcast was cut short as Damon turned off the radio. "Man, who wants to hear that shit? Stupid fucking rioters."

"Come on, man. I was listening to that."

"I don't give a shit what's happening in Philly. Sick, homeless people and pissed-off looters. Big deal. Fuck them." *Fuck them* was pretty much Damon's answer to anything that didn't directly concern him.

"Yeah, but what if it's something serious this time?"

"Like what?"

"I don't know, bird flu or something. How are we supposed to know if you keep turning the radio off every time the news comes on?"

"Yeah, right, or maybe terrorists, huh? Please. All *you* need to be worried about is dropping this package off so we can get our asses back to Baltimore."

"If you say so." Markus didn't agree with Damon, but he knew it was futile to continue arguing.

Lately, they had been more and more at odds over decisions handed down by Damon's father. This particular job didn't sit well with Markus at all. After something like this, there could be no going back to anything

9

resembling a normal life. A job of this nature would change a man. Though Markus had reservations, the time to speak on them had long passed.

Nearly an hour into the dense forest, crushed gravel gave way to rugged dirt roads. Unfamiliar territory slowly receded into a narrow, unmarked trail that resembled little more than a dirt path. Low-hanging tree branches closed in on the vehicle, once more scraping windows and ruining the finish. Their progress slowed as the dirt path gave way to thick mud. Finally, the car came to a stop. The vehicle's back tires had become impossibly buried in the sludge.

"I don't think we should have gone this far in, man."

"Not now, Markus."

Desperately trying to get free, Damon gave it more gas. Flooring it in frustration only resulted in spraying mud and rocks all over the car. It was no use; they were hopelessly stuck. Discouraged, they exited the vehicle only to find themselves standing in shin-deep mud.

Damon shouted and slammed his hands down on the roof of the car. "You have got to be fucking kidding me. Goddammit! Go get the package, man. We'll get rid of that shit right here."

"Here?" Markus asked, his hands in the air, face contorted in confusion. "What if someone drives by?"

"Really? Yes, here. Just fucking do it!" Damon shouted.

"Fine," Markus relented, knowing that at this point he had no choice but to see their boss's demands through, damn the consequences.

Sticky mud engulfed Markus's shoes. Each step was grueling. He struggled against the suction as he made his way to the trunk of the car.

Damon, still fuming, slammed his door shut, catching his coat in the process. Something hard tucked away in his pocket prevented the door from closing but managed to dent the car's body and chip the paint. "Fuck, now this is some bullshit!"

Markus surveyed his surroundings for curious onlookers, though the darkening forest could have held scores of watchful eyes and he would have never noticed in the waning light. As he opened the trunk of the car, a foot burst from the darkness, hitting him square in the face. Markus fell to his knees, screaming in agony. His smashed nose and busted lip gushed with blood. "Motherfucker!" Markus clenched his nose and doubled over in pain as a shirtless, handcuffed man leaped from the trunk and ran for the tree line.

Bullets whizzed by the bound man as Damon fired several rounds from his 9mm. None of his shots connected; the man quickly disappeared into the forest.

"Get up, Markus!"

"Fucker broke my nose." Searing pain blurred his vision as he regained his balance and rose to his feet.

Damon helped his friend from the deep muck. "We'll have more than that to worry about if he gets away. Let's move."

The two men trudged over the mud and gave chase through the unfamiliar and rapidly darkening forest. Branches flew by, whipping the men in their faces. The soft forest floor and slippery wet logs strewn about slowed their pursuit. Letting the bound man escape was unthinkable. Demetrius's displeasure with Damon as of late was not lost on the young man, and their present situation would only prove his father right.

Demetrius would often comment on how Damon had no drive, that the boy reacted to a situation as opposed to being the architect of one. Chasing the bound man through a forest in the middle of nowhere was a testament to that. Another thick patch of undergrowth tripped the men up. While struggling to push through, Damon realized that the bound man had eluded them.

A few months back, the bound man had gotten in over his head with the wrong people. A bad gambling habit and the expenses of a newborn child left him crushed with debt.

Just one more night at the tables. I can turn this around, he thought.

Three months later, with his bank account empty and absolutely no way to repay the seventy-three thousand dollars he owed the Greeks, he awoke to find himself tied up in the trunk of a car, terrified.

The bound man ambled through the woods. Duct tape covered his mouth, making it hard to breathe, and his long, tangled blond hair matted to his face and made it difficult to see. He weaved in and out of the trees, but being handcuffed behind his back was throwing off his balance. Branches smacked him across the face. Some only scraped the skin; others cut like razors. Ducking beneath a low-hanging tree branch caused him to lose what little balance he had, throwing him sideways into a pine. The impact snapped his collar bone. Agony sent him to his knees. His muffled screams were audible through the tape covering his mouth.

Exhausted and dizzy but not yet broken, the bound man found the strength to get to his feet and continue running. Thoughts of his wife and new daughter helped propel him through the twilight forest. If he could just keep running, those two thugs might tire and give up the chase. Heavy footfalls into the soft forest floor impeded his progress. His feet felt like bricks, and it was a struggle to maintain balance. Hopping over a large wet log, he mistimed his jump and came down on its slick surface. His feet yanked out from under him, and for a moment, gravity seemed to disappear. The bound man came down hard, face-first into a mud puddle, his feet stretched out over the back of his head. The sudden impact dazed him to the edge of unconsciousness. Adhesive mud caked his hair, gluing it to his face as he raised his head from the mud puddle. His sinuses burned as he sucked mud into his nose in a desperate bid for air. The bound man's head was almost clear of the filthy water when his face exploded in a shower of blood, gray matter, and skull.

Damon stood directly above the man, his gun still pointed down at his victim. A blank stare betrayed his apathy toward the deed.

"Holy shit. The guy's still alive!" Markus shouted in disbelief. He gasped in horror at the sight of the bound man lying at Damon's feet. Whereas moments ago there existed a man's face, all that remained was a blood-filled crater. Tiny bubbles erupted from the center.

"Let's go." Damon turned from his victim.

"We can't just leave him like this, man. He's still alive for Christ's sake," Markus pleaded.

"Then do something about it, but I'm leaving." Damon put his gun away and began the long trudge back to the car.

It relieved Markus that he didn't have to shoot the man first, though for his part he was no less guilty of murder. "Please forgive me," he whispered before shooting the man twice in the chest, then once more in what remained of his head. "Man, that was a tough son of a bitch, huh?" Markus said as he spun around. Fearing Damon might be listening, Markus thought it best to inject a moment of levity into the situation, lest his compassion be mistaken for weakness. That was something he'd prefer Demetrius not hear about. "Should we bury him?"

"With what? We left the shovels in the car."

Markus broke off a few low-hanging branches to cover the bound man's body. It was the least he could do, seeing as how they would leave him here, never to be seen or heard from again, his friends and family left pondering the fate of a loved one.

"Let's just go. No one's going to find him all the way out here in the middle of nowhere anyway or even know who the fuck he is if they do." Damon kicked one of his designer shoes against a tree, leaving a large chunk of mud behind.

"Look at my goddamn shoes, man. What the fuck!" He continued to curse their situation, more of a release of sorts than looking for any kind of validation from Markus, who was well aware of his friend's short fuse.

Markus looked on at Damon's display, then back at the man lying dead behind them. He was barely visible in the encroaching darkness. *We just killed a man*, he thought. *And all you care about is that your shoes got dirty.*

The lack of even the slightest bit of empathy on Damon's part over the murder disgusted him. Maybe the guy had it coming—maybe he didn't—but that didn't mean Markus had to like it. As a matter of fact, Markus was coming to terms with just how fed up he was becoming with Damon and this whole lifestyle. Part of him yearned to just get in his car and drive, not stopping until he reached some lonely, forgotten little town in the middle of nowhere, a place where he would be free to start over without the stigma of his past erecting walls he couldn't hope to climb. A pipe dream, really. His required loyalty to Demetrius would have to override any secret desires he might have once harbored. In that instant, hiking through the woods, Markus realized his life would forever be in the hands of someone else. Life and death decided by the whims of an old man with a cruel heart. Markus's destiny was not his own to decide anymore, if it ever was to begin with. The reality of it all was crushing.

One step at a time, they trudged through the forest, bumping against trees and tripping over large rocks. All around them, the Pine Barrens were alive, sounds of wildlife alien to two denizens of a concrete jungle. Their legs and backs were sore from what was surely thousands of footfalls into the soft forest floor. Hours of walking was taking its toll on them. They meandered through the dense forest. The bright moon overhead offered little benefit beneath the thick canopy. Frustration gave way to panic. The realization that they would inevitably end up spending the night in this unfamiliar forest so far from the streets of Baltimore terrified them both, although pride and ego prevented either from speaking on it.

Damon leaned against a tree. The full moon high above barely illuminated the forest floor. He struggled to read his watch again under what little light shone through the trees.

"What time is it?" Markus asked.

"I can't even tell. I haven't been able to read this thing for hours. This is fucking ridiculous, man."

"Face it, Damon. We are lost as fuck."

"Someone had to say it. Come on, I think the car's this way."

Hours passed, and the scenery never seemed to change until finally, as if a prayer had been answered, a break in the forest appeared in front of them. Beyond that was what looked like a clearing. They cautiously approached this discovery, inching ever closer until they hovered at the tree line. A tinge of hope began to swell. Breaking through the foliage, they found themselves at the edge of a field. Towering corn stalks filled the landscape as far as the eye could see.

"I think I see a house." Damon's eyes were adjusting to the luminous moonlight.

Relieved at the sight of civilization, even one as alien as a rundown farmhouse might have seemed to them, they emerged from the forest and stepped out into the cornfield. In the distance, illuminated by the bright full moon, the unmistakable silhouette of a small two-story house loomed on the horizon.

"Thank Christ, we're saved!"

Markus didn't exactly share Damon's enthusiasm. "We'll see. Let's not get ahead of ourselves. I can't make out any cars and the place looks dark. It might be abandoned." Markus *prayed* that the old farmhouse was abandoned. After the night they'd had, he feared for the safety of anyone inside who might attempt to stand up to Damon if the situation escalated.

Mindful to stay in shadow, they emerged from the cornfield, weapons drawn, and slowly crept onto the front porch of the house.

Markus peered into a blackened window for signs of life, though the bright moon made it nearly impossible to see into the darkened home. "I can't make out anything in there. You think anyone's home?"

Damon whispered, "Quiet." He gently pushed on the front door. The pair of them were surprised to find it unlocked.

Tentatively, they made their way through the opening and into the house, quietly making their way through the living room and heading toward a dimly lit kitchen. An old TV illuminated one corner of the small room. Its light revealed piles of dirty dishes, some with uneaten, rotting food on them.

On the television, a news reporter read from a jumbled mess of papers in front of her. Neither could hear what she was saying with the TV on mute, though. Markus nudged Damon's arm, bringing his attention to the TV. The crawl at the bottom of the screen read, "CDC – Pandemic strikes Northeastern United States – several cities under martial law – all nonessential workplaces have been closed indefinitely – all unofficial air traffic to and from the Eastern Seaboard has been grounded indefinitely – Baltimore, Philadelphia, and Richmond have National Guard units in place enforcing mandatory region-wide curfews – region-wide quarantine is being considered."

Markus whispered, "What the hell is going on?"

"I don't know." Damon checked the landline. "It's dead. Come on, we better make sure no one's home."

Silently, the men made their way to a staircase leading to the house's second floor. Aged, worn-out steps creaked and moaned under every footfall as the two men cautiously ascended. The stairs led to a very modest second floor that featured only two small bedrooms connected by a narrow hallway with a cramped bathroom tucked between them.

Damon opened the bathroom door. He peered inside to find three badly decomposed bodies, two naked, all three with gunshot wounds to the head and what appeared to be quite a few injuries.

Were they attacked by dogs? he pondered.

"What the fuck!" Markus yelled, pushing past Damon for a cautious glimpse at the grisly sight.

Damon put a finger to his lips, signaling the other man to be quiet.

They continued to the larger of the two bedrooms. Slivers of moonlight shone through the curtains, revealing the silhouette of a man and a woman lying in bed, barely recognizable in the darkness. The stench of rot permeated the air, and the buzzing of a thousand pairs of tiny wings rang in their ears. Damon pulled aside a thick hand-woven curtain, desperate to let in some much-needed moonlight.

Partially illuminated, the room revealed its appalling contents. A woman's corpse lay peacefully on the bed, hands folded against her belly, her white nightgown wrinkle-free as if fresh from the wash. A pillow rested atop her head. A black hole in its center betrayed the burns of a single gunshot. Barely visible in the dim light, a pool of blood had formed under the corpse, spreading halfway down the woman's body and staining the mattress.

A male corpse was dressed in jeans and a flannel shirt, his back against the headboard, though slumped forward. The man's head was nonexistent. His neck ended in a dried bloody stump, the remains of which adorned the wall behind him. The wall was spattered with bloody chunks of meat and bone of all shapes and sizes, forever dried to its surface. A shotgun lay across the corpse's chest, its finger bent and frozen awkwardly on the trigger. On a nightstand beside the bed lay a bible and a spent revolver.

"The fuck is this, D?"

Damon didn't reply as he took the suicide man's revolver and tucked it into the back of his pants. He pulled aside a dusty curtain for a peek outside. The bright full moon finally began to dip behind the tree line. The sun would begin its climb soon. He thought it best that they not be there when it did. Far too many questions they didn't possess answers to if someone were to show up looking for these people. "See if he's got any keys on him. Looks like they have a truck out front. I'll check the other room and meet you downstairs."

Damon stood just outside the door of the smaller room. A moist slurping and crunching emanated from the darkness. The eastern portion of the house remained in shadow. The moon offered no reprieve from the gloom this area was bathed in.

Slowly adjusting to the darkness, Damon recognized that he was standing in a child's bedroom. Two small beds in the center of the room were unmistakable. In each bed rested the body of a small child—a boy and a girl, specifically. Both were killed in the same manner as their assumed parents: single gunshot wounds to the head. Damon covered his mouth and leaned on the doorway for support, lest the gruesome discovery put him on the floor. A large shape came into view as the darkness began to betray its secrets. Damon strained to comprehend what his eyes were showing him. The silhouette of what appeared to be a man leaned atop the dead boy. His eyes continued to adjust to the darker room. He could discern that this man was filthy, covered from head to toe in dried blood and dirt. Similar to the bodies in the bathroom, this man appeared to have sustained massive injuries as well. Damon was sure the man's right arm was badly broken and dangling at his side. With that, it hit him, and all at once Damon realized what he was witnessing—the filthy man was chewing on the little boy's arm.

Damon screamed, "Get the fuck off him!" He fired two shots into the filthy man's chest.

Unfazed, the man lunged at Damon, forcing both men from the room. They struggled in the hallway, the filthy man furiously trying to bite and scratch at Damon. During the scuffle, both men crashed through the railing and tumbled down the stairs. As they fell, Damon lost track of his gun; it disappeared into the night. At the bottom of the staircase, Damon struggled with the filthy man, his putrid black mouth inches away from Damon's face.

A broken banister smashed against the filthy man's face, forcing the cannibal off of Damon. Markus stood above the man, repeatedly crushing his skull with the makeshift club. The noise of bone and meat grinding against the floor, combined with the man's horrid stench, caused Damon to unleash the contents of his stomach onto the wooden floor. The filthy man stopped moving, his head caved in against the unforgiving hardwood, the fingers of his broken arm still tapping an almost recognizable rhythm against the floor.

Markus dropped the gore-encrusted bludgeon to better help his friend to his feet. "Where the hell did *he* come from?"

"I don't know, but there are two dead kids up there." Damon brushed some dirt off his coat and spit onto the floor. "He was eating the little boy's arm."

"Bullshit." Markus scanned the darkened second floor from below.

"Go look for yourself. Sickest shit I've ever seen, that's for sure." Damon leaned hard against the wall to right himself and spit again.

Markus paced, confused and desperate for answers. "Well fuck him. He's not eating anybody now. So what do you think? He kill all these people? Was he just crazy?"

"I don't have the slightest clue, man, and to be honest, I don't even give a shit. Let's get the fuck out of here." Damon brushed himself off, his designer shoes scuffed and scratched beyond repair. His custom suit hadn't fared much better. "Did you find any keys?"

"No dice, but I did find these." Markus handed Damon a half-full box of revolver ammo. "Should we keep looking for those keys?"

"No, I just want to get as far away from this place as we can. As fast as possible. When I opened the curtains upstairs, I thought I saw some lights over the next ridge. Hopefully it's a gas station or something."

Unnerved, they abandoned the old farmhouse and followed the driveway out to a dirt road. Their silhouettes grew smaller in the distance. Damon and Markus were quick to put the small house and its occupants behind them. Off to the side of the road, obstructed by overgrowth and hidden from view, a dilapidated sign read, "Pepperbush 6 miles."

W.J. Hegarty

CHAPTER THREE

Pepperbush

Pepperbush lay safely tucked away in a far-off corner of the northern New Jersey Pine Barrens. It was a considerable drive from the nearest major thoroughfare, and travelers seldom found themselves there. On rare occasions, though, it happened, and those people were either expected or hopelessly lost. That was not to suggest its residents were country folk or simple by any means. Far from it for the most part. Pepperbush had no patience for lost tourists or thrill-seekers looking for explorable caves or some elusive devil; such things were frowned upon. The place was certainly no destination for adventure. Families chose to live there to escape metropolitan congestion, and if you didn't get it, you just didn't get it. Strangers were welcomed with open arms, but *please leave* was the unspoken rule of the day. Antique-shopping and sightseeing were met with reserved eye rolls and a polite push toward the next town. Ellicott City, one hundred miles south, was often suggested. "But we just came from Baltimore," was a vocal, confused disappointment often uttered by perplexed tourists. Similar sentiments were shared by visitors from Philadelphia, Washington DC, or even as far away as Pittsburgh. Some people just wanted to be left alone. Crisis or not, was any outsider ever really welcome in Pepperbush?

Pepperbush's remoteness helped keep trespassers away—until recently, when an epidemic of sorts was reported in Philadelphia, shortly followed by Baltimore and Washington DC. The talking heads would prattle on about the region's homeless population coming down with some sort of sickness and that viewers should keep their distance. The warning was laughable at first, as most people in the broadcast area wouldn't look twice at a homeless person, much less get close enough to touch one. Occasionally, one of these carriers—or "infected," as the media referred to them in the earliest days of the crisis—would wander close to town. How extremely ill people could get lost and wander that far off the beaten path to find themselves at Pepperbush's doorstep was a lie no one believed.

Twenty-three days had passed since reports of a viral epidemic of unknown origin began flooding the TV. The news first broke online four days before government officials acknowledged that there was indeed a serious problem in a handful of East Coast cities. Stories of quarantine and martial law reaffirmed to many citizens of Pepperbush that they were indeed in the safest place to ride out whatever was happening in major cities all up and down the Eastern Seaboard.

Being so far out of the way didn't exclude Pepperbush from the occasional passerby, even in quieter times. However, the current situation facing the region saw an influx of lost souls descending upon their quaint little town. These groups consisted mostly of handfuls of people who by mere happenstance stumbled across the quiet hamlet. They were weary travelers, most hoping to escape the big cities before they and theirs were exposed to whatever was afflicting the populace.

Twenty-seven refugees, as the locals came to call them, had found themselves the newest residents of Pepperbush. The lot of them were welcomed with open arms and given rooms in the Pepperbush Bed and Breakfast, the town's sole lodging. Having settled in for the duration of this pandemic, most of the refugees took up work around town to help pull their own weight. Jobs ranged from the mundane, like washing windows, to the vital, with town security firmly atop the list. Waste management, food preparation, and security were among the top jobs everyone living in Pepperbush was tasked with in those days. Volunteers from everyday citizens to the newest refugees worked twenty-four hours a day patrolling the perimeter of the town, always vigilant for the infected.

As a precaution to stem the flow of the disease, all regional transportation was temporarily suspended from New York to Richmond and as far west as Louisville. Schools were closed and all state-run services were halted indefinitely; within the first week, the lack of trash collection became an issue.

The Roaming

Fifteen days ago, Baltimore was officially declared a quarantine zone. No one except for FEMA, under the jurisdiction of the Department of Homeland Security, would be allowed to enter or leave the city indefinitely. The powers that be tried to hide the fact that Baltimore had been quarantined, but due to pressure from the media, stemming from thousands of first-hand reports coming in from the Internet, the government was forced to come clean.

Yes, Baltimore was indeed under quarantine; the government finally admitted as much. Everyone knew that already; the people just wanted their leaders to acknowledge it. What Pepperbush and the rest of the country at large were not ready for was the admission that Richmond and Washington DC were also under strict quarantine and that Philadelphia, New York, Atlanta, and Raleigh would likely be added to the list in the coming days.

The quarantines were one thing. After all, if hundreds of thousands, possibly millions, of people were catching some super-flu, then why not contain it? With admission of the quarantines came an explanation. FEMA was in complete control of the containment efforts by this point, and in an effort to quell public unrest, it released a breakdown of symptoms.

FEMA claimed that within twelve to forty-eight hours after contracting this "super-flu," those affected would in most cases turn on and violently attack those who were not infected—in most cases biting or scratching their victims. It was believed at the time that the virus was transmitted by the passing of bodily fluids.

"Do not let these people touch you," the media would warn ad nauseam. "Under no circumstance are you to approach the infected." *Infected* was a term the media would stick with when referring to these cannibalistic attackers. The term was upgraded to *carrier* seemingly overnight. The disease's new nomenclature brought with it a sort of foreboding among the populations in the quarantine zones. In the media's effort to scare people into compliance, the name change acted as a catalyst for widespread panic, inducing rioting and outright attacks on government office buildings. Authorities were facing an attack on two fronts: the growing number of infected and a panic-stricken populace hellbent on escape.

The first video footage broadcast nationwide of the infected indiscriminately attacking people was horrifying. There was no rhyme or reason behind the attacks. Men, women, children—no one was safe. The nation's brightest minds were at a loss; no one knew what would cause otherwise normal people to resort to such random acts of violence and savagery. Unbeknownst to the public at large, the videos being shown on

21

television were heavily censored. Their Internet counterparts, though, were another story altogether.

A local news station out of Philadelphia was the first to show video of National Guard troops opening fire on a large group of infected citizens. The attempted media blackout was officially at an end. Public outcry over the government permitting such violence against its citizenry fell mostly on deaf ears, though. Firsthand accounts were pouring into online forums at breakneck speed. The first batches of video evidence came from the Eastern Seaboard and quickly spread across the country. The image painted by the media's online counterpart told a far different story. Hundreds of reports with accompanying pictures and video couldn't be denied. Groups of police working with the National Guard were burning bodies by the thousands. Entire apartment complexes were sealed off in an attempt to contain the virus.

A news chopper captured what appeared to be hundreds of people on the roof of one of the sealed buildings. They were waving for help and flashing signs, attesting to the fact that they were not infected. The feed went live moments before dozens of carriers broke through to the roof in a mad dash for the people gathered there. Before the feed was cut off, many of the people pleading for help began jumping off the roof to avoid their attackers. All across the cutoff cities, countless people were shown to have been shot while trying to cross quarantine lines. Whether they were infected or not didn't appear to be an issue for those involved. The people demanded the truth; they finally had it, and then some.

The decision to pull the plug on the Internet was made shortly after footage showing units of National Guard and Army exchanging fire with each other was posted to the web. Apparently, a dispute over the treatment of civilians led to the altercation. The powers that be had finally had enough. Non-sanctioned reports and photography were hastening the spread of panic into otherwise safe zones. Until the outbreak was contained, and in the best interest of the citizenry, it was decided to pull the plug on the Internet.

Raids on the nation's major Internet service providers were conducted in hopes that most online communication would slow to a trickle. The few citizens that could still communicate via old channels were deemed irrelevant, as so-called experts concluded that less than five percent of the population was aware of the existence of such primitive computer programs. The deep web as well remained something even fewer people were aware of, much less knew how to access it.

The Roaming

The tactic was a near-complete failure, as only a handful of raids were even carried out. The manpower was of better use elsewhere. Large swaths of the populace were without Internet service to be sure, but at least seventy percent of the country was still operational. The flow of non-sanitized reports was momentarily slowed, though, and the government spin doctors got to work, quickly putting the blame squarely on the infected. They even went so far as to reveal video proof of dozens of carriers storming a local ISP headquarters, inadvertently burning it to the ground. For the most part, the population bought it. After all, there were more important things to worry about. Infected were spilling out into the suburbs.

Pepperbush had its first encounter with one of the infected seventeen days ago. Two miles from town, a local was hunting deer when he spotted a bloodied, naked man stumbling through the forest. Naturally, he thought the man was lost and in need of assistance, but when he approached, the man lunged at him. He swore the man was trying to bite him. The hunter claimed to have pushed the man down, hopped on his ATV, and hauled ass back to town. Rumor had it that he shot this stranger over fears of the infected, but no one would venture that far from town to verify.

This incident worried the people of Pepperbush enough to demand that the mayor do something to protect them from any more of these carriers just wandering in. In an effort to placate his constituents, a plan was devised. A twenty-foot tall wall consisting of massive trees, abandoned vehicles, earth, and rock would be erected around the main body of the town's primary living space. The cordoned-off area would contain most of Pepperbush's homes and businesses. Standing trees were no different from felled, the town built right around them along with a few abandoned buildings as well. The earth and rock had to come from somewhere, though. On the outer side of this wall, the construction crew dug a fifteen-foot-deep by twelve-foot-wide trench that served as a makeshift dry moat.

With the combined efforts of the locals and the refugees, it took eleven days to build their crude wall. The people of Pepperbush came to calling this makeshift defense "the berm." Construction of an extension to the berm was underway. When finished, the new addition would allow Pepperbush's single farm to be under the same protection as the rest of the town. Although the berm gave the residents of Pepperbush a much-needed morale boost in the security department, such a massive undertaking unfortunately cost them nearly all of their fuel reserves. In the aftermath of construction, the gas-hungry heavy equipment all sat on the outskirts of the farm, useless.

Ten days ago, one of the newest refugees came down with a cough. At the time, no one thought much of it, and life continued as usual. Sometime during the following afternoon, infection set in and she was found wandering Main Street. The town's sheriff happened to be one of the first on the scene. The infected woman was put down without much fanfare. This incident was enough to spur the people of Pepperbush into action. To protect the residents, it was decided that for the duration of this epidemic, no more refugees would be allowed to enter the town, with the added stipulation that anyone with so much as a persistent cough was to be placed under strict quarantine for an indeterminate amount of time. Everyone agreed and was eager to enforce this decision, including the refugees, who under differing circumstances would have found themselves on the receiving end of this new, harsh justice.

The first group of people was turned away from town eight days ago. It was a group of seven, two of whom were young children. One of the women in the group was coughing quite a bit and looked terrible. The guards explained that they were sorry, but they were not letting anyone else into town and the best they could do was give them some food and water. The group went along their way with little argument. That scenario would play out the same way three more times over the next few days.

Thirty-six hours ago, a group of eight bikers showed up at the gates, brandishing weapons and demanding to be let in. Lots of posturing from both sides mixed with an understandable fear of the unknown led to disaster. When the gunfire subsided, three of the bikers lay dead along with one of Pepperbush's newly appointed deputies.

In Pepperbush's long, proud history, nothing more violent than a drunken bar fight had ever transpired to shake up the community. That night there were four murders.

3:30am - Shearburn Residence

Vanessa kicked off her shoes and settled into the couch. Another long shift at the bar was over and she was left wondering about the futility of it all. The world around them seemed to be rapidly falling apart, but damned if that wasn't going to get in the way of the locals getting drunk on a nightly basis. Whatever was happening in Philadelphia and Baltimore surely couldn't happen here, right? Isolated incidents of infected traveling all the way to Pepperbush were becoming commonplace, not to mention last week's shootout verified for her that things were rapidly deteriorating, no matter what positive spin a handful of the town's officials wanted to put on it.

A few of her favorite websites were still up and running, though whatever was really happening in the region put a massive strain on the network. Large chunks of the Internet were unreachable. Even with the authorities blaming the outages on random mobs of looters destroying everything in their paths, something about the reporting didn't sit right with her and the few people she was still in contact with online. Vanessa had the opportunity to see one of these sick people up close. She didn't look to have the strength to open a door, much less ransack a service hub. And why would the rioters even do that if claiming to only want out of the cities was their only goal? None of it made any sense.

Long before this latest round of bullshit began, a friend got her involved in online gaming. It was called an MMORPG, specifically. She had no clue what that even meant and certainly no desire to try playing. Fast-forward five years later and she was a pro. Well, at least she was better than most of her friends, anyway. She would play for hours at a time, three or four nights a week. It was an addiction, some would say, but they didn't know the first thing about it.

Stay close-minded, she thought. *See if I care.* People lived to shit on things they didn't understand; it was the way of the world.

The game was Vanessa's one true escape from a town she couldn't stomach any longer, and she loved every second of it. Half of the fun of the game was the community and with that came the live chat always running in the bottom-left of the screen. They talked about everything and not just the gameplay. Real life, too. Movies, gossip, politics and religion, who's having a baby—you name it, they discussed it. In some sense, her fellow players were more real than most of these assholes in town. At least the gamers understood her, related to her. She logged onto the game. It was still operating.

Thank God, she thought. *Please don't deny me the one pleasure I have left.*

Vanessa sat back and watched the conversation unfold on her monitor. Hopping right in wasn't her style. She would observe and get a feel for the night's topics before commenting. Only a few weeks ago, when the first rumors of whatever this crisis was exploded across the net, the game was alive. The conversation moved so fast. Blink, and you were lost. Now the place was a ghost town. If a tumbleweed had blown past her screen, it wouldn't have surprised her.

Vanessa's username wasn't exactly thought-provoking. It was simply an abbreviation of Pepperbush, with the last two digits of her social security number added at the end. Easy enough. Besides, she wasn't the only one in-game with a lame username. At least she didn't slap a "69" at the end of it. Seventeen members were logged in, a shadow of the place's former glory when the servers were handling hundreds of unique accounts at once. Gone were the days of carefree conversation. No one cared who you were dating anymore or what the last movie you saw was. No one even played the game anymore for that matter; people just came to talk about the Eastern Seaboard Crisis, as the twenty-four-hour news cycles had christened it.

PprBsh84: Another day another one of those things near town yay
1313: that sucks
MandyLove: damn
spArkLe: getting more frequent there too huh?
PprBsh84: Yep 3rd one this week they say he was almost to the gates
dpPro: scary stuff
MonStar: my dad shot one last night he says were leaving soon but my mom doesn't want to
69kilr69: she probably sic 2 that's why
spArkLe: that was uncalled for
1313: go fuck yourself 69kilr69
MonStar: has logged out
PprBsh84: real nice
MandyLove: see what you did
69kilr69: just fucking around lighten up its getting bad here 2 you know
spArkLe: has anyone heard from JaGerMr today
SpaMMy: no
Admin: I haven't noticed him or Jennygurl logged in all day
MandyLove: sad
dpPro: fuck
PprBsh84: that makes 7 in the last 3 days
1313: they r probly ok
69kilr69: dont kid yourself
LukesMom: just stop it
spArkLe: go away
69kilr69: Im serious yall and so is this shit
Admin: everyone just be careful out there
dpPro: for real
PprBsh84: thats enough for me tonight guys work in the am be safe

LukesMom: goodnight
MandyLove: make sure to lock up
spArkLe: you'll be in my prayers
PprBsh84: has logged off
69kilr69: see ya
1313: take care

Vanessa sat her laptop aside, her options weighed days ago. As uncomfortable and alone as she felt in Pepperbush, she knew it was safest to stay and just ride this out, whatever it was, for now. Hell, she could always bond with the newcomers if it came down to it. *Queen of the refugees.* She allowed herself the briefest of chuckles. The idea forced a smile, a small pleasure too often denied as of late. Time for bed, anyway, as the bar reopened at nine. Five hours of sleep would have to be enough. Besides, what else was there to do, anyway?

W.J. Hegarty

CHAPTER FOUR

The Berm

An overworked, elderly farmer diligently checked rodent traps and sprayed for pests amidst a sea of corn stalks along the southern border of his farm. He knew how vital his crops were to the people of Pepperbush, though his humble nature would never allow him to speak of it. Although very likable, he would have never been confused for a family man. At first glance, he seemed gruff and even a little off-putting. If asked, his neighbors would have described Thomas as a humble, modest man who wasn't afraid of a hard day's work, not to mention that he certainly was not afraid of whatever fool thing the city folk had gone and got themselves wrapped up in, as he so often referred to the crisis.

Thomas lived on the outskirts of Pepperbush for his entire life, born when the town was no more than three shacks sharing ten acres of land. In the forties, when he was only a boy, his father taught him to work the ranch, and he grew to adore it. His love for life on the farm was not shared by any of his children. "No matter," he would tell them, and he meant it. "A child needs to make their own way in this world." Encouraging your children to follow in your footsteps was simply a product of an overinflated ego, he would say. "Do what makes you happy in this life because there's no guarantee of the after. This may well be all there is." That particular diatribe, or some variation of, was one of a few he was often heard repeating over the years.

Margaret, his wife of more than fifty years, passed more than a decade ago, leaving Thomas to a solitary existence. For the most part, he didn't mind living alone. Although he missed her immensely, he would never let it show. His children would visit on holidays, and of course, he received the obligatory but mostly random phone call. He enjoyed those moments and desperately looked forward to them, as fleeting as they were. At the end of the day, he was resigned to the fact he would most likely die alone. Thomas was content with the notion; he had lived a long, proud life and carried no regrets.

The outbreak rekindled a long-dormant sense of faith in the elderly family man. Thomas prayed daily for the safe return of his children. His son and two daughters moved away years ago and hadn't been heard from since before local travel restrictions began. When not tending to the farm, he spent most of his time at the town's main gates with the fleeting hope that maybe today would be that day when his children finally came home.

It was already late in the day; the farmhands were sent home early as a well-deserved break for their weeks of hard work. Stubborn as Thomas was, though, he would continue to work the field in their absence alone. He had enough food canned and stored away to feed himself for the rest of his days if he chose to go that route. Some would argue why you'd bother with anyone else if you had enough for you and yours. But that was what kept Thomas up nights. He enjoyed helping. Besides, what use did an eighty-seven-year-old man have with all that food, anyway?

Thomas was engulfed in a sea of corn stalks. His mind elsewhere, he was oblivious to a carrier approaching from a mere one hundred feet or so behind him. Sightings of infected had become all too common of late. It began with maybe one per week, perhaps a sighting every ten days or so. By then, the people that lived in and around Pepperbush were seeing these things more frequently. A half dozen or more reports of infected near town per week had become a reality.

This particular carrier had been wandering for quite some time, and it showed. The skin was torn from the left side of its face, revealing its putrid teeth and jawbone. Its clavicle protruded from its chest, the dried bone sticking straight up, jagged edges cutting deep into its jaw as the thing fumbled along. As was normally the case, the creature was filthy and covered with wounds. What set this one apart from the others spotted around Pepperbush were huge claw marks across its chest. They stretched to its mangled shoulder, culminating at a fleshy stump where an arm used to be. This unfortunate carrier probably startled one of the few black bears that dwelled in the wilderness surrounding Pepperbush. In recent years, bears had made a comeback region-wide. Though sightings were rare, they weren't unheard of.

Unaware of the danger just a few feet away, Thomas continued his work, methodically checking each plant for bugs or rot. With each shaky footfall, the creature stumbled closer to the farmer. Flies buzzed around its milky-white eyes. Its mouth hung agape. Chipped and broken teeth were a glimpse into its violent journey. With its sole good arm raised, its prey in sight, the infected was ready to pounce. A barely audible low hum emanated from the throat of the creature. If Thomas had seen the thing approaching, he would have noticed it looked almost excited in its proximity to the old man.

The infected closed in as Thomas stood to stretch his back. Rustling corn stalks caught his attention at the last moment. Startled, he turned in time to see the infected's head explode in a shower of brain and skull, accentuated by a fine red mist that dissipated as quickly as his would-be attacker dropped. Thomas fell back onto his ass and nearly choked on a mouthful of chewing tobacco. Relieved to be alive, though still lying in the mud, he turned toward the berm and sent a thankful wave to the guard half a football field away. He wiped his brow with a grin. Had Martha or God forbid one of the children witnessed his carelessness, he would have never heard the end of it. Thomas brushed himself off as he regained his footing. The crops could wait until morning. Maybe he needed a break, after all.

Fifty yards from Thomas's location, the closest guard stood atop the berm, rifle in hand. He took a moment to tip his hat toward the thankful farmer before returning to his binoculars. From his vantage point, the guard had a good view of the southeastern portion of Thomas's fields. Working in conjunction with the next watch post one hundred yards farther down the berm, these two lookouts kept the southern half of the farm well protected from most unwanted intruders. Expansion of the berm, when completed, would offer the farm the same protection as the rest of the town. Until then, the farm needed around-the-clock surveillance. Pepperbush's lone means of renewable resources were far too important to go unprotected indefinitely.

Southwest of Thomas's farm, near the opposite side of town, two men patrolled the outer perimeter of the berm. The sun had set by then, the moon nearing the treetops. Boundary lines inside and out of town were constantly safeguarded by groups of two, usually armed with rifles or, sometimes if they were lucky, shotguns. Mostly they were armed with their own weapons, though more than a few were stuck with what could be afforded by those who decided such things. All that really mattered was the ammunition the gun held and whether you felt comfortable with the number of bullets in your pocket.

Tobias's dog sauntered along a few meters ahead of the men. He was a Yellow Lab named Dusty. The dog was apt to jump at squirrels and chipmunks, harmless as they were. Though Dusty had never actually been tested against carriers, the dog's presence gave the men a well-needed if never spoken of sense of security while out on patrol. Tobias's young son, Tommy, worried every night when his father would take the boy's dog out beyond the safety of Pepperbush and its reassuring light. The conversation rarely went much further than Tobias's wife Isabelle assuring their son that his father and Dusty kept each other safe. The idea of his father and his dog coming home in the morning usually put the boy at ease. His college-age daughter Lillian had no such qualms. She knew her father would never take unnecessary chances, which included putting Dusty in harm's way. The two of them would come home safely every night; she was sure of it.

Tobias and Danny hiked the same route nightly since patrols were put into effect shortly after the first carrier was sighted near town a few weeks prior. The men had been close since they were kids. After high school, Tobias went into real estate. He was marginally successful as an agent while Danny went off to work as a general contractor. The old friends would partner up years later, flipping houses. Tobias would secure the properties, and Danny would renovate them. The business was going well until the crisis. Now, in their early forties, both men were relegated to glorified guard duty, a position neither was adequately trained for, though both were eager to help Pepperbush in any way that they could.

His rifle's weight dug its coarse shoulder strap into Tobias's neck, adding to his discomfort. He still wasn't accustomed to lugging the thing around. It seemed he spent more time adjusting the uncomfortable strap than scanning the horizon for threats. He didn't take the situation lightly, though, far from it, as adjusting himself and the strap was an extension of his usual nervous ticks. Tobias never was very familiar with weapons, guns in particular. His uncle took him shooting a few times as a child, but the lessons never took. His discomfort was interrupted by Danny's newest thoughts on courting the local bartender.

"I don't care what you say, Toby. Vanessa *is* into me."

"She's a bartender. Her livelihood depends on people liking her; you're reading way too much into it."

"Nah man, you just don't get it." A thunderous boom silenced Danny. The men looked to the sky, but it was already gone.

"You think they even know we're here?" Danny asked, straining for a glimpse of the jet.

"Why would they? This place barely registers on the map. Besides, they're preoccupied with Baltimore and Philly. They don't have time for us." Tobias's mind was elsewhere.

"Oh well, screw them, then. Anyway, I think I'm going to swing by Mother Leeds after shift tonight. You should meet me there."

"Oh no, no way. Isabelle would have my ass if I'm out all night again," Tobias said as he shook his head no. "Besides, Vanessa's not interested, Dan."

"How do you know?" Danny was irritated. He was quick-tempered and easily angered. He read Tobias's lack of support as implied malice.

"She's just not, okay?" Tobias shrugged off his friend's concern. He'd heard this story more than once over the past few weeks since the world turned upside down. It was almost humorous to him in light of life as they knew it being pretty much over.

"Yeah, well, we'll see about that." Danny laughed off Tobias's misgivings. After all, what did Tobias know, anyway? He'd been married for what might as well have been a lifetime by then. "I'm still going to the bar tonight."

"Don't say I didn't warn you." Tobias was through speculating over Danny's infatuation. There were more pressing concerns than bedding a bartender. The sooner he could get off his chest what had been at the forefront of his thoughts over the last couple of nights, the better. "You know, my boy climbed to the top of this thing without a problem the other day," Tobias said matter-of-factly while glancing at the berm.

"Yeah, we chase kids off of it every day. That's pretty fucked up you let *your* kid play on it, Toby," Danny jabbed.

"That's kind of my point, Dan. This thing has never even really been tested." Tobias threw a fist-sized rock at the berm, causing a mini avalanche of dirt and small stones that wound up coming to a stop at the men's feet. "Mayor Lancaster's got his head up his ass if he thinks a pile of dirt will keep these people safe."

"I don't know, Toby. We haven't seen any deer wander into town since the berm went up. Hell, if it keeps the wildlife out, you know it'll keep those things out."

"That's just the problem. I don't know that for sure, and anyone who says they do is fooling themselves or outright lying. Has it ever occurred to you that maybe the deer are staying away *because* of the infected?" he

33

asked, not expecting a response. Tobias stopped walking and gestured to the forest surrounding them.

Danny cleared his throat. His horse cough echoed into the night. For the first time since their shift began, not even the birds sang anymore. Not so much as a cricket was chirping. Except for Dusty's panting, the night was silent. "I hadn't really thought about it." Danny straightened himself a little at the revelation.

"It's not just the deer, Danny," Tobias continued. "Raccoons and squirrels, even the birds don't come around anymore. The hunters are traveling farther away every week to even spot a deer, much less shoot one. Whatever those things are, the animals know to stay away from them and, as a result, us." Tobias pulled Dusty close. Almost on cue, the dog let out an empathetic whimper.

Danny straightened himself looked to the forest and back to the berm. "You know what? Maybe the next time we find one of those things, before we shoot it, we should get it to climb the berm. See if it can make it up over the top. We just won't tell anybody."

"Wow." Tobias shook his head. Something near a smile began to form on his troubled face.

"Oh, come on, it's only an idea. You don't have to be a dick about it."

Tobias stopped poking the berm and placed his hand on his friend's shoulder. "For the first time in a long time, Danny, I couldn't agree more."

CHAPTER FIVE

Mother Leeds

Little more than eighteen months ago, following the death of her husband, Vanessa became the sole owner and operator of Mother Leeds Bar and Grill. Clint had been diagnosed with an inoperable brain tumor just under two years prior. Mercifully for the young newlyweds, the end came quickly, and as fast as their marriage began, it was over. Clint inherited the bar upon his father's passing and always planned to hand it down to his children someday. This was, of course, not to be.

The roof of Mother Leeds was adorned with a statue of the Jersey Devil. Clint never believed in the legends—"superstitious bullshit," he called them—though Vanessa wasn't so sure.

"It could be out there somewhere. What's the harm in believing?" she would reply when asked.

Her childlike wonder and awe at times was a huge attraction for Clint; he loved her all the more for it.

The couple met when he was on a business trip to Baltimore. If love at first sight was real, then this was it. Within a year, they were married and Vanessa found herself living in Pepperbush, proud co-owner of a modest drinking establishment at the edge of the world. Clint saw to his day job from home on his laptop while Vanessa ran the bar. The coupled lived in bliss, their little slice of paradise.

Fast-forward two years and Vanessa found herself alone, with very few friends and no family to speak of, still very much an outsider in Clint's hometown. Three weeks ago, just before the town was closed to outsiders, two men from Baltimore showed up at the bar, exhausted and dehydrated, their designer clothes ragged and filthy. They introduced themselves as Markus and Damon. Apparently their car got stuck in the mud and they wandered for more than two days before they stumbled upon Pepperbush. Vanessa welcomed them with open arms. The relief to see someone from back home all the way out here in northern New Jersey was only a part of it. A few more outsiders added to the already swelling numbers of the refugees made her, at least appearance-wise, seem to belong.

The men were not aware of what was transpiring over the past week or so back in Baltimore and other big cities up and down the East Coast. After about an hour glued to the TV, the men decided to leave their car in the mud and stay in Pepperbush until whatever was happening ran its course. They were lucky, she imagined. Those two must have wandered out of the city in the earliest days of the crisis when large gathered groups were still being chalked up as protesters and rioters. Vanessa offered them the loft above Mother Leeds for as long as they needed it and jobs if they were interested. Markus welcomed the opportunity to pull his share, whereas Damon said he would think about it. He was still considering the offer.

Vanessa was restocking the bar when a bell attached to the front door signaled another customer's entrance.

"Be with you in just a second. Have a seat anywhere you like," she said without so much as a glimpse in their direction.

Sam removed his worn cowboy hat before picking a stool at the farthest end of the bar, closest to the largest window at the front of the building. He glanced around the room sprawled out in front of him as he leaned his rifle beneath the bar to his right before taking a seat. He always made it a point whenever visiting Vanessa to secure a seat in this area as the large mirror behind the bar allowed him a near three-hundred-sixty-degree view of the place. It saved him the trouble of having to twist his neck and scan for anything out of the ordinary, but more importantly, he didn't want people to know he was watching them—always.

"No rush, darling. Take your time." Sam dropped his G's but always spoke deliberately and with a kindness in his tone, emphasized by a quiet country drawl.

"Oh, hey, Sam. I didn't realize it was you!" Vanessa's eyes lit up at the realization that one of the few people in town she truly considered a friend had come for a visit.

Stocking the bar could wait. Sam deserved a proper greeting and at least the bulk of her attention. After a lingering hug that lasted a little longer than the older man was comfortable with, Vanessa leaned over the bar to pour Sam a draft, his favorite light beer. Most of her customers didn't drink the swill. "Light bullshit," most called it—the nice ones, anyway. Vanessa didn't particularly care for it, either, but Sam loved it, and that was all that mattered. She didn't have the heart to tell him that this was the last keg of the stuff.

She reached back over to the server's side of the bar to pour Sam a beer. Standing on her tiptoes while stretching the width of the countertop gave her just the distance required to reach the tap. She'd poured beer like that a thousand times, as most of the regulars were more than happy to have her do. Her long brown hair flowed down to the bar top and curled into a pile just beside the line of taps. The effort pulled her white tank top up slightly, exposing the small of her back and the top of her white panties peeking out of her low-cut jeans. Vanessa's smooth, flat stomach pressed firmly against the cool bar top. The fringes of her shirt soaked up spilled beer. She would curse her carelessness later.

Sam wouldn't even so much as steal a glimpse at her; her natural beauty wasn't lost on him, though. Far from it. Sam knew Vanessa held him in close regard, though he was the nearest she had to a father figure and he'd die before jeopardizing that bond.

"Here you are, Sam." She slid the already sweating glass to him. "And don't worry. As far as anyone else is concerned, this keg is empty," she added with a wink.

Sam chuckled before taking a long refreshing pull, nearly blushing from the attention.

"Oh, it's okay, Van. No need to hold onto the stuff on my account. You do what needs doing around here. The world's not over yet." He took another extended swig, followed by an "ah" that perked up the ears of customers at the other side of the bar.

Vanessa smiled and shook her head as foam dripped from Sam's thick mustache. He managed a long smile of his own for the girl as she returned to cleaning the bar.

"You're in here kind of late Sam. What's up?"

"Meeting with Tobias. The man's looking for a little perspective, I reckon."

"Anything I should know about?" Vanessa stopped what she was doing long enough to gauge that the next words out of Sam's mouth would most likely be lies.

"I'm sure it's nothing to worry about, sweetheart. So how are you holding up?" Sam changed the subject as gently as he knew how.

"Oh, you know. Another day in paradise." Vanessa shrugged and sat a bottled beer for Tobias in front of Sam. "Here he comes now. I'll check up on you guys in a bit."

"Thanks, Vanessa. Take your time." Sam tipped his hat as Vanessa made her way down the bar to check on her other patrons.

Sam was a fairly tall man in his mid-fifties, rarely spotted without his worn Stetson and equally weathered boots. A thick gray handlebar mustache was unable to hide the warm smile he was quick to offer. His shoulder-length salt and pepper hair was known well around town, though these days, it was more salt than anything else. He was a kind but stern man, quick to tell you like it was and set a man straight if need be. Pepperbush's new head of security was wisely chosen, as Sam knew his way around a fight but more importantly was well respected in the community. Even the surliest of its residents would think twice before engaging him.

Sam served two tours, the second of which saw him on the ground during Operation Desert Shield. While on patrol one evening, the man next to him stepped on a landmine. His friend was blown to pieces, near vaporized just feet from Sam's position. Sam took a good dose of shrapnel and spent the next few weeks in an Italian hospital just off the coast of the Mediterranean. Most of the wounds were little more than superficial, but the worst of it was a large sliver of metal that lodged under his kneecap, nearly severing his lower leg. Months of physical therapy in one VA hospital after another granted him the use of the limb, though he never fully recovered and still walked with a pronounced limp as a result.

It was decided in the earliest days of the crisis that additional security patrols would not be run by the police, as they were already overextended. Sam was asked by Sheriff Marisol to head up this aspect of town security to keep the mayor's corrupt men away from such a critical position.

Sam agreed that the mayor and his men were not to be trusted, especially with security matters. Over the past few weeks, Sam personally handpicked each member of the new security detail with his old friend Ron appointed as a second in command of sorts. By now there were close to thirty men answerable to Sam only, their prime concern being berm patrol. Constantly rotating shifts ate up most of their time, and truth be told, he could have used more men. One of Sam's most trusted happened to be Tobias Burke, who asked Sam to meet him here for some advice and a possible offer.

Tobias hung his coat by the door and joined Sam at the far end of the bar. He stored his rifle next to Sam's before the two men exchanged a handshake.

"So how goes it, Tobias? An uneventful shift, I hope," Sam asked as he motioned toward Tobias's waiting beer, his grin momentarily returning.

"Thanks, Sam. Nothing worth mentioning. What's the scuttlebutt today?"

"Well, Miss Reynolds called again." Sam gave an eye roll Vanessa could have seen from the other end of the bar had she been paying attention.

"Oh no, let me guess: they're in her attic again? Or is it her basement this time?" Tobias shook his head.

"Her garden. She only recently moved some of her crops from her greenhouse. Apparently the infected have been eating her tomatoes."

Neither man could hold his laughter. The idea of infected making their way from Philadelphia only to rifle through an old woman's garden for produce turned out to be just what the men needed to take the edge off.

"Is that so?" Tobias finally responded as he straightened back up to a modicum of seriousness. "Well, I suppose I could stop by on my way home and talk to her. I think she's just lonely, is all."

"I'd appreciate that, Tobias." Sam took a long, slow drink from his mug. When his face came back out of the glass, his demeanor had changed. What nearly passed as a smile a moment ago was replaced with a somber expression. "It's not all humorous news today, I'm sorry to say." Sam curled his lip. He blinked and held his eyes closed just long enough for Tobias to realize the tone of their conversation was going to change, and not for the better. "John and Beatrice Parker committed suicide last night." Sam lowered his eyes. "Looks like he drowned old Beatrice in the bathtub, squeezed in beside her, and cut his wrists. I guess calling it a murder-suicide would be more appropriate. Hell of a way to go."

"Jesus, I hope for their sake it was fast. How many does that make now?"

"Too many. We should keep this one to ourselves for as long as we can."

"Oh?" he replied, taken a little off guard by the request. Tobias was at a loss. It wasn't like Sam to be shifty or shady. He was always right up-front with everything. If the man wanted to hold back information as big as this from the town, he must have a good reason.

"I know what you're thinking, and yes, the town deserves to know, but not right now. They need some good news for a change."

"You'll get no arguments here."

"So what's on your mind, son? *You* called *me* here and I'm the one spilling all the gossip? Drinks in the middle of the week can mean only one thing. You're fretting over something, so out with it."

"There's no easy way to put this, so I'm just going to say it. Tonight, I'm going to see what Isabelle thinks about leaving Pepperbush."

"I assume you mean leaving town for good?"

"I do."

"You sure that's wise, son, what with your family and all? You know the berm should keep the infected out of here, right?"

"Oh come on, Sam, you know as well as I do that the berm has never been properly tested."

"Go on."

"I'm saying we have a false sense of security here *because* of the berm. For the most part, everyone's acting like we're immune to whatever the hell's going on out there. We put down more and more of those things each week and it's only a matter of time until they show up in numbers that we are simply not ready for."

Sam interjected. "The closest city we saw on TV that was a mess would be Philadelphia, and that's a hundred miles away. Those things don't look like they could travel that kind of distance."

"Sure, we're out in the middle of nowhere by city standards, but I don't think we're far enough off the beaten path to stay safe indefinitely. Besides, the ones we're seeing have to be coming from somewhere and we don't even really know what the hell those things are truly capable of."

"Then there's the whole supplies issue. I mean, while we're at it we might as well put everything on the table, Tobias."

"You're right. We don't have a clean water supply anywhere near here. Access to the aquifer is forty miles away. If the wells dry up—or worse, get contaminated—there will be a lot of thirsty people in a matter of days."

"And then there's the matter of Thomas's crops. They won't sustain us forever. When the food supplies run out, I'm confident we'll find that the produce and livestock won't last very much longer."

"What are we going to do if the power grid fails? You saw the cities. They were completely blacked out, not to mention Baltimore was a goddamn war zone last time the news was kind enough to show it."

"I won't argue that, Tobias. We're living on borrowed time here, even if the rest of the town refuses to acknowledge it. Seeing as you felt the need to pull me aside and discuss this past dinnertime, I assume you have a plan?"

"Well, I'm thinking we should head to the coast. At least that way we're not potentially surrounded and we would always have the ocean to retreat to if things got bad. Here, if something were to happen, I just don't know."

"Sounds feasible, but what do you propose we do about it? Three hundred people are a lot of bodies to relocate on short notice."

"I'm going to check around town and see if anyone agrees with me. If I can get enough people together that want out, I'm going, and I think you should come with us, Sam," Tobias suggested expectantly.

"I hear ya, son, and I'd be lying if I said similar thoughts hadn't crossed my mind, especially after Dennis was shot."

"Yeah, I've been thinking about that night, too. So what is it, Sam? Can I count you in?"

"There's one more thing to consider, Tobias. Mayor Lancaster will fight ya on this. Count on it. He won't take kindly to you upsetting the balance."

"Tough. He may own this town, but he certainly doesn't own the people in it." Tobias was adamant.

"I think I've heard about enough, Tobias." Sam ran his fingers through his thick mustache and his stubbly beard. "Look, you get your people together, son, but quietly. Once word gets out about your plan, it won't be easy going with the mayor and his lackeys fighting you tooth and nail. You can be sure he'll do his best to shut this down fast."

"He can try all he likes. My mind is made up, Sam. Besides, what can he do to stop me?" Tobias shrugged.

"Slander, discredit you at best. At worst, well, we're not going to let it come to that, now are we? I'll keep them off your back, for now. They don't want any part of me, but you're going to want to move fast. The quicker we're on the road, the better for everyone involved."

"Agreed, so I can count you in?"

"Absolutely. I had to be sure you were serious, is all." Sam gestured to Vanessa for two more drinks.

"Be right there, Sam." Vanessa remained upbeat, though what little of Sam and Tobias's conversation she overheard concerned her. Before fetching their drinks, she slid a tray of finger foods over to her newest employee. "Markus, you want to run this over to table twelve?"

"No problem, Van. Seven's burgers are almost up, too. After that, you mind if I catch a smoke?"

"Of course not. You've earned it, sweetie. Thanks."

Markus carried his tray of food to the waiting diners while Vanessa delivered two beers to Tobias and Sam.

"Two more, boys, one bottle, one draft." Vanessa winked at Sam. "So what are you guys whispering about over here?" Vanessa planted her elbows atop the bar, her chin resting in her upturned palms.

Deflecting the comment, Sam inquired about the damage done to Mother Leeds, the fallout from a gun battle between a group of bikers and Pepperbush's stressed security less than a week prior. "How are your nerves holding up?"

"You mean today or just in general?" Vanessa replied with a shrug.

"You know what I mean." Sam motioned to a cracked windowpane, haphazardly taped up, and a handful of stray bullet holes just above eye level behind the bar. "I'm talking about last week's shootout a block from here."

"I won't lie, Sam, it scared the shit out of me. I heard all the yelling from here, took the customers into the back room, and made them lie down."

"Smart. You probably saved lives." Sam eyed the damage. Beside him, Tobias gave an approving nod.

"Maybe, poor Markus, bless his heart. He shoved me to the ground and jumped on top of me after the first shot." Vanessa smiled. "Unnecessary for sure, but appreciated nonetheless."

"Good kid, that one. So how are the new guys working out anyway?" Sam asked, happy to change the subject.

"Oh, *he's* great, and boy did I need the help. You know with all the new mouths to feed and all. Plus, it's kind of nice to have someone from back home to talk with, present circumstances aside."

"Familiarity can be a great comfort when the world keeps piling on."

"Yeah, really. What are the chances of two guys from Baltimore winding up here at the northern tip of the Pine Barrens of all places?"

"Crazy times we're living in, girl. Crazy times indeed."

Tobias didn't join in their conversation. Instead, he drank his beer in silence while he peered through the window out onto Main Street. He noticed a middle-aged woman pushing a double stroller with three small children in tow, and for a moment he wondered how in the hell this idea of his was even feasible with so many people's lives at stake. His thoughts inevitably drifted to Isabelle's face and his children's smiles. He realized that that was enough for him. His family's safety was paramount. If it came down to it, no one else mattered; he'd get his family out alone if he had to.

On his way out to the street for a cigarette break, Markus held the door for an elderly couple no doubt looking forward to enjoying a meal together. The cynic in him pondered if it would be their last as he scanned distant shadows for carriers. Lately, though, his thoughts were more positive, and of course this pleasant couple and the town at large would be just fine. Pepperbush had a good thing going here. He believed in it wholeheartedly.

"Welcome to Mother Leeds, folks."

"Oh, thank you, dear," the old woman replied with a smile.

"It's my pleasure. Enjoy your meal, ma'am," he said as he closed the door behind the old couple.

Markus lit a cigarette and leaned against the front of the building. He rested the back of his head against the cool bricks, and sweat dripped from his brow. This new life he discovered with the people of Pepperbush was the most peaceful time he could remember. Amid society crumbling more and more each day, Markus was content in this quiet little town so very far from home.

Taken in under Damon's father's wing at a young age was something Markus felt he could never properly repay. The life of a young man living on the streets of Baltimore could be tough under the best of circumstances. Without Demetrius's guidance during his formative years, Markus was sure he would have become yet another statistic in the sad circle of violence that claimed so many of his friends. Damon never told Markus why his father took such a liking to him, if he even knew. If remaining loyal to Damon in some small way showed Demetrius his appreciation, then so be it, although the urge to shun that lifestyle and all who perpetuated it stirred in Markus's gut.

The day he and his best friend stumbled across this place forever changed his life. The men were sure that these hicks, as Damon put it, would not be very welcoming to a couple of city boys. Quite the contrary, as it turned out. The citizens of Pepperbush welcomed them with open arms. Gone were the cold stares and the uneasy feelings of impending violence of Westside. All of that was replaced with warmth and a friendly sense of welcome that at first was alien to the two strangers. In the weeks since they arrived, Markus had come to call this place home. If he had any say in the matter, he would never leave.

A brutish, heavyset man sat alone at the opposite end of the bar from Sam and Tobias. Much to Vanessa's dismay, he was a regular. His obese belly hung over his belt, separating him from the bar top by at least a foot. A worn-out yellow ball cap adorned his unkempt head of hair. More than a week's worth of beard growth and bad teeth rounded out the appearance of a man angry at the world and everyone in it. Jim was always an asshole. The fact that he was Mayor Lancaster's muscle only made him worse over the years. The apparent collapse of the outside world seemed to have triggered something in the man. If it was at all possible, he was worse now than ever before. Half of the townsfolk feared him; the other half simply avoided him. Jim had been especially hard on Vanessa since the passing of her husband. Unfortunately, his acrimony only escalated under the developing regional crisis.

"What are they, the only ones in here, or am I invisible? Bring that sweet ass of yours over here. I need to talk to ya, girl." Jim chugged down another shot of whiskey. Overflow spilled down his bloated neck.

"Dammit, I hate that asshole. He comes in here every goddamn night now." Vanessa wasn't looking for attention but thought it prudent to make Sam aware of her trepidation.

"You want me to go have a word with him, darling?" Sam offered.

"No, Sam, I'm a big girl. I can take care of myself. Thanks, though." Vanessa's smile momentarily faded as she returned her attention to the brute.

"About damn time. My drink ain't gonna pour itself," Jim sneered.

"Coming right up, James." Vanessa hated this part of the job. Every evening like clockwork, Jim would wander into the bar for a few hours before doing God knows what the man got himself involved in on a nightly basis.

"How many times I gotta tell ya, sweetness? Call me Jimmy," He slurred.

"Sorry, Jimmy. Here you go." Vanessa handed off his drink with a noticeable frown.

"Ah, forget it. What's in a name anyway, right? Speaking of names, why did you keep your old man's name anyhow?"

"Out of respect, I guess. Why does it matter anyway?" Her brow furrowed and the hairs on the back of her neck stood at attention as she wiped down an already cleaned part of the bar, away from even the slightest eye contact with Jim's gaze.

He breathed heavy, mouth agape, eyes penetrating the girl from across the bar. With each sigh of his massive frame, spittle exhaled upon his beard and the bar top. "I gotta say, my point is it's been a mighty long time since your man up and left ya. I know you must get lonely up in that house off of Sweetfern Lane all by yourself. Why don't you let old Jimmy come by later and keep ya warm?" Jim chuckled as he threw back another shot of whiskey.

"I've told you before, Jim, Clint didn't leave me. Why don't I get you a sandwich or something, huh? Maybe some coffee?" Vanessa offered, desperate to change the conversation.

"I don't need no goddamn sandwich!" Jim snatched her up by the wrist, pulling her in close to his sweaty bulk. "Lemme look at ya, girl. Ooh wee, ya ever notice how the sweat collects 'tween your tits there? Mm-hmm, why don't you let old Jimmy take care of that for ya?" he slurred. Jim moved in close toward Vanessa's chest and inhaled a long deep breath before slowly pulling his head back to a raised position, his eyes closed in apparent euphoria. "Now there, girl, if you give old Jimmy just—" Jim was cut off mid-thought. The room spun for an instant before he found himself on the bar's cold hardwood floor.

Towering over the humiliated man, Markus leaned against the bar to better make eye contact while he righted Jim's barstool. "You're going to have to be more careful, Jim. These floors can get pretty slick."

Jim wobbled to his feet, yelling and smashing his fists against the bar on his way up. "You motherfucker. Ya kicked my stool out from under me."

"You must have slipped, Jim. It happens more often than you would think. We really need to look into a new floor wax before someone gets hurt. Here, let me help you outside. The fresh air will be good for you," Markus offered.

"Get your goddamn hands off of me!" Jim yanked his arm free. "You and all those other refugees don't even belong here!" Jim pounded his fist down on the bar again and pointed to Vanessa. "You set me up, you little bitch. You told that big bastard to do that, didn't you?"

"Jim, I did nothing of the sort, and you know it," Vanessa tried to assure the man.

"No wonder your man left ya. He was right. Good for nothing dirty little whore." Jim spat in Vanessa's face and grabbed her by the front of her tank top, yanking the girl nearly over the bar in the process.

Instinct took control as Vanessa sent a barrage of fists into Jim's face before he could react, bloodying his nose and lip.

Jim pulled his other arm back. In mid-swing, he was pulled away from Vanessa and sent careening down the front of the bar, beer mugs and stools tumbling along with him.

Sam had Jim by the collar. He was sliding the heavy man down the slick edge of the bar top. Safely away from Vanessa, Sam yanked Jim away from the bar. He punched him twice in the face before throwing him back to the floor. "You lay another hand on that girl and it's the last thing you'll ever do!" Sam leaned in and hit him again, this time opening a wide gash above Jim's left eye. "Get this piece of shit out of here, Markus!" Sam forced Jim up and into Markus's waiting arms.

"We ain't through, girl. That's for damn sure," Jim stammered. He scurried to his feet, correcting himself before Markus could grab him and turned toward Sam, face to face with his assailant. "I ain't gonna forget this,

Sam. You best believe we gonna settle up." Jim stormed out of the bar, kicking stools and chairs along his way.

"I'll be waiting, you fat tub of shit." Sam turned his attention to Vanessa. "You alright, darling?" He held out his hand, attempting to wipe the spit from her cheek.

"I hate this fucking place, Sam. What am I doing here, goddammit?" Vanessa ran into the back room, no longer able to hold back tears.

Sam placed a confident hand on Markus's shoulder. "Get after her, son."

"She'll be alright, Sam. Vanessa's a tough chick. Excuse me, fellas." Markus shook Sam's hand and nodded at Tobias before disappearing into the back room after Vanessa.

Tobias apologized to the remaining customers who hadn't fled during the altercation.

Sam gestured for Tobias to look out of the front window at Jim pushing his way through innocent bystanders in his mad dash away from the bar. "You paying attention, Tobias? This ain't an isolated incident. The whole town's got cabin fever. Hell, just yesterday I broke up a fight in front of Tabitha's antique shop of all places."

"The fact that the antique shop is open at all proves my point, Sam. These people are fooling themselves if they think they're not in danger here." Tobias looked at his half-full beer and put it down on the bar.

"There's more to it than that, Tobias. The second Mayor Lancaster realizes the old rules truly don't apply anymore, he'll let Jim and the boys off their leash. Troublemakers will be the first to go, and you damn well better believe you'll fall straight into that category once word of your plan gets around."

"Believe me, I've thought about that. Jim and the rest of Lancaster's thugs already act like they own the place. Things are escalating, and one way or another, whether it's a bunch of infected or Lancaster and his men officially declaring a dictatorship, we're going to have a fight on our hands. I'd rather my family avoid both. As far as I'm concerned, it's just another in a laundry list of reasons to get the hell out of here as soon as possible." Tobias took note of the elderly couple leaving the bar. Their warm meal sat untouched at the table behind them. *What a waste,* he thought. But not only about the food, which was an issue all its own. This town should be coming together to weather the storm, not fracture. These random acts of violence kept the town on edge. Pretty soon no one would leave their homes for fear of what might happen. Now more than ever, he knew he was right.

Markus slowly approached Vanessa. He had grown to know her well enough to realize if she was upset enough for tears. Jim must have really gotten to her. "Hey, why don't you knock off early? I'll take it from here," he offered.

"No thanks, Markus. What am I going to do, go home and watch the world turn to shit on TV? I may as well stay here, right? I *will* take a drink, though. Hand me that bottle, would you?" Vanessa pointed out a bottle of Absinthe imported from Switzerland years ago she was saving for the right occasion. The European variety had a higher wormwood content, allowing for a better effect. Last bottle of the stuff in the bar, as it turned out. "Now is a good a time as any."

"Don't be afraid of that asshole. We all know he's just a bitter piece of shit." Markus set up two glasses, gently poured a little ice water over the alcohol, and waited until the disappearance of the dark line at the top of the combined liquids revealed the perfect mixture. The bar was out of sugar cubes, so they would have to do without.

"I'm not afraid of Jim, Markus. I'm crying because I'm frustrated. For whatever reason, he's just got it out for me. I don't know what his problem is. He never liked Clint, for one, and he used to just be rude to me. Now I just don't know what's going through his head. It seems like since things changed, it's like he's lost his mind, almost as if he thinks the rules don't apply anymore."

"Maybe they don't." Markus handed her a glass.

Vanessa sat back in her chair while she slowly sipped her drink. "Yeah maybe, but he better find someone else to push around because I'm not going to put up with it for much longer."

W.J. Hegarty

CHAPTER SIX

Neglect

Isabelle was fast approaching forty. Thirty-eight to be exact. A few delicate lines on her face conveyed a sobering reminder that at twenty-two, her daughter Lillian was the same age Isabelle was a lifetime ago when Tobias proposed. Since they married so young, the temptation to stray remained steadfast in Isabelle's fantasies. To never know the touch of another man or experience the carefree lifestyle of a young woman in her prime gnawed at her as of late. Current circumstances only hastened the feeling that maybe she *should* stray or leave altogether. On the one hand, she viewed Tobias and her children as all that was good in the world. The thought of imposing such pain upon her family became unbearable at times.

Trapped at home since the crisis began, boredom encouraged her mind to wander. She would often leave the doors unlocked. The thought of a dozen filthy intruders, not too dissimilar to the ones she saw on TV, cornering her in the bedroom filled her with anticipation. Nowhere to run, she would be at the mercy of her attackers. Animalistic impulses controlled her as one by one a steady stream of shadowy figures had their way with her, the ravenous horde holding back no longer as they swallowed her up in their lust.

Isabelle possessed a myriad of fantasies to busy herself with, not all of them pleasant. The ones where she hurt people, or worse, scared her the most. Her thoughts inevitably drifted back to her children's faces and a smiling Tobias so eager to please and keep his family safe. A sense of guilt sometimes washed over her, chilling her to the bone. The moment ruined, she slipped her hand out from between her legs and pulled the covers up around her neck. Was it guilt she felt, or something else entirely?

Tobias entered the room after another long night on patrol. She could sense it exhausted him. Once again, she would be up all night alone, lying there with only her mind for company.

"Hey, Izzy. Let me take a quick shower. I'll be right out." Tobias was near asleep on his feet, with hardly a glance toward his wife.

Typical, she thought. *Why should tonight be any different?* Isabelle turned away from the view of him showering to gaze out the window, faceless attackers once again at the forefront of her thoughts. There was a time when she would lie there and watch Tobias shower. No longer. Isabelle continued her exploration, returning to parts of her body it seemed Tobias had lost all interest in. The people in her mind were becoming real for her. In some respects, they knew her better than her husband ever did. She would drift off mid-storyline, wake a few minutes later, and reflect. *How long has it been? Minutes or hours?* She could lose herself if only—Tobias coughed. It echoed from the steamy bathroom. She was irritated with her husband for interrupting, especially if all he was going to do was bitch and pass out. *Just go to sleep, Tobias.*

Tobias discarded his damp towel and crawled under the covers. She didn't care anymore whether or not he realized that the end of the world also heralded the end of their marriage.

The Burkes settled in for the night, taking up familiar places in their bed. It became a ritual. Every night after Tommy was asleep, Tobias and Isabelle watched the news for any sign that maybe the crisis in the cities had passed. Light from the TV illuminated their weary faces. The woman on the screen repeated the same message she or someone like her read every night. *Don't go out alone and stay away from anyone that looks sick.* One location was secured while another was not.

Isabelle lit a cigarette. The smoke bothered Tobias immensely. Just a few weeks ago, she would have never considered smoking in the house, much less in the bedroom. It seemed the collapse of society didn't end at their doorstep, after all, no matter what her husband thought. "Did anything exciting happen at work today?" Isabelle asked reluctantly.

"Just Danny."

Isabelle rolled her eyes as she exhaled long and slow. "Let me guess, Vanessa?"

"Yup." Tobias situated himself away from the path of drifting smoke.

"Huh." Isabelle shrugged. At least Danny knew how to show interest. She looked again to the darkened window while taking another long drag.

"Right." Tobias's full attention was on the TV, as usual.

Isabelle dropped the cigarette butt into a discarded rum bottle at the side of the bed. Smoke wafted from the glass as the butt rolled around the bottom of the bottle until finally landing in a tiny pool of liquid, extinguishing it with a sizzle. "Okay, enough brooding already. I know the look. What is it?" Isabelle honestly didn't care what his answer was. She had heard it all before. Tobias didn't trust the mayor, Danny was an idiot, and this person and that person... *Enough!* When he wasn't complaining, he could be overbearing. She imagined herself punching him square in the face and telling him to shut up and fuck off.

Tobias turned to Isabelle, and for what seemed like the first time in weeks, it felt like he wanted to speak *with* her, not *at* her. "You ever wonder what's really going on out there? I mean out *there*, the rest of the state, the country, hell, the rest of the world, even?"

If it wasn't so dark and she hadn't drunk so much earlier, looking back on this moment come morning, she would have sworn Tobias was tearing up. Isabelle tried to feign concern. Tobias had become so detached from her he wouldn't notice, anyway. She wasn't frightened, though she would play the part. "I try not to think about it too much. With the kids and all, I... Look, we have a good thing here, Tobias. Lots of friends, plenty of food. We're safe from those things."

"That's just it, Isabelle. I'm not sure how safe we really are." Tobias turned down the volume on the TV, just loud enough for Isabelle to stop worrying about Tommy waking. It was the same instructions displayed at all hours of the day: *do this, don't do that*. Isabelle touched her husband's hand, and he turned the television off altogether.

"The TV says the same shit it's been saying for days now, Izzy. We have seen nothing new in almost a week. For all we know, the TV station's equipment was left playing on a loop. They could have abandoned the place weeks ago, or worse."

Isabelle stared at Tobias for a moment. "Don't talk like that. If the kids hear you say those things, you'll scare the shit out of them."

"Good, it *should* scare them. We should all be scared. We, us, this whole goddamn town is not ready for the kind of attacks we saw on the news. If just a handful of those things ever made it over the berm unnoticed..." Tobias briefly paused. He looked to his wife, then out to the hallway leading to the children's bedrooms, and finally back to the black television screen.

"What are you saying, Tobias?"

"I'm saying we should take the kids and get the fuck out of this town."

11:15pm - Town Outskirts

Moonlight shone through the foliage, dotting the forest floor in random splotches of white. The contrast between light and dark played tricks on their eyes, but Danny was used to it. Growing up hunting these woods, you became familiar with the territory and conditions or went hungry. That was true now more than ever. Almost every night since the town went on lockdown, Danny brought an inexperienced hunter out into the forest to show them their way around a gun. Sometimes, if they were lucky, they would also be shown how to clean a kill. Just over a month ago, hunting this close to town would have been rewarded with a night in jail and a hefty fine. Things had changed.

Steven would have been nearly finished his junior year of high school had a region-wide epidemic not ground the everyday trappings of civilization to a halt. The boy drew a breath and exhaled slowly, his target in sight. A medium-sized doe grazed in the moonlight, its young fawn in tow. Under normal circumstances, shooting the younger deer would have been forbidden. Times were growing desperate, though, and every wild-caught meal took a little strain off of Thomas's farm. At least the doe would live to breed again. The fawn left alone would surely die. This catch, though modest, would feed many for days. Tonight's hunt was vital. The men lay in the dirt, waiting.

Steven had his shot lined up. Danny lay beside him in the dark, whispering soft words of encouragement. "That's it, kid. When it's in your sights and you think you're ready, take a breath, hold it, and slowly pull the trigger."

Steven was ready. The fawn was in sight. *All I have to do is squeeze the trigger and I'll be a hero, at least for a few days*, he thought. He would hand-deliver a portion of the spoils to Cindy Peterson. Her dad didn't like him very much, but too bad. No one turned down a free meal. Not now, at least.

The doe was in range. Steven remained calm and confident; it was time to prove himself.

A carrier burst from the shadows and latched onto Steven's arm. Danny rolled the opposite way and was quickly on his feet. In the distance, the deer disappeared into the night.

Steven screamed while jumping to his feet. "Shit!" Long hours lying prone cramped his legs. He quickly lost his balance, falling backward on top of the creature. His rifle discharged as they landed. "Oh God, help me! Help!"

Danny stumbled backward into a tree as the boy's rifle fired again. This time the bullet caught Danny in the throat. Steven was lying on his back on top of the infected, unable to escape its grasp as a second carrier appeared from the darkness. The infected beneath Steven latched its jagged teeth down on the boy's neck. Blood sprayed onto the thing's decaying face as it tore free a large section of meat. The second carrier, excited by the commotion, joined its companion and pounced atop the boy. This second one chewed ferociously on the soft flesh of Steven's exposed belly. The creature's ruined jagged teeth were like razors and easily dug a hole into the young hunter's stomach. Its prize reached, the infected gorged itself on the boy's warm, wet entrails.

Danny slid down the tree, clenching his throat and gasping for air. Blood escaped from his neck and mouth. His eyes went wide and his lips trembled. He could only watch as Steven struggled to free himself from his attackers.

Infected ravaged Steven's body, dislodging large chunks of flesh. His clothes and the ground beneath him were drenched in blood, making the soft earth even slicker than before. As the two infected struggled for dominance over their meal, Steven's warm intestines spilled out onto the cold forest floor. Steam rose from the boy's emptied cavity.

Danny's eyesight was fading as the torrent of blood from his neck dwindled to a trickle. Across from him, Steven's arm reached out. His fingers seemed to play in the soft dirt. The boy's lips still moved, trying to form words that Danny could not make out—a result of *his* weakened state or the boy's he would never know.

Danny willed himself to escape. A surge of adrenaline shot him to his feet, and he stumbled toward one of the rifles. Still clenching his gushing neck wound, Danny managed to run a few feet before collapsing back to the ground. He'd lost too much blood. The wounded man rolled onto his back, still clenching his neck. With his free hand, he reached up toward the full moon. In the clearing, its light accentuated the sticky crimson covering Danny's body. His arm felt like bricks and came down hard, back to the earth, slapping against a decayed, partially skinless foot.

The third carrier wasted no time chewing into the soft flesh of Danny's wounded neck. Danny struggled but to no avail; he was far too weak to fight. The infected bit off a mouthful of Danny's fingers in its quest for the man's warm crimson throat. Bloody nubs that moments ago were full digits scratched desperately at the attacker's face with no effect other than removing a few chunks of rotting flesh and the monster's ear. No longer strong enough to struggle, Danny fixed his eyes on the starry sky. The life drained from his body with a final spurt of blood onto his attacker's face. A pair of shooting stars caught Danny's attention as the world went black.

CHAPTER SEVEN

Conviction

Town Hall was filled beyond capacity; the majority of the residents of Pepperbush had gathered there in response to Danny's and Steven's deaths. An emergency meeting was called to debate town security and attempt to alleviate fears that the ever-looming regional crisis had finally reached their doorstep. Philadelphia, the closest hot spot and less than one hundred miles away, dominated most of their minds. By this point the populace had become desperate for anyone to calm their frayed nerves.

Mayor Donald Lancaster stood behind the podium at the front of a small stage, flanked by close associates on either side of him. Before him, packed in shoulder to shoulder stood a room full of nervous residents. He looked pompously down at the helpless masses, as he'd been known to refer to them, both figuratively *and* literally. He surveyed the crowd with contempt in his eyes, masked by an almost jovial demeanor. Behind a thick white mustache, the man wore a smug grin the likes of which could make the hardiest man in the room question his convictions. Mayor Lancaster portrayed himself as a sophisticated southern gentleman; the fact that he resided north of the Mason Dixon Line did nothing to dull the man's swagger. For twenty-four years Lancaster had been mayor of Pepperbush with very few instances of a challenger come election time, much less one that stood any chance of winning. A perfectly pressed white suit and matching bowler had become synonymous with any appearance from the man, no matter how trivial.

In such a laid-back town, it was easy for a silver-tongued former used-car salesman to gain a foothold in local politics. Upon the results of his first election, he never looked back, and through the years, the man acquired quite a few close associates. Lapdogs or cronies, as some more outspoken townsfolk referred to them. Joshua and Phillip had each been at Lancaster's side for more than two decades. Phillip was Pepperbush's only judge while Joshua owned the town's sole bank. And then there was Jim, the mayor's muscle. With an animal like that and two corrupt politicians on his payroll, it was no wonder half the town thought all but the first election was rigged.

Mayor Lancaster leaned into Joshua as the crowd settled. "Just a moment is all it should take to quell these savages." He smirked, his mustache hiding his disdain.

The crowd would have mostly been unable to read the men from across the room, though Joshua covering his mouth with his hand could have revealed the apathy Lancaster held toward the town's issues.

Lancaster tapped on the microphone as his cocksure grin receded. The microphone's feedback brought the majority of the room to attention. "Good people, let me begin by assuring you there is absolutely nothing to fear. We are in no more danger than we were last week or the weeks before that. An unfortunate incident befell our proud community this evening past, and as troubling as it may be for all of us. We must continue ever forward. Believe me when I say that I feel the loss of one of our own as deeply as the rest of you." Mayor Lancaster carried himself with a faux mournful tone most in attendance didn't read. Or they were simply too shaken up for it to register. "As far as those abominations are concerned, well, the occasional straggler does not herald the end of our community."

A few random claps and a "here-here" by Phillip helped drive the point home. As far as Mayor Lancaster was concerned, the entirety of the audience was with him.

"And a fine community it is, I might add," he continued. "Our walls are strong, our people resolute. We don't share the decadence and sin which brought this hell upon our fine nation's cities." Mayor Lancaster's tirade was cut short.

A faceless woman yelled from the crowd. "His name was Danny, and why don't you tell that to his sister, or did you even know his name?" Her outburst caused many who were silent to voice similar concerns.

"Have you seen the news lately? Baltimore's a mess."

"Philly doesn't look much better."

"I haven't seen my dog in a week."

"We're not safe here."

"You can't protect us."

Uninterrupted voices continued to express their concerns. Lancaster remained silent throughout the tirade, allowing Joshua to attempt damage control.

"This outburst is quite unnecessary. The lot of you, show your mayor the respect he has earned," Joshua fired back at the crowd. "We *will* have order."

Ever the statesman, Lancaster took the opportunity to mediate, even if it meant casually throwing Joshua under the bus.

"Oh, that's quite alright, Joshua. I understand the good people's concerns all too well." Lancaster returned his attention to the crowd, in particular the woman who initiated the outburst. "My dear, last evening's tragedy was an isolated incident to be sure. We all know the risks associated with hunting in the forest, especially at night."

Tobias interjected with a poor imitation of the mayor's dialect. "And that's why some of us don't hunt at all, sir. It is far too dangerous, right?" His imitation of the mayor's condescending tone and southern drawl resulted in a few nervous laughs from the crowd.

Standing at the back of the room, Sam smiled, slightly shaking his head back and forth in quiet approval. He was joined by Isaac, one of Pepperbush's scant few police officers.

Lancaster straightened himself immediately. His smug grin receded as he unfastened and rebuttoned his vest. "I beg your pardon, sir," the mayor fired back, practically condemning Tobias's ridicule.

Tobias stood. "With all due respect, Mr. Mayor, you haven't left Pepperbush town limits since the berm was put up. The truth of the matter is, we are seeing more and more of those things every week." Tobias held his hand up as if to gesture, *Now what?*

Someone else in the crowd stood, followed by another, and more still.

"Tobias is right, sir. My boy and I have put down six of them bastards in the last ten days." Glen's only son looked up as his uneasy father joined the slowly increasing number of citizens voicing their concerns.

"It wasn't very long ago when we might only see one of those things a week," another anonymous woman added, causing the crowd to once more erupt in protest.

Joshua stepped forward again. "People, people, calm down, please. Would you listen to yourselves?" He attempted to quell the crowd for a second time.

Lancaster patted his lackey on the back of his shoulder and again took the microphone. "Okay, okay, let's not cause a panic here today, Joshua." He pointed Joshua back to his seat. "These trying times are a burden for us all," Mayor Lancaster said. "We cannot let one isolated incident crumble our resolve as we have ample defenses in the berm and—"

The mayor was cut short as the seeming ringleader of the protest spoke again.

Tobias waved his arms at the crowd. His slow, deliberate gestures quieted the room. Finally, it seemed as though he had the attention of his peers. It was clear to him that these people only needed a slight nudge in the right direction. They could see through the mayor's deception; they only needed someone to speak for them. "Defenses which have never been properly tested, sir. I don't want my family to find out the hard way when hundreds of those things come pouring over the top of the berm in my sleep." Tobias looked around the room.

Curious, worried faces had given way to nods of approval. Slouched shoulders that betrayed a lack of confidence became stern, almost daring the mayor to continue his lies.

Mayor Lancaster's snide grin had given away completely to contempt at Tobias and all he was insinuating. "Let's not overreact now, sir. I am well aware that Mr. Danny was your close friend, and for that, I deeply apologize, but that is no reason to get these good people all riled up. Now, you must admit, hunting at night is a very foolish thing to do, especially in these cautious times we have found ourselves faced with. Can we at least agree upon that, Mr. Burke?" Lancaster stood his ground. This upstart had succeeded in dividing the room. The mayor knew damage control was his only remaining play.

"Spin it any way you like, Donald. Until *you* personally have to deal with one of these things, you quite frankly don't know what the fuck you're talking about." Tobias kept his eyes on Lancaster and his cronies, even as Jim rose from his whiskey stupor and took a few determined strides toward the edge of the stage.

Portions of the crowd applauded while others gasped. Most were silent as the mayor looked on in disgust, blushing from embarrassment.

Jim eyed the stairs at the far end of the stage that led down to the crowd. "If you don't like the way we do things here, boy, you know the way out of town."

Mayor Lancaster motioned for Phillip to halt the brute's progress. "Now, now, let's not get carried away here, Jim." He chuckled. "Mr. Burke is just scared and a little confused. Aren't you, son? Nobody's going to do anything

58

foolish, now are we?" Mayor Lancaster responded carefully while absorbing the crowd's reaction.

Tobias scanned the room, surveying the crowd. Eager eyes fell upon him, desperate for a fresh strategy or at least reassurance that everything would be okay. It was obvious to Tobias that many in town shared his misgivings of the berm and the false sense of security it afforded.

The mayor's lies were transparent and angered or frightened more than a few of those in attendance. They might not have spoken up very loudly, but it was written all over their faces. They were afraid and desperate for a new leader they could turn to, one they could rely on. Tobias realized he would never have as good of a chance again to gain the town's attention and, more importantly, its trust. Unless Tobias was willing to risk his family's safety all alone while on the road, he had to convince at least some of these people that he was right.

"That's exactly what I'm saying, sir. Your precious berm is pathetic, and I realize that people are trying as best they can, but our defenses are a joke. Pepperbush is a death trap waiting to happen. I'm taking my family as far away from here as possible." Tobias turned his attention from the mayor and back to his fellow citizens. "You've all seen the news. There haven't been any updates for a week now. Those stories on CNN, Fox, local—pick any one of them and they're playing on a loop for Christ's sake. Admit it or not, you know it's true. I'm willing to bet the TV and radio stations have been abandoned for days now. Hell, for all we know, the big cities are completely gone. No matter what Donald Lancaster or his cronies say or how much dirt they pile up, we *are not* safe here." Tobias turned and faced Mayor Lancaster. "My family and I are leaving Pepperbush. *Anyone* who wants to come with us is more than welcome."

Glen and his son stood. Glen was the salt of the Earth type. He was the guy who was always thinking about the next job and how to better use his time to get the most work squeezed out of every day that he could. He was a strong family man with strong values and unshakable ethics. Glen was asked by Tobias early on if he would be interested in picking up a shift or two on berm-perimeter duty. Surprisingly for Tobias, Glen declined. "Absolutely not" was Glen's response. Every minute he was away from his home, his wife and son could be in harm's way. The thought of leaving them alone even for a minute in this new world never crossed his mind, not for a second. His family came first, period. For the man to even be here now while half of his family was left at home without him there for protection revealed his concern over current affairs. "Where would we go, Tobias?" he asked with heavy eyes.

"Well, Glen, there are plenty of islands down south. If we can make it to the ocean and find a boat, I think we'd have a real shot at finding a safe place without any of the infected roaming around."

"What about a boat, Tobias. Where would we find one?" Vanessa's eyes went wide at the prospect of leaving Pepperbush for good and not on her own.

"Cape May Harbor, Vanessa. Hundreds of boats dock there at any given time, and it's only about a two-hour drive from here."

Jim snickered and returned to his seat. "Long as the roads are clear."

"If the roads aren't clear, we'll just have to take care of that ourselves, now won't we, Jim?" Tobias fired back. "The more people we have with us, the easier situations like that will be to handle *if* it even comes to that." Tobias returned his attention to the room. "For anyone who is interested, please do not hold back. Come talk to me. Most of you know where I live, and I'm on berm patrol every night for those of you that don't."

A large portion of the crowd seemed receptive to Tobias's plan.

"I'm in."

"When are we leaving?"

"Sounds good to me."

"Gonna need to check with the wife."

Mayor Lancaster was near shaking. His face flushed, his eyes wide, he turned to Joshua, who casually shrugged. Uncertainty had overtaken the man. He waved Joshua off as he returned his attention to the crowd and more specifically to Tobias. "Mr. Burke, I must protest. I simply cannot allow you in good conscience to up and leave Pepperbush under the guise of some hairbrained scheme. This entire endeavor is foolish and downright childish if you ask me." The mayor responded with a nod to his lapdogs, who stood and clapped. A desperate move by desperate men trying in vain to regain the room's trust. "Supplies and manpower is what *has* and what *will* continue to keep these people safe. Anything and anyone you would take with you on some grand journey to the sea would only serve to weaken this town's resolve."

"I didn't ask for and I don't need your permission, Donald. I'm leaving. My offer applies to everyone, including yourself, Mr. Mayor." Tobias turned back to the crowd. He held his opened palm high for all to see. "Five days." He looked around the room while flashing his hand high above his head for the benefit of anyone who didn't hear so well. "We are leaving in five days!" Satisfied that his point was made, but more importantly not wanting to overdo it, Tobias squeezed through the crowded room and exited Town Hall. Many sets of eyes followed him out the door as whispered conversations became a roar. The room was divided seemingly right down the middle as the people in attendance argued for or against Tobias's plan.

Mayor Lancaster's contempt for Tobias was unmistakable as he slammed his fist onto the podium and stormed off stage. He had lost control of the room. For the first time in a very long time, his smug grin was nowhere to be found. Joshua and Phillip scurried off as well, close on the heels of their master, while Jim remained on stage, his eyes affixed to a particular spot in the crowd.

During Tobias's tirade, when Vanessa spoke up, it caught Jim's attention. He stood there like a man possessed, staring at the woman. Had anyone been close enough they would have noticed spittle forming at the sides of his mouth or the slight bulge in his jeans as he watched her exit the small building. Preoccupied with the day's events, no one noticed Jim adjusting himself in full view of the audience. Most of the townsfolk were too busy filing out of the building and carrying on conversations of their own.

As the citizens emerged onto the streets, they continued talking among themselves. A new light was shone on their situation and most knew a tough decision lay ahead: stay in the relative safety of Pepperbush, hiding behind an untested defense, or join Tobias for an uncertain future on the road. At any rate, there wouldn't be much sleep tonight.

11:30 pm - Police Station

Marisol was losing the struggle as she dragged a heavyset man into a holding cell in the back of the police station. She was the opposite of frail. Her biceps were proof of that. Deadweight was difficult to move, no matter how strong you were. The unconscious man reeked of far too many days of heavy drinking and not nearly enough showers. Marisol didn' t have a clue where his clothes were. His dead weight made it nearly impossible for the woman to hoist him onto the cold metal slab. Just as well, those things weren't exactly the height of comfort in the bed department. She sat a bucket and a bottle of water beside him and covered him with a coarse blanket better suited to moving furniture than a peaceful night's rest. It was better than sleeping it off in the streets. Floyd was getting fall-down drunk on an almost nightly basis since the Berm went up. The implied cutting-off of the outside world hit the man harder than most. Marisol quickly turned her head and held her breath as he mumbled. So close to her face, his breath nearly made her vomit.

"I can't understand a word you're saying, Floyd." Marisol tucked a small pillow beneath his head.

"I'm sorry, Sheriff," he slurred, barely intelligible.

"Yeah, yeah, I know you are, Floyd. Just sleep it off. We'll talk about it in the morning." Marisol closed the cell door behind her. She didn't bother locking it.

"Ma'am, don't you want to be shutting that door proper?" Corey pointed to the cell door.

"Floyd's harmless, Corey. He'll wander out of here in the morning and we'll pick him up again in a few days. If that's how the man chooses to deal with this mess, who are we to argue?" She rubbed her hands together as if to signify that she had washed them of the responsibility. What was she supposed to do? Keep him locked up? Then what? Her wisdom wasn't exactly lost on the young police officer.

She reached for a bottle of hand sanitizer. The cool gel oozed between her fingers. One man's stench quickly washed away. If only the rest of her problems were so easily removed. Marisol inherited the position of sheriff of Pepperbush from the late John Ballard. Although not fully trained at the time of his passing, she had served as a deputy for so long working side by side with him that her confidence in her new position was well-founded. That sentiment was certainly shared among her fellow peace officers.

Mayor Lancaster, on the other hand, despised Ballard's grooming of Marisol as a replacement. His argument that she was too young, not to mention a woman, never registered with Ballard. Lancaster's disapproval of Marisol came down to one simple factor: her Hispanic heritage. Although clever enough to talk his way around it for his constituents, Lancaster's charm did not affect Ballard. After all, the two men were products of the turbulent sixties, both quite familiar with the ever-present racial divide of the times. If Lancaster insisted on clinging to that old-school racist dogma, so be it. Ballard would have no part of it. Marisol was the best officer for the job, period. Ballard knew it, the other officers knew it, and the citizens of Pepperbush not only loved her, but also respected her. A more qualified replacement simply did not exist.

At twenty-one years old, Corey was by far the youngest officer on Pepperbush's police force. He was a good kid and admired by his peers, the quarterback of his high school football team, and an Eagle Scout. Corey was the guy all the girls in town talked about and every mother wanted her daughter to date.

"How are you holding up, Corey?"

"As well as can be expected, ma'am, circumstances and all." Corey was double-checking the locks on the gun cabinets, a wary eye kept toward Floyd.

"Only a month out of the academy and the world goes to hell, huh? Didn't think it would be like this, did you?"

"Isaac's been showing me the ropes. I'll be honest, ma'am, aside from turning people away at the gate and the occasional infected that the guards miss, this whole peace officer gig has been a piece of cake." Corey smiled from ear to ear.

The young man's positive outlook was refreshing, though for his benefit, Marisol would never show it. "Don't get complacent, kid. We all saw Philadelphia and Baltimore on the news. If cities like that can self-destruct, it could happen anywhere."

"I guess you're right, Sheriff. It's just hard to imagine that kind of insanity coming to a small town like Pepperbush, is all." Corey shrugged.

Isaac interrupted, looking sullen like usual. His partner was away, visiting family in a DC suburb when the outbreak took hold of the East Coast. Shortly after quarantines were put into effect, he lost all contact. It had been nearly three weeks since his phone last rang. "No disturbances at the meeting, ma'am, although Tobias Burke seems adamant about us leaving town. He says it's not safe here anymore."

"Who's *us*?"

"Well, everyone, I assume. He left an open invitation for anyone in town who wants to form a caravan and head east to come talk with him."

"That couldn't have sat well with Mayor Lancaster." Marisol's brow furrowed.

"Oh, it certainly did not. He and the mayor got into a bit of a squabble. For the first time since I can remember, the mayor seemed to be almost at a loss for words," Isaac said with a smirk. His disdain for Mayor Lancaster was plain to see.

"Almost wish I could have seen the look on that pompous ass's face when he realized not everyone in Pepperbush is at his beck and call."

"It was a sight for sure. It may be advisable to keep an eye on Jim, though."

"How's that?"

"It may be nothing, but he and Mr. Burke had a few words. Nothing serious. It's just... I don't know. There's been something in that man's eyes since this whole thing started. Like I said, it's probably nothing. Just thought you should know."

"Instinct, Isaac. Instinct. Always go with your gut." Marisol looked at Corey and pointed to her head, then returned her attention to Isaac.

"I'll send Seth over to the Burkes' place in the morning. They're friends. If Tobias thinks he has a problem with Jim, I'm sure he'll let Seth know about it. Anything else I should be aware of?"

"That's about it, ma'am. Otherwise, it's been a pretty uneventful evening."

"Good to hear. I like uneventful. Isaac, before you go, have you heard anything from DC? Any headway on contacting Mitch?"

"No, ma'am, absolutely nothing. It's been nearly three weeks since I've heard his voice. To be honest, I'm beginning to fear the worst." Isaac lowered his head a bit and began flattening nonexistent creases in his pants.

Marisol held her hand on his shoulder for a moment until Isaac eventually met her gaze. "Hey, when it's just you and me, it's Marisol, okay? Forget that 'ma'am' bullshit. Keep your head up, Isaac. There's no reason to give up hope yet. Refugees are still showing up and we are nowhere near the big cities. The rescue centers around DC are probably filled to capacity. I'm sure Mitch is just fine. Give it time. You'll be reunited before you know it."

"Thank you, ma'am. If that's all, I think I'll be heading home for the evening."

"Get some rest, Isaac. I'll see you in the morning."

"Goodnight, Sheriff." Isaac closed the office door behind him.

Marisol sat down heavily into her chair. She wasn't lying; uneventful *was* nice, but the trick was keeping it that way. Of course, there was no way to guarantee things would stay calm, not before this mess and certainly not now. Your best bet was to ride it out, adjust course when need be, and get up when you fell down, but no matter what, through it all, you had to keep pressing forward. At least that was what she'd tell Corey. Remaining positive was one thing; being realistic was something else entirely. This town was in for a reckoning—she could feel it. The only question was, could she and a handful of police officers keep the peace if Pepperbush exploded?

1:48 am - Mother Leeds

Over at Mother Leeds, it was almost closing time. Vanessa was dead on her feet from another sixteen-hour shift. She tied off a couple of beer-soaked garbage bags and unlocked the back door. "Taking out some trash, sweetie. Be right back," she yelled to Markus, who was busy stacking chairs near the front of the bar. Vanessa dragged the heavy garbage bags over to the dumpster, dropped them in, and wiped the spilled beer off her hands onto her dirty jeans. The exhausted woman turned to head back when an arm yanked her from her feet into the darkened alley behind the bar. *This is it. Those things have already gotten into town*, she thought as she was slammed against the brick wall.

A thick forearm pinned her by her throat. She felt a sweaty hand inside her shirt and pawing at her breasts. This was no carrier.

Barely able to breathe or speak, she pleaded with her attacker. "Jim, please," Vanessa gurgled, clawing at the man's arm in vain.

"You gonna laugh at me now, bitch?" Jim pushed even harder on her throat.

"Can't breathe," Vanessa choked.

"Huh? What's that ya say? I can't hear ya. Not so uppity without Sam or your big black boyfriend around, are ya?" Jim slurred, eyes glazed over in a combination of alcohol and rage.

Vanessa couldn't respond; she struggled less and less, moments from blacking out.

"A whore like you. Yeah, yeah, you gonna like what old Jimmy got for ya." Jim pawed up and down Vanessa's back.

She struggled, but Jim had his free hand firmly on her ass. He used it to pull her close. His tongue greedily molested her neck and cheek, progressing further until at last he covered her mouth with his, desperately trying to pry her lips apart with his invasive tongue.

"Come a little closer, cock tease." Jim adjusted his grip, fumbling with one hand to force Vanessa's tight jeans a little lower. He suddenly stopped, released his grip completely while racing to protect his balls. He had left himself exposed.

Vanessa wasted no time crushing his manhood with a repeated barrage from her rock-hard knee. Her would-be rapist fell to the alley floor, writhing in the muck.

"You bitch. You fucking bitch," Jim cursed at Vanessa as she wound up and kicked him in the balls again.

"If you ever!" She kicked him in the balls once more and Jim vomited down the front of his shirt all over his fat belly. "Fucking touch me again!" She kicked him in the mouth, then pulled the beaten man up by his collar. She spat in his face before unleashing an avalanche of blows against his head. His nose exploded against her knee. Blood gushed as an open faucet poured down his face. "I'll fucking kill you!" She pushed him down hard. His head bounced off the pavement, knocking the beast unconscious.

He moaned once before she kicked him in the jaw a final time, sending two teeth tumbling beneath the dumpster. Satisfied the point was made for Jim to leave her alone, Vanessa backed out of the alley, leaving her unconscious attacker in the dirt. For the first time since the crisis began, Vanessa found herself hoping some carriers would find their way into town. Maybe they would clean up this mess.

Back in the bar, Vanessa slammed the door closed behind her and kicked the mop bucket across the floor.

"Hey, are you okay? What happened to you?" It was clear to Markus that Vanessa's disheveled appearance was not the result of simply taking out the garbage.

"I'm fine. Really, I am. Just had a scare, that's all."

"One of those things? An infected, in town?" Markus reached for an ax tucked behind the sink.

"No, nothing like that. I had another run-in with fucking Jim."

"That motherfucker!" Markus shouted. "I told that redneck piece of shit never to show his face again." He was heading toward the back door, ax in hand, but Vanessa stopped him mid-stride.

"No, no, no, don't worry about it. I took care of it this time. When he wakes up, he'll know what happened to him, and the last thing he'll want to do is talk about it. Trust me."

"You chased that fat prick off?"

"Damn right I did. And he's got the bruises to show for it. He won't be back anytime soon."

"That's my girl." Markus pulled her in for a one-armed hug while still clenching the ax, his attention fixed firmly on the back door.

CHAPTER EIGHT

Blackout

Vanessa was home by 3:00 a.m. After she convinced Markus not to take the ax out behind Mother Leeds and put Jim down like a wild dog, *he* convinced *her* to reach out to Marisol. The sheriff came alone; she was furious, so much so that she didn't bother to put her uniform on. She cuffed Jim so tight his hands were beet-red before she had him in her squad car. Markus got the impression that Marisol would have preferred to put a bullet in the grotesque filth right there on the spot, throw him in the dumpster, and be done with it. Instead, she drove Jim out beyond town limits and left him at an abandoned local convenience store with the stipulation that if she ever saw him again, that it would be the last time anyone did. Perhaps she went easy on him, but if she set the precedent now that vigilante justice would not only be tolerated but would be carried out by those sworn to uphold the peace, and by Pepperbush's sheriff no less, that could open the floodgates for the town's citizenry to put the rule of law aside. Pepperbush could slide into lawlessness no better than a Wild West frontier town.

The first thing Vanessa did was shower, always, though tonight's was more significant than usual. She would cleanse away not only the grime from another long day, but with it, the burden of Jim's misplaced ire was washed away as well. Vanessa was able to reset, to begin anew. She toweled off and stood in front of the mirror, leaning heavily on the sink for support.

Dark bags under her eyes grew more pronounced daily. She couldn't keep going like this. Something had to give. Her hands were already sore from the beating she gave her attacker, her knuckles cut up and bruised. By morning, her hands would be near useless. She discarded her towel and slipped into a T-shirt, another item atop a growing pile of dirty laundry. One more chore added to the list of jobs to take care of with no time in which to do them.

Only one beer left in the fridge, fuck. She meant to bring some home, but with the evening's drama, it was no wonder she forgot. Leaving it behind was probably for the best, as inventory was running catastrophically low at Mother Leeds. At the rate things were going, she would be completely out of booze before month's end. Food, too, for that matter.

The couch accepted her; she fit perfectly in the indent worn in after years of habit. Vanessa cracked her knuckles before turning on her laptop and opening the game in her browser. It was loading; somehow, she still had Internet access. She had no clue how it was even possible when a good eighty percent of the web was down. More often of late, a well-known poster would disappear. After a few days, the group would stop talking about them, none wanting to admit what they all knew. Whoever it was on the other end either had to flee or they were dead, although some held the hope that maybe the poster's power grid finally shut down and everything was otherwise fine. If anything, the back and forth became a way to talk themselves out of the fact that another friend was gone for good. Her heart sank when the screen read, "Two other members currently logged on. Zero guests."

PprBsh84: hey guys
69kilr69: sup
spArkLe: good to c you r still here
69kilr69: shits bad just been us all day
PprBsh84: damn guys what happened
69kilr69: you know
PprBsh84: I guess I do dont i
spArkLe: the last time 1313 was here she said she couldnt wait to

Vanessa's screen went black along with the rest of her house. For a fleeting moment, she assumed that Jim was responsible and armed herself. He couldn't be. It was impossible; he was miles away. It wasn't until she reached a second-floor window with the best vantage point over her property that she accepted that it wasn't Jim at all. Her entire street was out. As far as she could see, it was pitch-black everywhere. Not a light shone in town. Pepperbush had finally lost power.

4:10 am - Security Headquarters

Although not very ambitious, Ron was meticulous to a fault. He was never one to follow through on ideas of his own, and this had always been a sore spot for his family, his wife in particular. However, place a problem in front of the man, and he would grind out the details night and day until the issue was solved. When Sam suggested a separate security force be set up in the wake of the Baltimore-DC quarantine, Ron immediately began the process of interviewing potential candidates. His intimate, almost investigative interviewing style worked well in establishing which applicants truly felt the need to help from those who merely wanted a free gun and a little authority or simply an excuse to get away from their families for a few hours a day.

Within forty-eight hours, Ron had a list of more than two dozen candidates for Sam to assemble his security force from. The idea behind this team was to have a separate entity not hampered by town politics, the safety of Pepperbush its only concern. Of course, this incensed Mayor Lancaster to no end. The idea of an independent group of locals brandishing weapons and answerable to themselves only was, in his eyes, the earliest stages of a coup.

Marisol and the police, on the other hand, welcomed the idea with open arms. Since the earliest days of the outbreak, her small band of police officers and her sole deputy, Seth, had been overwhelmed, be it from bored locals fighting with refugees or Ms. Reynolds insisting that someone was breaking into her house every night at three in the morning. Cabin fever had set in and its symptoms had quickly spread. Stretched as thin as she was, Marisol welcomed the extra hands. Hell, she even encouraged it.

All fourteen volunteers for the security detail were handpicked by Sam himself, with a little nod this way or that from Ron's fastidious stack of notes. The security force quickly became more than a simple perimeter sweep. In addition to overseeing the refugee-acclimation process, Sam took charge of the berm project as well. Although vocal during the initial planning stages that such a structure wasn't a viable long-term solution, he conceded that for the time being the berm was better than nothing. The project would also give Pepperbush's residents something to think about and discuss other than the growing crisis only a few hours away in nearly

69

W.J. Hegarty

all directions. With Sam and his security force working in tandem with Marisol and the police, the citizens felt a sense of safety not shared since before the outbreaks began.

The security office itself was nothing more than a repurposed post office. No mail was coming or going, so why not put the place to use? It had plenty of space and was secure. Three men stood watch out front, ready at a moment's notice to receive direction or help when the need arose. Inside, Sam and Ron discussed how to better utilize the resources they had instead of requesting more, should the need arise. The conversation was cut short when the lights went out.

Pepperbush went black from Town Hall to Main Street. Every light in town was out. Within moments, the roar of a handful of personal generators starting up cut through the silence.

"Man, that was fast, Sam. Some of these people never sleep."

"Do you blame them?"

"Can't say that I do, but I'm not sure all that noise is such a great idea."

"You're probably right. Grab a few of the boys and send them door to door. Tell them to pass along that we need to conserve fuel and save the generators until we have a better idea of what's going on. And for God's sake, make sure they don't start shooting at everything that moves."

"I'm on it, Sam." Ron rushed out of the building and waved for a group of the men to join him.

Sam's radios had battery backup, so his men staying in contact wouldn't be an issue. His radio buzzed with static before revealing Bernie's voice from the other end.

"Hey, Sam, everything went dark up here by the gate. How's it look on your end?"

"We lost power, Bernie. That's all. The whole town did by the looks of it. We knew this was coming sooner or later. Nothing to get too excited over."

"Roger that. I'll get back to my rounds then. If you need me, just holler." Bernie tucked his radio away. His trek's halfway point, the gate, was within sight.

4:40 am - Burke Residence

At the northernmost section of Pepperbush, the Burke residence and its entire street were just as dark as the rest of town.

Isabelle was awake when the power failed; it put a smile on her face. Tobias would wake and leave, thinking he was some kind of hero of the

70

people if he ran around town barking orders and looking concerned. *Fine, they can have him*, she thought. *I prefer to be alone, anyway.* Spiteful, she lay there unmoving for close to a half an hour before waking her husband to inform him of current events. The idea of him having to play catch-up when the situation was already under control was amusing. "Tobias, wake up. The power's out! I've been trying to wake you for ten minutes, but you wouldn't budge."

Tobias leaped to his feet. He pulled aside a curtain and peered out into the darkness.

"The whole street's out. Stay calm, Izzy. We knew this was coming! Check on the kids. I'll find candles and make sure everything's fine outside." Tobias hastily dressed and disappeared out of the room.

She wouldn't see him again for hours. With any luck, he'd pass out sometime around noon at Sam's ridiculous security shack. *Thank Christ*, she thought. Isabelle threw the covers off and felt her way down the hallway to the kids' rooms. For Tobias to assume that she was worried or scared just increased her annoyance. *Treat me like I'm your fucking equal, you prick. You wouldn't talk to Sam like that.*

Lillian's room was the first in line. Isabelle palmed the door's handle and paused. Their daughter hated being barged in on. Privacy was a big deal for her, and being twenty-two years old, she didn't want to live with her parents, anyway.

A part of Isabelle wished Lillian never even came back from school. Had she not been home on holiday when the crisis hit, she would have been stuck on campus. It might have been safer than Pepperbush. *If the girl wants her privacy, she can have it.* Isabelle released the doorknob and moved on to her son's room. Tommy was only six years old, young enough that he shouldn't be left alone these days but old enough to know that something was wrong. People weren't acting the same anymore; he took notice early. Isabelle quietly crept into his room where he was already awake and staring intently at his door.

"Those bad men are here, Mommy." Tommy was almost in tears. He sat alone on his bed, wrapped in a sheet. A tiny flashlight inside illuminated his makeshift tent.

"No, they're not, honey. Daddy and his friends chased them all away. The lights went out. That's all." Isabelle crouched down to better see into the tent.

"They're not coming?" he asked while rubbing the sleep from his eyes.

"Not tonight. I promise. There's nothing to be afraid of, sweetie." She attempted to reassure the child.

"Don't leave, Mommy. Sleep in here tonight," Tommy pleaded.

"Okay, sweetheart, I will. Scoot over." Isabelle squeezed into the tiny bed.

Snuggled up tightly next to his mother, Tommy wrapped his little arms around her waist. With his mother inside the tent along with the flashlight, Tommy felt a little more at ease, and as soon as his dad returned home, he knew he would be safe again.

4:54 am - The Gate

At nearly five in the morning, Bernie was halfway through his shift patrolling the berm. Bernie was tall, lanky, and maybe a little disheveled. He had the look of clumsiness about him but wasn't usually. No one wanted to pull graveyard shift, but he would much rather sleep during the relative safety of daytime hours, anyway. His motives for seeking the overnight shift weren't wholly selfish, though, as he realized that most others who saw to this aspect of town security had families to look after. Spending as much time as possible with loved ones was more important now than ever, he believed. He came upon the berm's sole gate. It was nothing more than a school bus reinforced with corrugated metal that blocked a ten-foot-wide gap in the berm. The edges of the earthen fortification were held in place at either end of the exit with lines of six-by-six timbers cemented into the ground.

"Now's a good a time as any to take a leak." Bernie made sure the shoulder strap on his rifle was securely in place before undoing his pants.

The zipper on his favorite pair of jeans was always getting stuck. It was a pain in the ass to deal with, but he'd never throw these things out, as worn-in and comfortable as they were. At last, he was free, and not a moment too soon, he let his stream go on the bus's tire not half a second after getting it out of his pants. Relaxed for a moment, he took a second to stretch his neck, rolling the back of his head across his shoulder blades from one side of his back to the other, joints cracking along the way. He opened his eyes for a quick look at the stars. They seemed to shine a little brighter these days, or maybe he just never took the time to look at them before. Movement caught his eye, and he dared not breathe. Standing on top of the bus, directly above him, a blackened figure stared back, it too frozen in place.

"Oh shit," he shouted on reflex and cursed himself for the mistake. Bernie fell back on his ass, his stream arcing in the air with him. He was up quickly and darting toward an adjacent alley, one hand fumbling to pull his wet pants up, the other haphazardly aiming his rifle. A single shot rang out from his weapon. The round deflected harmlessly off the side of the bus, missing its intended target by at least a car length. A second shadowy figure rose in the darkness, followed by another. Within seconds, as far as he could tell, half a dozen more were on top of the bus.

Bernie tripped over a trash can as he dove into the alley. His bare thighs scraped against the pavement. At that point, he had forgotten about his pants entirely and was busy fumbling with his gun. He took a second to catch his breath and calm his trembling hands. Peeking around the corner, he saw that a sizable group now stood motionless atop the bus. The frightened man whispered into his radio. "Sam, are you there?" Bernie stammered.

"Right here, son. How does it look out there tonight? It's pretty dark, I reckon?"

"Goddammit, Sam! I need backup at the gate right fucking now!"

"Easy now, Bernie. What do you see?" Sam snapped his fingers for Ron's attention.

"They're getting over the gate, man! They're getting over the goddamn gate!" Bernie bellowed.

Sam turned to Ron, who was already peering through binoculars out into the darkness. "Where is he? Can you see him from here?"

"Too dark, Sam. I can't even make out Mother Leeds, much less the gate."

"Bernie, you still there? Answer me dammit!"

Tobias slammed the door to the security building shut behind him. "Sorry about that, Sam. The wind caught it. I thought I'd swing by and see what's going on. The power is out up at the north end. The whole town's out, I take it?"

Ron answered for Sam. "Yeah, that's what it looks like. Other than that, it was quiet until a minute ago."

"What's going on?" Tobias removed his jacket and placed his rifle on the rack with the others.

"Bernie just called in. Says he sees something out by the gate. It's probably just his nerves, power out and all," Ron suggested.

Tobias reclaimed his rifle as fast as he had set it down. Sam took notice while again trying to raise Bernie over the radio.

Bernie remained backed against the nearest wall, lying in the muck and filth of the alley. He finally managed to pull his pants mostly back up. Not an easy task with only one soaked hand as he held his rifle in a death grip with the other. All the while he never took his eyes off the shadows on the bus. He peered through his scope, but it was too dark to make out anything more than the stirring of vague shapes in the darkness.

"Sam, I've got five—no, no, no, make that seven. I've got seven carriers climbing over the bus," Bernie sputtered into his radio.

"Do not shoot them, Bernie! Do you hear me? Do not fire your weapon!" Sam ordered.

"They're climbing down! Sam, they're getting in. I gotta do something!" Bernie's radio turned on and off repeatedly as he struggled between his rifle and communicating with Sam.

Sam was exasperated at Bernie's apparent lack of reasoning. He holstered a sidearm and slung a rifle over his shoulder as he headed for the door. "Is that guy fucking kidding me, Ron? Infected can't climb the side of a goddamn bus!" Sam yelled, his radio still open for Bernie's benefit.

Bernie was confused as he listened to Sam over on his end. Bernie was cognizant enough to realize that, yes, he *was* panicking, but he *must* have heard Sam wrong.

"Hold your goddamn fire, Bernie! I'm coming down there. Do not shoot anything! Do you copy?"

"But, Sam..." Bernie whimpered after dropping his radio in the muck, frozen.

Ten yards from Bernie, the dark figures began dropping from the top of the bus and spreading out.

Rifle in hand, Sam darted out of the security office in a mad dash for the gate, yelling into his radio the whole time. Tobias and Ron followed. They checked their weapons and made for the gate as well.

"Hold your position, Bernie! Don't do anything until I get there. I'm on my way!" Sam shouted.

"I know I can hit one of them from here. I can maybe get two more before I gotta make a run for it," Bernie whispered.

"Those aren't carriers down there, man!" Sam screamed into his radio.

Bernie squinted hard, trying to better see into the shadows as the dark figures quickly closed in on his position.

"Are you listening to me, Bernie? For God's sake, man, you're looking at survivors!"

The shadowy, dark shapes dropped one by one from the top of the bus and formed up defensive positions in the vicinity of the gate. Nine battle-worn soldiers trained their weapons on the terrified man. Bernie climbed to his feet out of the filth with his hands raised in surrender. His rifle fell to the ground along with his pants, exposing his shriveled manhood again to the cold night air.

The lead soldier moved forward, his AR-15 trained squarely on Bernie, inches from the man's forehead. "Who's in charge here?"

W.J. Hegarty

CHAPTER NINE

Reality

Just before sunrise, the soldiers were being treated to a warm meal courtesy of Grace. The dining room of her bed-and-breakfast was devoid of customers this early in the morning. Mayor Lancaster, Tobias, and Marisol had relentlessly questioned them since their arrival in town less than two hours prior, Sam silently observed. The soldiers were ragged and worn out. Weeks of fighting this unconventional enemy had taken its toll on them, and it showed. What remained of their gear after the long trek to Pepperbush was in shambles. None of them were kitted-out by that point. Only three tactical vests made it this far: they had abandoned most of their gear along the way.

"Could I top off your coffee, Mr. Takashi?" Grace asked.

"Please, ma'am." Takashi held his empty mug out for the old woman with a slight nod. For a moment, the older soldier closed his eyes. "Thank you, Grace."

His gesture didn't go unnoticed to the old woman; she smiled back and poured the cup. Her coffee pot clinked against his ceramic mug. It took both of her hands and most of her concentration to pour the hot liquid without spilling any.

Takashi steadied her shaking hands with his. "Don't worry, ma'am. Everything will be fine." He limped back toward his unit. His fatigues were torn open at the knee, and bloody bandages showed through. They were wrapped around the majority of his lower thigh.

Takashi's unit consisted of a ragtag group of nine soldiers culled from the remnants of various branches of the United States military and even a lone member of the IDF. This unlikely group was forced together in a mad dash to flee the overwhelmed and overrun city of Philadelphia. All of their dress and gear—what was left of it—looked like it had been through the wringer. The lot of them were filthy from combat and living off of the land or out of abandoned structures. Those who could all sported new beards of varying lengths and thickness.

Radzinski was the lone Marine of the group. He was tall, broad, and muscular. Gruff in appearance with the bad attitude to match. "The reality of your situation is that you people think you're safe, but you're not." He leaned over his plate like a bear, shoveling more food into his mouth as he continued his criticism of Pepperbush's defenses. "Let me ask you something, Sheriff. How many of those things have you had to put down at once? Three, six, a dozen? Wow, try liberating a stadium full of refugees just to find out they've all been dead for a week."

"That's one of the perks of living in a small town," Marisol added.

"And what's that, sweetheart?" Radzinski didn't bother to look at the woman as he spoke. Instead, he continued to gorge himself as fast as Grace could offer more food.

"One upside is that we don't have to deal with strange assholes very often."

Radzinski raised his head from his plate and smiled wide. A small sliver of bacon hung from his lips. "Hey, hey, check it out. I like this one. You got a little fire in you, huh, senorita?" He nudged Garrett, who chuckled at the exchange.

Sam crossed his arms in quiet contemplation.

Visibly shaken by Radzinski's comments, Grace nervously offered the soldiers more breakfast. "Would... Would anyone care for some more eggs or bacon?"

Takashi spoke for the group. "No, thank you, ma'am. This was more than enough."

Most of Takashi's unit acknowledged the hint and rose from the table without hesitation, though a couple were slower on the uptake. One in particular had a few more thoughts he needed to get off his chest.

Still not finished his rant, Radzinski shoved his plate away. His utensils tumbled to the floor. "Thousands of those things came pouring out of that fucking stadium. They're slow, sure, but you get enough of those bastards piling up and your fucked. When we opened that door, six men got swallowed up before we could even get a single shot off."

By then, the rest of the soldiers had finished eating. A couple of them had already left the establishment.

Radzinski poured himself a cup of coffee and lit up a cigarette before continuing. "By the time we got reorganized, five more of us were down or compromised."

Tobias interrupted. "Compromised?"

Miller spoke up. He was unkempt from weeks in the field and on the run. His fatigues were singed. The burns stopped just below a blood-spattered brown T-shirt. "Yeah, compromised. That's what we call it when someone gets bitten."

"I hate that fucking term," Radzinski said. "You get bit, I'm putting a fucking bullet in your head. End of discussion."

Garrett gave a somewhat approving shrug and a nod in Radzinski's general direction on his way out the door. Garrett was a peer of Takashi's who was working as an instructor prior to the crisis. Now he was only one of a handful of beat-up soldiers who were lucky enough to make it out of Philadelphia alive, and he had the road-wear to prove it.

"See, I'm not alone in this, Miller." Radzinski felt vindicated by the older soldier's silent approval. "If it comes to it and I have to put you down, no hard feelings."

"No one's saying you are alone. I just think these people have heard enough for now, Radzinski."

"Well, I don't think they have," Radzinski fired back. "What do you think's gonna happen when they get a few hundred of those dead motherfuckers piling up on that pathetic dirt pile out there, huh?"

"I don't know, but right now's not the time to discuss this."

Everyone else in the room went quiet. Tobias and his fellow Pepperbush natives were curious as to where the two soldiers' conversation was heading.

Takashi could sense that some of their hosts were anxious, even frightened. Grace appeared on the verge of a nervous breakdown and was barely holding it together. "That's enough, Marine. Everyone, fall out. Get some rest. God knows you've earned it."

"Yes, sir," the Marine and the Army captain responded in unison.

Miller and Radzinski collected their belongings and headed for the exit. Miller shook his head in disgust at Radzinski's outburst.

Radzinski insisted on having the last word. "What? Do something."

Jeremiah remained quiet throughout the meal, silently assessing their situation all while rubbing a crucifix between his fingers. He was brought up in a very religious town in the south. He was raised the son a preacher of a Gospel Church, so faith had always played a significant role in the medic's life, though the hell he'd experienced over the last few weeks had shaken that faith to the core. On his way out of the bed-and-breakfast, Jeremiah yanked his crucifix from his neck. "Why have you forsaken us?" he whispered, the words barely audible as he hung his grandmother's crucifix on a cross by the door.

One by one, the soldiers filed out of Grace's place while expressing their gratitude for the meal and hospitality.

Before Takashi could leave, Sam pulled him aside. "A minute of your time, Colonel?"

"What can I do for you, sir? Sam, right?"

"How long?" Sam asked sternly.

"I'm not sure I understand your meaning." Takashi's response was not very convincing.

"How long did it take you and your men to get here?"

"You have to understand, sir, we were moving at a pretty good pace and those things tend to be slow, very slow."

Sam stopped the colonel mid-sentence. "How long?" he insisted.

Takashi remained silent for a moment before answering. He knew what he wanted to say but thought it best to wait a few hours and let the shock of a group of soldiers randomly showing up wear off. *The hell with it*, he thought. Full disclosure was agreed upon before they even set foot in Pepperbush. Telling them now or later really made no difference in the grand scheme of things. "Twenty-four to thirty-six hours."

Mayor Lancaster ceased his eavesdropping. "Jesus H. Christ, you led them right to us. We would have been just fine if you hadn't shown up!" he shouted. "I told you people we were just fine. No outsiders, no problems. Now look."

Just outside the door, Radzinski heard the exchange and decided it best to insert himself into the conversation. "Excuse *me,* sir, but we didn't even know you people were here." Radzinski pointed at the mayor.

Takashi picked up the conversation. "We were about five klicks out when we saw your lights."

Radzinski couldn't help himself; he got in the mayor's face. "We went out of our way to come warn you people. Shit, for all we knew, you were already dead. Just so we're clear and to avoid any misunderstandings, if it was up to me, we would have kept going."

Miller returned as well. "That's why it's not up to you."

Takashi pointed at the door. "Stand down, Marine. That's enough! You *will* maintain discipline. I told the both of you to fall out. I won't say it again." Takashi continued as his men complied in silence. "There was no way of knowing if the carriers following us would have passed you by or if they would have been drawn to your location. We couldn't take that chance."

Mayor Lancaster had a suggestion of his own in light of this newest revelation. "I think it best if we keep this little turn of events to ourselves—only for the time being, of course. Wouldn't you agree, gentlemen?"

His subordinates were quick to agree, offering reasons of their own why the townsfolk should be kept in the dark. Takashi and his unit had other plans for Pepperbush, it seemed.

Takashi replied without missing a beat. "Absolutely not. These people have the right to know exactly what's going on and that they need to protect themselves accordingly."

Tobias was overflowing with contempt for the mayor. "What part of imminent danger isn't registering with you?"

Jeremiah addressed the mayor as well. He had a monotone, clinical way of speaking. His fellow servicemen often called him a robot for it. "Perhaps you weren't listening. Colonel Takashi told you that your home could be hours away from attack and you would hide this information from your community?"

Mayor Lancaster attempted to save face. "No disrespect implied, Colonel. I was merely suggesting that we don't cause a panic, is all. Why don't we talk about this a little further before jumping into commitments that can't be undone?"

"No offense taken," Takashi said. "I plan to formally address your town in a few hours. I would appreciate it if you didn't make me go door to door with what I have to say."

Marisol spoke on the town's behalf. "Consider it done, sir." She radioed back to the police station, entirely disregarding Mayor Lancaster's thoughts on the matter.

Sam offered assistance as well. "I'll give my people a heads up. They'll help spread the word." He nodded for his men who were in attendance.

"We're on our way, Sam," Tobias said as he and Ron left.

Sam turned to Takashi. "Does 9:00 a.m. at Town Hall work for you, Colonel?"

"Thank you, Sam, 9:00 a.m. it is," Takashi added with a look of contempt in the mayor's direction.

Mayor Lancaster went ignored. His fellow townsfolk and these new strangers alike were making plans for *his* town and leaving him no say in the decision-making, all right in his face. He stormed out of the bed-and-breakfast, cursing under his breath. His cronies followed quickly behind him. The group of would-be elder statesmen pushed past Rachel.

She was another of Takashi's unit, a bubbly, short-haired redhead. Her arm was bandaged up at mid-bicep, and red bled through the wrappings. "What was that all about?" Rachel asked. She might or might not have purposely gotten in his way, pretending to not see him as she picked food scraps from her teeth.

"Our esteemed mayor thinks he knows what's best for *his* town," said Marisol.

"His town?" Rachel chuckled.

"Very little happens around here without his say so."

"Interesting." Rachel's eyes followed the mayor out of the room.

Soraya leaned against the wall outside of Grace's place, one leg tucked up behind her on the wall. Her fatigues and ragged brown tank top looked as if she had fallen in a mud pit. Her tight bun was bedraggled, and stray hairs fell in her face and down her back. She carved an apple and fed herself the slices from the blade, all the while staring with contempt at the mayor and his lackeys as they passed. She caught enough from the conversation with Mayor Lancaster to begin forming a picture of the man in her mind. "Piece of shit," Soraya said in Hebrew with a glare that could have burned a hole straight through the man.

Though Mayor Lancaster couldn't understand the foreign language, he knew well enough from the inflection that she wasn't introducing herself. He hesitated for the briefest of moments but thought better of the exchange and continued on his way. He didn't even bother with one of his usual quips, although he would certainly commit her face to memory.

Standing beside Soraya was Aiko, a Navy medic. She was tending to a wound in the Israeli's side while her patient casually ate. Aiko wore a long, straight black ponytail that was caked solid with dried blood. The mess soaked through her clothes and left a reddish-brown trail down the back of her white T-shirt.

Like Miller's, both Soraya's and Aiko's pants were burned, leaving them with intact but still dirty and blood-soaked shirts, almost as if the trio had been on fire and had to abandon their tops and gear.

"Let him be, Soraya. He's just scared. In shock, most likely."

"You are probably right, Aiko, as usual."

The Roaming

The youngest and final member of Takashi's unit, Broderick, exited the building in time to catch the near exchange. He was the cleanest of the group, though not by much. "Old-timer probably thought they would be safe out here in the middle of nowhere. Shit, I would have."

"I am not so sure. Something about him I do not like," Soraya replied. "I do not trust his look."

W.J. Hegarty

CHAPTER TEN

A Warning

From all outward appearances, Emily's general store looked like it had been looted. What little supplies remained were spread all over. The noonday sun peeked through dusty windows, highlighting antiques and collectibles used for trade in recent weeks, which were piled up in no discernible order. It was hard to imagine that an old woman in the earliest stages of Alzheimer's could operate a business alone, but she managed. Surprisingly enough, no one took advantage of her diminished capacity, even in these uncertain times. The piles of items left in trade were a testament to that. Family heirlooms and irreplaceable items of sentiment littered her store, having been traded off for one last round of vital supplies.

Isabelle browsed the offerings while shaking her head in frustration as Tommy sat in an aisle and played with an antique wooden toy car. Isabelle was fond of Emily. The sweet old woman had been kind and gentle for as long as she could remember. As a child, she visited this very same shop with her own mother. Even then Emily seemed old. Ancient, really. Watching Emily's mind slip away these last few years upset her. She had always been patient and understanding with the old woman, but lately, with all that was happening, Isabelle had lost most of her patience for Emily's dementia. "Useless junk. Why didn't I get down here days ago?" she reprimanded herself, placing a turn-of-the-century oil lamp back on the shelf.

"What's that, honey? Not much left, I'm afraid," Emily said apologetically as she slowly made her way to a flashing neon open sign in the front window. "Not much sense leaving this on, I suppose." Emily unplugged the sign and locked the front door.

"Any idea how long until the power will be back on, Emily?" Isabelle asked, not expecting an answer.

"No one's sure, honey. Word around town is it could stay on for another month or five more minutes," Emily said as she plugged the sign back in and unlocked the door.

"What happened? I was just here Tuesday and you had plenty of things left. And where's Thomas's produce and all the venison? There was more than enough to go around."

"Well, between the power failure and those soldiers arriving last night, the whole town seemed to panic. Did you know there was a line around the corner when I opened up this morning?"

"No, I didn't know that, Emily. How could I?" Isabelle said sarcastically.

"That's okay, dear. How could you?"

Isabelle shut her eyes. If she tried hard enough, she could just barely manage to tune the old woman out long enough to collect her thoughts.

"I'm expecting a truck in the morning anyway, but don't tell anyone, dear. I want it to be a surprise. Carlos is here every Friday with my order. He hasn't had a day off in thirty years, bless his heart."

"Oh, okay. Well, I'll come back tomorrow then." Isabelle was not in the mood to humor the senile old woman. Everyone in town was well aware there were no more trucks coming. Not tomorrow and not next week, either. As far as Isabelle was concerned, there were no more trucks coming, period.

Isabelle and Tommy walked down Main Street. She would have preferred to drive over taking the forty-minute walk each way, but Tobias didn't want to waste the fuel. Just in case, he would say. She rarely argued over those matters; the logic wasn't lost on her, though she didn't have to like it. Isabelle's gray spaghetti-strap dress blew in the breeze, whipping around and snapping at the air. Of course, Tobias warned against wearing something so impractical on the off chance they needed to up and leave town at a moment's notice. They wouldn't have time for her to change into something that offered a little more protection. *Whatever, Tobias*, she imagined. *Go play town savior with your friends. I'll wear whatever the fuck I feel like wearing since you've left me to play single parent.*

They turned off Main Street and walked through an alley beside Bob's Hardware, the usual shortcut back toward the northernmost cluster of homes. Two college-aged men followed closely behind, their obnoxious conversation broadcast for all to hear.

"Yo, last night was crazy, bro. I told you to come out," the louder of the two said.

"Shit, man, my mom was being stupid, whining about it not being safe. I wasn't trying to hear that shit, dude. I said fuck it and went to bed," the other replied, already disappointed that he missed out before even hearing the story.

"Ah, you missed it, bro. All night those chick bartenders were doing belly shots off each other. I'm telling you, it was hot as fuck, dude."

"Oh man, goddammit! See, I knew I should have come out anyway. Fucking bullshit."

"Yeah, I'm telling you, man, a few more drinks and they'd have been going down on each other right fucking there in front of everybody. Dude, and when they started making out, I swear—" The louder one's anecdote was cut short.

Isabelle turned and grabbed the kid by his collar, slamming him against the brick wall. An arm to his throat, a hand firmly clenched his balls. She squeezed hard while pressing against his neck. Tears welled up at the corners of his eyes. Isabelle's face was twisted in a sudden fit of rage, eyes wide, face flushed. She breathed heavily in the young man's face. Her warm breath oozed over his cheeks and mouth. Her teeth were so close to the boy's skin he was sure that, any moment now, this woman would tear into his flesh just like one of those things on TV. "That's my daughter you're talking about, you little piece of shit," Isabelle growled.

The second boy promptly backed away from her. "What the fuck? Let him go, lady. You're hurting him," he pleaded. "Stop!"

"Stop?" Isabelle snarled. "I haven't even started yet. Shut your mouth or you're next." She returned her attention to her prey. "Even think about her again and I'll rip these little things off. Do you hear me?" She clamped down harder and began to twist. The corner of her lip quivered as the boy trembled beneath her grasp.

The loud boy whimpered as his legs gave out from beneath him. She followed him to the ground, clamping harder and harder on her target for the duration. Isabelle released her hold a few seconds after he hit the pavement. The loud boy immediately scrambled to his feet, assisted by his friend. Then the two quickly ran off.

"You fucking crazy bitch," the second boy yelled back as they disappeared down an alley, away from Main Street.

Isaac caught the tail end of Isabelle's altercation while stopped at an adjacent streetlight. He wasted no time rushing to Isabelle's side. "Everything alright, Isabelle?" He scanned the alley for signs of the young men Isabelle chased away.

"Oh, it's fine, Isaac. Just a couple of kids that don't know when to shut their mouths."

"Okay then. Well, no harm, I guess. Where you headed?"

"Back home. Grace's store's been ransacked. I guess we'll just have to make do with what we have stored away until this blows over."

"Oh, Isabelle, I have more than enough food at my place if you and the kids need something," Isaac offered.

"Thanks, Isaac, but no, we've got more than enough. You know, Tobias is always prepared. Overgrown boy scout that he is."

"The man *is* relentless with it, isn't he?" Isaac added, chuckling with an eye roll.

"He is. Trust me. Truth is, I really just needed to get out of the house for a while. Being stuck inside all day, every day is getting to me."

"I imagine it would, but at any rate, I can give you guys a lift. It's not a problem, really. I'm heading in that direction anyway, sort of."

"No thanks, Isaac. I think we'll walk today. Nothing else to do anymore anyway, right? Besides, I think we'll stop at Nisha's house for a bit. I haven't seen her in a few days."

"You do have a point there, Isabelle. There really is nothing to do anymore, is there? Well, if you need anything, please don't hesitate," Isaac offered a final time.

"I won't. Thanks, Isaac."

Isabelle and her son continued their trek north. They walked in silence until they finally broke through a wooded shortcut out onto the road that led home.

Tommy was fidgeting most of the way until curiosity finally got the better of him. "Mommy, why did you hurt the man?" Tommy stopped walking and tugged on his mother's arm.

Isabelle crouched down to eye level with her son. She pulled him close, and she wrapped his tiny hands in hers. "He was a bad man, Tommy," she said with sincerity. "And when you see a bad man, it's important to hurt him before he hurts you."

11: 25 am - Burke Residence

Tobias and Seth finished up a late breakfast. Lunch, really, by that point. Isabelle left a couple of plates in the oven before heading down to Main Street for some shopping with Tommy. The men sat back in their chairs, sipping hot coffee and still reeling from the morning's revelation.

Seth spent six years in law school, unhappily going through the motions because that was what he was supposed to do with his life. His parents both toiled away in the service industry, the latest in a long line of blue-collar workers. The backbone of the country, as his father liked to describe it. They put in ridiculous hours and hoarded every spare penny to put Seth through college. It was in their hands to break the cycle started generations past of working like a dog for sixty years and dying broke. No, their son would not suffer through that lifestyle as well. Whatever it took, they would pay for his schooling and put him on his way to a better life than theirs.

Only a semester away from graduation, up late studying evenings, tired and in desperate need of a break, he would walk to the local convenience store for a much-needed cup of coffee and a decent conversation. Seth looked forward to his chats with Mohammed. The friendly late-night clerk always served as a welcome respite from the monotony of his studies. Mo, as he insisted his friends address him, immigrated to America three years prior in search of better opportunities. Seth wasn't the prying type but learned in passing that Mo had given up a lucrative career as an attorney back in Egypt to come to America. That struck Seth as odd. Why would anyone choose to give up the relatively comfortable life that a lawyer's salary afforded just to up and move somewhere else, to go largely unnoticed behind a counter? Mo would explain to him over the course of a few months that material wealth was the lie that we'd all been fed: eating up every last drop, striving to have more than your neighbor, was the trap we were all stuck in.

"What point is all the money in the world if you are miserable?" Mo would say. "Life should be about doing what makes us happy, consequences be damned."

Seth would dwell on those conversations for months until it finally reached the point when, without him even realizing it, his favorite moments during any given week were his talks with Mo. Seth had a few questions about life in Egypt that had been on his mind for weeks now. He was determined to get the answers before Mo dominated the conversation, as he was apt to do. As he rounded the corner from the backside of the building, flashing lights caught Seth's attention. Blue and red beacons danced across the parking lot, reflecting off the shattered glass of the storefront. He rushed into the shop, which by then was filled with police officers taking notes and speaking with witnesses. His friend was nowhere to be found. A blood-soaked white sheet covered a large mass behind the counter. "Please, no!" Seth pushed past the officers for a better look. A hand lay protruding from the shroud, its wrist adorned with a trinket lovingly prepared by a child. There was no mistaking it: his friend Mohammed had been murdered.

Seth spent hours talking with the police. No leads, of course. The convenience store owner, cheap bastard that he was, had no equipment hooked up to the hollow cameras on the wall. Mohammed's murder would go unsolved. It was over money, no less. Seventy-six dollars and change to be precise. Something inside Seth changed that evening. What started as grief evolved into a sense of purpose. Mo's voice echoed through Seth's mind.

"Being happy should be the priority, not a mere dream that's cast aside, crushed by the weight of a standard of living someone else chose for you long before you were born."

Weeks passed, but the store was no longer the same. Without Mo, Seth had no need to return. Seth changed his routine and began walking to the police station once a week for any updates on his friend's case. His sojourns became more frequent until Seth found himself visiting his new friends on a nightly basis. It wouldn't be long before he dropped out of law school altogether and signed up for the academy. His parents would be heartbroken, but Mohammed was right: Seth needed to be happy, and happiness for him was in helping people. What better way to help the community than as a police officer? Seth never looked back. From time to time, he still thought of his old friend Mo. It often brought a smile to his face; the old guy was right all along.

"Scuttlebutt around town is you had some words with Lancaster last night."

"News travels fast, huh? Good, he's nothing to worry about. Just a bitter old man, last of a dying breed, really." Tobias topped off Seth's coffee.

"That may be the case, but he's still dangerous. The mayor and his cronies shouldn't be underestimated, Tobias."

"Thanks, I'll keep my eyes open." Tobias shrugged.

"I'm just saying, man, tread carefully with those people, Jim especially."
Seth knew that Marisol *disposed* of Jim, though he kept that detail from
Tobias. Best that his friend kept his guard up.

"Well, if he's so bad, why don't you go arrest him?" said Tobias half-
jokingly.

"Go fuck yourself, Toby. You know I can't just put him in lockup for
being a prick."

"I know, I know. I'm just busting your balls, man. Look, I'll be sure to
stay away from Lancaster and his crew, but I'm serious, Seth. I'm out of
here as soon as possible. You should think about joining us."

"I have. I am. I mean, I agree with you, Toby. If something happens,
we're in some serious trouble here. Look, I gotta split. Tell Isabelle thanks
for breakfast. You take it easy, rabble-rouser." Seth hurried to the door.
"Hey, I'll see you at the briefing, alright?"

"You got it, Seth. I'll see you there."

Tobias watched his friend drive off under an overcast sky. In the
distance, the horizon grew increasingly dark.

W.J. Hegarty

CHAPTER ELEVEN

Canvass

Miller was making the rounds, checking in on what remained of Takashi's unit. More than two dozen souls fled Philadelphia with them, a mix of soldiers from various branches of the military, some local first-responders, and a handful of citizens. Of that group of survivors, nine soldiers were all that remained. The journey had claimed nearly all of them.

Pepperbush had adequate defenses in the berm, but Miller was fairly confident in his assessment that the earthen wall was never truly proven. His first stop was Sam's security headquarters. Miller had met the man briefly this morning, though he thought it wise to get Sam's viewpoint on town security one on one.

Sam greeted Miller at the door with a firm handshake and a warm smile as he led the young captain into his office. Tobias was present, standing by a large map of the East Coast.

"Captain, I'd like to introduce you to Tobias Burke. He's a member of my security detail."

"It's nice to meet you Tobias."

"Likewise. If I could get a moment of your time, Captain, I'd like to run something past you."

"I've got time."

Over the next hour, Sam and Tobias explained for Miller the local politics, a brief history of Pepperbush, and the undead threat from their view out in the middle of nowhere. But that was all a primer to prepare Miller for his idea of flight to the sea. The plan, sound as it was, got thrown into disarray at the prospect of an unknown number of carriers less than two days away.

"This plan sounds feasible, Tobias. I like the sound of it. Listen, I'm off to check up on the rest of my unit, but I'll let Colonel Takashi know what you said, and we'll take it from there."

12:07 pm - The Berm

Miller and Rachel were twenty-eight and twenty-seven, respectively. They grew up together, went to the same high school, and afterward enlisted. The two of them went through boot camp at Fort Sill. Afterward, Miller was assigned to Colonel Takashi's unit in Afghanistan while Rachel went off to a spec-ops unit in South America where she would serve beside Radzinski. They would keep in touch through the years, frequently sending email back and forth, calling on birthdays, and, when it worked out, visiting on holidays. They were the vanguard of a young generation of career military. Miller was a newly minted captain while Rachel had recently received lieutenant stripes of her own. They hadn't spoken in months until by happenstance both were deployed to Philadelphia. Once they were on the ground, the situation deteriorated quickly. There was no time for pleasantries before they were well and truly in the shit. Now safely behind the walls of Pepperbush, the two young soldiers found time to catch up, to take a breather.

Miller climbed the ladder to a watch post at the southernmost tip of the berm. On the platform above, Rachel was familiarizing herself with their new surroundings, getting the lay of the land from Bernie, one of Pepperbush's roaming sentries.

"As far as you can see, and then far past that, we're surrounded by forest. The closest anything is twenty miles down the road. General store with a single gas pump."

"Fuel? That could come in handy." Rachel almost lit up at the revelation.

"It did. We ran their reserves dry building the berm."

"So you're telling me that the only fuel in town is whatever is left sloshing around in your gas tanks?"

"That's the long and short of it, yeah."

"Good to know."

Bernie gave Miller a hand up. "Captain."

"Bernie." Miller wobbled a bit when he reached the apex. "These things are a little rickety, huh?"

"No concrete for the posts. We just buried them in the dirt." Bernie returned his attention to Rachel on his way down the ladder. "I need to get going. Perimeter ain't gonna watch itself. You holler if you have any questions."

"I will, Bernie. Thank you."

Miller took a spot beside Rachel, surveying the dense forest. "He seems like a friendly one."

"Nice enough." Rachel held Miller at arm's length. "Let me get a look at you. Everything happened so fast. God, it's good to see you, Miller." They hugged hard and long. Rachel laughed and backed off. She waved out her shirt and brushed her other hand past her nose. "Careful, I reek."

"Weeks on the road will do that. I'll take *your* stench over theirs any day." Miller gestured to the wilds beyond.

"You've got a point. Immanent death aside, it feels nice to be able to slow down, take a breather."

"I know. Philadelphia was a clusterfuck of epic proportions. I can't imagine what the rest of the country is going through right now."

"Yeah." Rachel was eager to move on to another subject. Why rehash the past few weeks? Miller and everyone else in their unit just experienced the same hell. Talking about it wouldn't make it go away. "So you seeing anyone?"

"No time, you?"

"Eh, a date here and there, nothing serious. How are the folks?"

"I wish I knew. I talked with my mom a few days before touching down in Philly. She said everybody was good. Big sis and little brother are still arguing over whose name should go above the bar. Mom says they should just use the family name and be done with it. I guess that makes too much sense. Dad was still busy with the dam project. They hope to be up and running by the end of summer. Renewable energy for the entire city. Clean drinking water to boot. They'll be completely self-sufficient, nearly one-hundred-percent off the grid. It's impressive for a city of that size. Honestly, that whole project is so far past my purview I wouldn't know how to explain it properly if I tried. But no, I haven't spoken with him or anyone else in months. Now I never will."

"You don't know that."

Miller slowly nodded. Rachel wasn't sure if he was agreeing with her or standing firm that his assessment was unshakable. They stood in silence for a beat before Miller changed topics. "You ever think of Trevor?"

"That asshole? Not often. Last I heard he was assigned to a listening post in Alaska. Serves him right. Huh, fucking Trevor. What the hell made you think of him? Boot camp feels like a lifetime ago."

"Tell me about it." Miller gestured to Radzinski, who was passing a few blocks away. "Like you said, he's an asshole."

"Yeah, that guy *is* a dick, isn't he?"

"So how does it look out here?" Miller took the binoculars for a view of the forest.

"Not a peep. It's quiet."

"Good. I'll take anything positive at this point."

Rachel stared off in the distance, trying to determine where exactly they came from. "Did we kill these people, Miller?"

"God, I hope not."

1:15 pm - Bed-and-Breakfast: Triage

Miller met Jeremiah on his first tour in the Middle East. Both men were serving under Takashi, and though Jeremiah was standoffish, the two became fast friends. Jeremiah was similar to Miller's father in the sense that his current task consumed him. His goal took over his entire being until the man and the mission were inseparable. Miller respected the work ethic but knew the pitfalls of such a state of mind. He often had to force Jeremiah to relax or to even socialize with the rest of their unit for a few beers and just unwind.

Aiko and Jeremiah were Navy medics assigned to the front lines in Philadelphia. What remained of their units combined with Colonel Takashi's shortly after the FOB fell. Aiko was in her final year at Bethesda, and Jeremiah was back for retraining when they met. A year later, they were secretly engaged. Their privacy kept until the fall of Philadelphia, when it became apparent there was more between the two of them than camaraderie. Jeremiah was on leave from his station on the USNS *Mercy* when he was recalled and ordered to hook up with a Marine unit in the Philadelphia area. An outbreak of some kind nearing a tipping point was the rumor among medical professionals. That theory made the most sense in the face of so many troops active on U.S. soil.

Enlisting wasn't Aiko's first choice or even the second. Biology was her passion. She dreamed of attending medical school and one day being at the forefront of some Earth-shattering breakthrough. Unfortunately, her parents couldn't foot the bill and she was turned down for every scholarship she applied for. Aiko had never considered military service, but as her options dwindled, she became desperate, imagining herself toiling away at a nine-to-five. She loved the medical field and would do whatever it took to achieve her goals. While she was studying a first-responder's manual, a recruiter came by. At first, she was opposed to the idea and brushed him off, though not before accepting a little literature.

It can't hurt to at least read it, she thought.

The options really didn't sound so bad, not to mention until that point she had no idea the military would pay for schooling. This was all she needed to know. Three years later she found herself deployed to Philadelphia. Something about mass riots. It didn't make sense, but there she was.

The medics were given an area off to the side of Grace's as a makeshift triage. Some of their unit needed proper care now that they were off the road. While they were set up, the medics offered to look at anyone from town with an injury, seeing as Pepperbush was lacking in the medical care department.

Aiko had just finished cleaning Soraya's bandaged side. She was on her way out, back to the main dining area of the bed-and-breakfast, as Miller passed. He and Soraya exchanged smiles that lingered a little longer than those with their fellow unit members. Aiko was tending to the colonel; his knee was bad. Takashi could still walk, but running was out of the question.

"How's he looking, Aiko?"

"His knee is dislocated. He shouldn't be on it at all. If I had access to a wheelchair, I'd strap him to it. It's honestly a small miracle that he even made it this far."

"I'm sitting right here, you two." Takashi grit his teeth as he wobbly rose from his chair.

"Sir." Aiko attempted to steady her commanding officer.

"Enough. I'll keep my weight off of it as best I can. I'll be of no use to anyone if all I'm doing is barking orders from a chair for the next two days."

"And if we have to carry you out of here because you damaged your leg further by being stubborn?" Miller was ready to act if Takashi looked like he was about to fall, but he kept his distance.

Takashi would have none of it. "I said that's enough. What can I do for you, Captain?"

"Sir, I've spoken with a member of Sam's security detail, and according to him, a large contingent of Pepperbush is in favor of leaving. In fact, he was in the final stages of preparation to do just that. Our arrival threw a wrench into the works."

"Does he have a destination in mind? Just hitting the road seems more like delaying the inevitable."

"He thinks we should head for the ocean, find a boat that can carry everyone, then head south for the islands."

"Not bad. I'll take it under advisement, but first things first. We need to address the town as a whole, inform them of what's coming. We don't have the time or the resources to commit to a full-scale evacuation. If the carriers reach us while we're in the middle of the evac, these people will scatter. For now, it's best that we fortify the town's defenses and get these people up to speed. When we've put down the undead threat, then we march to the sea."

Sam stood in the entranceway, just out of earshot. He leaned on the doorframe, tapping his fingers above his head against decades-old wallpaper. Dusty knickknacks adorned a shelf just above his reach. Sam couldn't wait for Takashi to offer a proper briefing. He had to know. He had to know now.

"Colonel. A word?"

"Of course, Sam."

Miller made eye contact with Sam. The recently appointed head of Pepperbush security was anxious. He needed answers that couldn't wait for a formal briefing. Miller thought it best to let him speak with Takashi one on one. "I'm heading out, sir. I'm going to continue canvassing town and finish checking up on the rest of the unit."

"Dismissed, Captain."

Sam nodded at Miller as he passed, his attention squarely on Takashi. "Philadelphia, just how bad was it?"

Takashi studied the man. Sam had a stern gentleness about him. Concern was obvious; that was a given. While some might only have their best interests at heart, Takashi surmised from just one look that Sam kept Pepperbush and all of its residents at the forefront of his priorities. He could handle the truth. Sam wouldn't abandon these people at the first sign of trouble. The colonel sized him up in less time than it took to form the thought. "I won't mince words here, Sam. Philadelphia is gone. A line was drawn in the sand. If the horde approached I-95, the Air Force would initiate a bombing run, blow all those things back to hell. They did it, alright. Everything from North Broad Street to the Delaware River was completely erased from the map. The carriers in the immediate vicinity were vaporized, and every living thing in a twenty-block radius was killed. By nightfall, there were four times as many carriers coming for us. We didn't stand a chance."

"Your superiors made it worse," Sam said with a certainty that lacked any judgmental undertones.

"Yes and no. People were trapped in the city with no way out unless they could travel on foot. Thousands chose to walk out of there. Hundreds of thousands stayed behind. All that the bombing run accomplished was to speed up the process."

"And the rest of the country?"

"The last good intel I received said that DC had fallen and the Capitol Building was in flames."

"Jesus."

"It's safe to assume that most, if not all, major metropolitan areas nationwide have suffered a similar fate."

1:30 pm - Bed-and-Breakfast: Dining Room

Soraya usually spoke near-perfect English, though when deep in thought or caught off guard, her speech became broken. Miller found it a cute quirk, but others were annoyed by it, especially Lev, who was embarrassed to be in her presence when she slipped up. He felt it was an affront on their superiors' behalf to have sent someone with such a handicap to represent the IDF as a whole. To hear him speak like this broke her heart. At least he only lambasted her in private where her tears could remain her own. After Philadelphia, Lev wouldn't be disparaging her anymore. In fact, he wouldn't be doing anything at all.

Soraya sat alone at the main dining table of Grace's bed-and-breakfast. Most of her unit was out scouring the town for weak spots in its revealed-to-be lax defenses. Spread out on the table in front of her were the remnants of two broken radios she disassembled in the hope she could salvage one working device out of the mess.

The bed-and-breakfast typically didn't host many guests. A few out-of-towners would stumble in during any given month, and that was fine, but the place was mostly used as a getaway of sorts for the residents of Pepperbush. It was common to have a couple stay a night or two on a special occasion or just as a change of scenery. Now, though, the place was filled to capacity with refugees. Normally, Grace would feel overwhelmed by the crowd; these days, she welcomed the company.

Grace shuffled about in a mauve dress and little matching shoes that were synonymous with the woman. She was tidying up the guests' area. Whenever she was nervous, she would clean. After the conversation she overheard the soldiers having, this place would be spotless twice over by the end of the day. "Could I get you anything else, dear?"

"No thank you, ma'am. I am full." Soraya rubbed her belly.

"I don't mean to pry, but may I ask what you're fiddling with there, honey?"

"This pile of scrap used to be a radio. It took a bullet for me back in Philadelphia, probably saved my life." She rubbed her side. "The radio took the brunt of the damage, but it still hurt like hell. It may not look like much now, but if I can get it working again, maybe we can get in contact with command and agree on a rallying point."

"Oh my, that sounds confusing. I'd better returned to my chores. This place won't clean itself." Grace smiled and returned to her cleaning. "If you need anything else, I'm just a shout away." Grace wasn't really interested in what Soraya was doing; she merely wanted to let the young soldier know without having to come out and say it that she was welcome. It was just her way.

"Thank you, Mrs. Grace."

Miller gently closed the door behind him, the old woman who ran the place seemed on edge. No need to upset her further with another earful of dire conversation. He took a seat beside Soraya and began stripping the second radio for her. "Hey."

"Hello, sir." Soraya smiled, though she didn't rise from her task.

"How are your ribs feeling? Any better?"

"Much better, thank you. Aiko was right: I was being stubborn. It is fine now. I just needed rest."

"Good. You think you'll be able to fix one of these things?" He looked over the pile of components, unable to make heads or tails of any of it.

"I believe so, yes. These things no difficult can piece." She stopped. It was happening again, and thanks to Lev, now she was aware of the problem. It embarrassed and frustrated her, making it worse.

"It's okay. Just calm down," Miller said gently as he took her trembling hands in his. "Breathe and take it slow. There's no need to get yourself worked up. It's only a radio."

"I am okay, sir. Just need to fix radio."

"I know what's been bothering you, but you did what you had to do back there at Hall Station," Miller insisted. "Lev was out of control. He could have killed us all. It was him or everybody else. You did the right thing, Soraya."

"I know, Captain."

"Please," he said warmly. "It's just Miller. That's what my friends call me."

"Thank you." Soraya allowed herself the briefest of smiles. "Miller." She pronounced his name *mee-lor*.

As worn as Miller was from the road and what he and his unit had gone through since Philadelphia, he still found it adorable when Soraya said his name. She never failed to brighten his day, even when he was at his lowest.

3:10 pm - Mother Leeds

Mother Leeds was unusually empty for such a warm afternoon. The majority of the regulars were most likely at home, pondering the latest Town Hall meeting. Vanessa normally didn't work the afternoon to early-evening shift. That was her time to relax, so she would leave the bar in Lillian's capable hands. Vanessa came to trust the girl explicitly over the years and the two became quite close as a result. Vanessa refused to let anyone work a shift alone, so a few days a week, Lillian's best friend Cindy would fill in.

Cindy's family moved to Pepperbush the summer before she was to start high school. She and Lillian hit it off from the start and remained best friends since. "I'm going to head home and feed the dogs. I'll talk to you later," Cindy said as she wrapped up her apron and punched the time clock.

"Cool, thanks. I'll swing by after work. The last thing I need is to stay home tonight. Who wants to watch their mom get hammered?" Lillian laughed. Her mother was no drunk. Isabelle was just having a rough time with where current circumstances landed her, not to mention that Lillian's father spending every night out on berm patrol ate away at her mother's patience.

Lillian and Cindy slowly grew apart during the past few years. College opened Lillian up to a larger world, one that she had every intention of experiencing, whereas Cindy was content with small-town living. Cindy had aspirations to work with her mother at the box factory in the next town over, but otherwise, she seemed content to never leave. The girls still remained close; they always picked up right where they left off no matter how long they'd been separated. It was inevitable, though, that one day Lillian would leave Pepperbush and her best friend Cindy behind for good.

Radzinski sat alone at the bar, his rifle at arm's reach and his pack on the stool beside him. Various gear spread out around him kept any curious townsfolk from approaching. "Give me another. The good stuff this time." He tapped his finger on the bar and gestured for the top-shelf liquor.

Lillian had just the drink in mind: a twenty-year-old Scotch that they hid behind the swill.

Radzinski turned his head ever so slightly, taking in Lillian's figure as she reached for a bottle from the top shelf. Her shorts were small enough for the bottom of her ass to peek out just an inch below the fabric. Stretching for the bottle, they rode up even farther, revealing more skin, her left cheek almost completely exposed. *Maybe this town's not so bad, after all.* He lit up another cigarette and waved for Lillian to hurry back.

Lillian caught his glance but ignored it, as she was familiar with advances from horny customers. She poured the crude soldier two fingers and smiled. New faces in town were always a welcome sight, no matter the circumstances. She was used to the attention her tight skimpy uniform would attract. Show the customers a little skin, flirt with them just enough, and they'd keep coming back for more. Vanessa had told her once, and the lesson stuck. It made perfect sense to her. Living on campus nine months out of the year, Lillian was well aware of the lengths a desperate guy would go to for the attention of a pretty girl. That experience dovetailed well into a part-time job at Mother Leeds.

During the summer when home from school, Lillian worked at Vanessa's bar for a little extra income, but mostly to escape the boredom she felt living in such a small town so far from what she considered normal society. One more year to go and she could apply for a teaching position in Philadelphia or even Baltimore, for that matter. Anywhere but here, she thought. All her life, she dreamed of moving away from Pepperbush for good. These simple people with their simple problems were nauseating to her. Currently, though, with what was happening in the cities and with these soldiers showing up, she wasn't sure if she would ever return to school, much less have a chance at the future she had planned for herself.

Lilian replaced the bottle of Scotch with something a little less expensive. The good stuff had to last. "So how bad is it out there?"

"You don't want to know, kid. Just leave the bottle." Radzinski offered nothing. Pretty girl or not, he wasn't about to get cozy with the locals.

"I'll leave you to it then. Let me know if you need anything else."

In the earliest days of her employment at Mother Leeds, one of the first things Vanessa taught her was not to pester the customers. If they wanted to be left alone, she shouldn't bother them. Find someone else to talk to or straighten up the bar; the customer would let you know if they needed something. Oftentimes, the waiting would get customers to open up.

Occasionally that method would backfire and they would leave frustrated and angry. It was rare, though.

A second soldier entered the bar; it was Captain Miller. He quickly scanned the patrons until his eyes fixed on Radzinski at the far end of the bar. "Radzinski, what in the hell do you think you're doing?"

Radzinski pulled his face from the bottle long enough to make eye contact. "What does it look like I'm doing? In case you haven't noticed, it's the end of the fucking world, Miller, and we keep finding ourselves right in the shit." Radzinski downed a shot and set his glass up for another. "Cheers."

Miller stepped between Radzinski and the prying eyes of the rest of the bar. "I need you focused. In less than two days, this town is going to be crawling with infected. You're no good to me *or* these people if you're hammered." Miller slid the Jameson's just out of arm's reach.

"Oh, we're going to play *this* game, huh? I've had three shots, and this is only my second beer for Christ's sake. Calm the fuck down." Radzinski shook his head and reached for another cigarette.

Miller cut the distance between them in half.

"You will address me as 'sir.' Am I clear?"

"Please. Takashi only field-promoted you to make sure he stays in charge if that leg winds up sidelining him. As far as HQ is concerned, you don't outrank me, so you can go wave that discipline flag somewhere else." Radzinski leaned back as far as the stool would allow. The angle provided a clear shot to blow smoke in Miller's face.

The good of the mission and the advanced timeframe was not lost on Miller. For the time being, keeping the unit intact was the priority. Disciplinary issues could wait. The clock was ticking on what could very well turn out to be another sustained battle. Despite the glaring lack of respect for the chain of command, Miller approached the situation from a different angle. "Look, if we can speak man to man, I don't want to be in your face like this, I really don't, but we have to keep it together here, Radzinski. These people need our help, and if we're at each other's throats, we're no good to anyone."

"Save it. You've got two choices here, Miller. Back off or I walk the fuck out of this town. Some of the others may even come with me. How's that make you feel?" Radzinski rose from his stool. He looked down on Miller with a grin as he stood a solid six inches taller than his commanding officer. "Now, if you've finished waving your cock around, I'm going to sleep for a few hours."

Radzinski swallowed the rest of his drink, gathered his gear, and withdrew from the conversation, leaving Miller angry and more than slightly embarrassed. If that little scene had played out in front of the unit and not a handful of civilians, he feared he would have lost all credibility in the eyes of his subordinates. Radzinski was getting harder to deal with by the day. Unfortunately, that would have to remain an issue for another time.

Garrett entered the bar from the kitchen area in the back. Walking with a heavy foot, he cleared his throat, quietly announcing his presence for the young captain. A hothead arguing with a young officer that passed him in rank was rare but not unheard of. A little reassurance would do Miller good, he thought.

"Garrett." Miller greeted the older soldier with a nod. "What are you doing in here? I never took you for much of a drinker," Miller asked, pulling up a barstool.

"Don't drink. Quit the stuff when you were in grade school." Garrett took a conservative sip from a small bottle of water. "I've been scouting locations to dig in for the shit. The roof of this bar is the perfect spot to set up my nest. This place has got a clear line of sight to the gate. Plus, I'll be able to offer covering fire for at least a portion of the front line, provided the weather cooperates."

"That's a relief. God knows we're going to need all the help we can get tomorrow. So how much of that did you hear?" Miller came out with it, face partially flushed.

"Enough to know Radzinski's losing it. Don't take anything he says to heart, kid. Long and short of it is he's an asshole. Pricks like Radzinski come and go and there's not a damn thing you can do about it, now especially," Garrett offered. "The best you can do is focus on the ones you know you can count on. Eventually he'll burn himself out and fall in line or go AWOL. Either way, fuck him. He's a good fighter, no question, and we'll need the manpower down the road and most assuredly when those things get here. But that's as far as it goes."

"Yeah, you're probably right. I definitely don't have time for this shit right now." Miller stood, slung his rifle, and offered a quick wave to Lillian, who returned the gesture. "Well, if you're all set here, I'm going to keep moving."

"I'm good, sir," Garrett responded. "I'll be looking for a few volunteers to help keep this place secure and give me a hand. We'll hunker down and ride this motherfucker out, Captain."

"Good luck, Garret." Miller left and hit Main Street with a light jog, onto his next destination.

Back inside the bar, Garrett politely waved Lillian over. "Can you spare a minute, sweetheart?"

3:45 pm - Bed-and-Breakfast

Broderick sat alone beneath a wide bay window at a far table toward the front of Grace's. He leaned his elbows on his knees, head down in his palms. This was the nearest semblance of a break, or time to simply unwind, that the young soldier had in weeks. The horrors he witnessed just getting here finally overwhelming him. Soraya stood above Broderick, hand on his shoulder and trying to comfort him. She wasn't much older. Twenty-two to be exact. She was keeping it together; some were just better at it. Quicker to adapt.

"I don't know what's gotten over me. Crying like a baby."

"Let it out. It is nothing to feel embarrassed about."

"Thanks, Soraya. If anything, you're the one who should be upset. I'm sorry about Lev."

"Do not be. Lev was no good." Soraya rolled her eyes at another mention of Lev.

Yes, both she and Lev were Israeli. That didn't make them friends. They were strangers in a strange land, coworkers at best. Lev clearly held disdain for Soraya; he never tried to hide it. Sure, they were both chosen for the troop exchange. It was a high honor, but that didn't make either of them exempt from insecurities and prejudices. Maybe Lev simply didn't like serving with her. It was becoming less common but still a reality that some men just didn't want to serve with women.

Soraya would comfort Broderick for now. She didn't have time for this. He needed to snap out of it fast. Preparations needed to be made, fortifications checked. Pepperbush needed to be brought up to speed, and here she was holding someone's hand. She should have kept tinkering with the radio and ignored his sobs. As if answered from on high, Soraya heard her commanding officer coming.

Grace surprised Takashi with a hug as he limped from the makeshift triage. He went wide-eyed at the gesture but returned a hug of his own all the same. "Good afternoon, Grace. Thank you again for the wonderful meal this morning."

"My pleasure, Mister Takashi. Could I offer you a coffee while you're still here?"

"I'd love a cup, Grace. Thank you."

Soraya and Broderick leaped to attention when they heard the colonel's voice.

"At ease. Have a seat, please." Takashi motioned to the chairs beneath the window. Pepperbush's expanse lay beyond.

Outside of the window, people came and went about their days, ignorant to the fact that these soldiers' arrival was a harbinger of doom. Takashi felt a growing swell of remorse that his unit's mere presence shattered the tranquility of this once peaceful town. If asked, most would not fault the colonel for leading an army of undead to their doorstep, though the sentiment wouldn't quell Takashi's guilt. In less than thirty-six hours, two days if they were lucky, these people would be fighting for their lives. Takashi had no way of being sure if any of them would survive the coming onslaught, including his unit. Everyone left in his command had a job to do. Keeping them focused could mean the difference between life and death. The population of Pepperbush depended on it. "We need to discuss what comes next."

CHAPTER TWELVE

Understanding

By dinnertime, Town Hall was filled far beyond capacity. Nearly every man, woman, and child turned out for whatever news Takashi and his men had to offer. The appearance of nine battle-worn soldiers in their quiet little town rightfully unnerved these people. It started with a few whispers, a comment here and a response there, but quickly turned into full-blown conversations until the assembly room was filled with panicked voices. The citizens of Pepperbush, who for so long hid behind the false sense of security the berm provided, were in no way prepared for the implication of Takashi's unit showing up at their doorstep.

Marisol approached the podium. The concern etched on her face only added to the growing trepidation of the crowd, which remained vocal. Various people shouted questions in unison. Their loud voices blended together in a cacophony of nearly unrecognizable ramblings.

"What's happening, Sheriff?"

"Why is the army here?"

"Are we being evacuated?"

"We're being quarantined, aren't we?"

Marisol began with an unfamiliar tremble to her voice. "Everyone, if you would please quiet down, we'd like to get this briefing started, but first I have an announcement to make concerning Colonel Takashi and his unit's presence in our town."

107

W.J. Hegarty

Behind her, Colonel Takashi stood, waiting for her to finish. He was prepared for his own address to the uneasy crowd. Miller and the other soldiers stood behind him at attention. Their stern looks solidified the people's dread that an ominous announcement lay ahead.

Radzinski stood far off at the end of the dais, displaying his typical disregard for proper posture. He rolled his eyes with every eager question from the crowd. The Marine obviously held these people in contempt.

"This isn't good." Miller leaned in for Takashi's benefit, careful to keep his comments from the people's eager ears.

"No, it isn't. We're committed now, though, Miller. Focus. These people need us. We don't have much time."

Marisol turned the podium over to Takashi. The crowd began to calm as the stranger took the stage.

Takashi grew up poor in an Indiana suburb; he was born during the Kennedy administration to first-generation immigrants. The colonel was intimately familiar with small-town politics and their penchant for distrusting outsiders. His family scraped by as best as it could by stretching every last dollar as far as possible. Takashi's parents had a rough go of it as immigrants in a turbulent era, a direct result of losing everything after spending time in a Japanese internment camp as young adults during the Second World War. Tales from those trying years were the catalyst for Takashi enlisting. He felt compelled to prevent something similar from ever happening again. If such fear manifested itself on American soil once, it could raise its head anew. Takashi wanted to put himself in position to make a difference. Maneuver to the front lines, fighting as the voice of reason against such atrocities. At least the people of Pepperbush were letting strangers in. That was a good sign that they might actually be receptive to what he had to say, despite a few sideways glances and hushed accusations.

"Thank you, Sheriff." Takashi smiled at Marisol as she nodded and made her way back to the side of the stage. She situated herself between Mayor Lancaster and Sam.

"Good morning," Takashi began sternly. "I would like to begin by addressing a few questions you may already have concerning my unit's arrival in your town. There are many rumors floating around that I would like to take this time to dispel. Some are very much true. Most, though, are not, I'm afraid. First off, we are *not* here to put your town under quarantine or martial law, *nor* are we here to evacuate you. Any type of curfew restrictions or lack thereof will remain in the capable hands of local law

108

enforcement. We are not here to exert any form of control over your community. We *only* want to help."

An audible sigh of relief sprang from the audience. Dozens of frightened faces gave way to relief and even a few smiles.

A group in the corner erupted into nervous laughter, the sight nearly bowling Radzinski over in amazement. "Are these people for real?" he asked Garrett.

"Quiet. They have no idea the shitstorm that's headed their way," the seasoned, older soldier replied as their commanding officer continued.

Takashi tried his best not to acknowledge Radzinski's comment. The Marine's reaction, though, was apparent for anyone with eyes on the man. "As you may have heard, the men standing before you were cobbled together from the remains of various units deployed to Philadelphia twenty-three days ago. We have been out of communication with command for more than a week. As far as I know, we are the only survivors of the Philadelphia siege."

Another audible gasp erupted from the crowd, much louder this time. Again, conversations escalated.

"If I could have your attention for one more moment, please." Takashi was drowned out by the nervous crowd. He let the frightened citizens get their misgivings off their chests for a few brief moments before speaking up, louder than he was accustomed to. "We were followed here," he said bluntly.

Immediately, the crowd went silent.

Takashi continued. "A large group of infected have been following us since Philadelphia. We managed to keep a good distance ahead of them for the first few days. Unfortunately, they don't tire. When we slept, they kept moving."

"So you led those things right to us," Mayor Lancaster interrupted, never one to miss an opportunity to assign blame, righteously or not.

"As I told you this morning, Mayor Lancaster, had we been aware of your location, we would have avoided this area altogether. Circumstances as they are, we were miles past your town when we noticed your lights flashing. If not for your power failure last night, we would not be here."

"And you expect us to believe that?" Mayor Lancaster accused.

"Believe what you will. My primary concern—my *only* concern—is making this community aware of the danger." Takashi turned from Mayor Lancaster and redirected his attention once again to the crowd. "We believe this group of infected numbers in the thousands. We estimate that they are currently between twenty-four and thirty-six hours behind us."

The crowd remained silent, fixed on every word from the colonel's lips. Their individual arguments and suppositions momentarily were quelled.

Mayor Lancaster wasted no time with an obviously prepared rebuttal. If the people of Pepperbush let an outsider over-speak their leader with tales of ghouls, then what kind of leader was he? He elbowed past Takashi with a backup microphone at the ready for just such an occurrence. Mayor Lancaster pointed at Takashi, then flailed his arms wildly toward the colonel's unit. "You and your people come into our great town all high and mighty, waving your guns around, and we're expected to, what, acquiesce? I am afraid not, sir." Mayor Lancaster returned his attention to his constituents. "We have been safe right here in Pepperbush for the duration of this madness—madness I'll have you know people like the good colonel and his fellows here brought to Philadelphia and other cities across our great nation." He turned back to the soldiers, his eyes wide and his face reddened. His upper lip trembled, exposing grinding teeth. No longer able to hold back, spittle spewed with every word. "I'll tell you, good citizens, it is a sham. All of it. Time and again, those who would call themselves your betters would have you bow to their every whim. I say no more. We will not do as you say, sir!"

A few members of the audience began to nod in approval. Others cheered their leader. Some got up and left, sure to give the soldiers in attendance a condescending sneer on their way out of the room. Lancaster had won back at least a small portion of the crowd.

"I have kept you safe this long," the mayor continued. "And I will continue to do so. Our defenses are more than adequate to contend with a few slow-moving science experiments people like the good colonel's superiors have burdened *our* country with." Mayor Lancaster turned his attention to his cronies. "This way, gentlemen. I've heard more of this foolishness than I care to for one evening." Mayor Lancaster stormed out of the building, his lapdogs following closely behind, the lot of them exchanging congratulatory assertions under their breath.

A sizable portion of the crowd was relieved at Lancaster's refusal of Takashi's warning. These people left with the mayor.

Soraya turned to Miller. "I should hit him, yes?"

"Do I want you to? Absolutely. Should you? Probably not."

Takashi ignored the outburst for the sake of those that remained. He had seen it all before: one frightened man afraid of losing what little control he had over his tiny corner of the world would say or do just about anything to keep that control. One man's ego-stroking wasn't important to him. Saving as many of these people as possible was paramount. Takashi addressed those that remained. "As I was saying..."

The handful of citizens that remained returned their attention to the colonel.

"Hundreds, possibly thousands of infected are coming *here,* to *your* community, from the direction of Philadelphia. I suggest that every home and business south of Main Street relocate to the northernmost territory as soon as possible. We need to move fast. *All of us.*" He gestured to the people in attendance as well as his own. "My unit has been briefed on town security and the procedures you already have in place. The police, with assistance from Sam's security force, will help organize the transfer, but we will need every able body to lend a hand with preparations," Takashi said, though what remained of the crowd again burst into unsure questioning.

There were a few gasps from the crowd as reality struck. These people were in no way prepared for a full-fledged assault. Most of the people in Pepperbush saw Philadelphia and Baltimore sacked on their televisions, but over the weeks, they had become complacent. Horrors like those would not—could not—happen here. It seemed that they were wrong. A portion of the townsfolk left the meeting at this revelation, no doubt to secure their own property and loved ones. Perhaps they had contingency plans of their own.

"Can you stop them?"

"Are reinforcements coming?"

"Can they get into my house?"

Many questions arose, most of which Takashi ignored while he motioned for Marisol to take the stage. What remained of the dwindling crowd quieted slightly as a trusted face approached the podium.

"We've discussed options," Marisol began. She looked back to Takashi, then over to Sam, who gently nodded in agreement. The three of them had spoken earlier, though the agreed-upon plan still didn't sit well with her. Marisol cleared her throat. She closed her eyes for what felt like an eternity, far longer than she was comfortable with in front of the waiting masses.

To Miller's surprise, the people remained calm, after all. Of all the speakers who took the stage that night, Marisol was the only one everyone trusted without fail.

She continued. "Over the next six hours, we need to relocate everyone south of Main Street to the northernmost homes."

"Is that absolutely necessary, ma'am?" Glen asked, his hand partially raised as he stood.

"Unfortunately it is, Glen. And for what it's worth, I'm sorry. If what Colonel Takashi and his men have told me is accurate, then there is most likely a small army of those things almost at our doorstep."

A teary-eyed woman spoke up. "How can you be sure? Maybe they'll just go right on past. They might not even see us." She slumped back down into her seat, breathing heavily. Her husband tried his best to calm her.

Marisol covered her mouth with her hand and quickly dropped it back to her side. "I... I can't," she stammered.

Miller pulled the sheriff aside. He didn't envy Marisol's position in the slightest. These were people that she was mostly friends with. They trusted her and she was telling them as gently as possible that some, possibly all of them, would be dead in less than two days' time.

"Ma'am," Miller spoke up, addressing the frightened woman in the crowd. "We don't know for sure, but it's safe to assume that the infected followed us here."

Radzinski smirked at Miller's display of compassion.

Glen stood. His hand remained steadfast on his son's shoulder. "What can we do to help?"

"Simply put, we need volunteers, sir. Anyone who knows their way around a weapon is vital. Even just a passing knowledge will be extremely helpful."

Glen nodded in agreement. His boy lowered his head.

"Rifles and shotguns are preferable, but any weapon will be an advantage for us. In the meantime, Sheriff Marisol and her police officers will help to coordinate the relocation effort."

Sam, Seth, and Tobias met up just outside of Town Hall, away from their question-laden peers.

"Looks like we have a change of plan, son." Sam stroked his mustache as he watched the crowd thin.

Seth was pale. "I'll be honest. I didn't think they were going to have *good* news for us, but I didn't see *that* coming."

"You don't have to tell me, guys." Tobias was dumbstruck. "This changes everything."

"I trust you'll do the right thing here, Tobias?"

"If you're suggesting I might pack up the family and take off tonight, forget it, Sam. I'm nervous, not suicidal."

"Glad to hear it." Sam kept a watchful eye on the crowd filing out of Town Hall. "I think our best bet for now is to ride this thing out with Takashi and his people. Let's play it by ear for now."

"Agreed," said Seth.

Tobias gazed toward the red horizon. "Takashi and his unit just being here should be all the proof anyone needs that we should get the hell out of this place. I just hope it's not too late."

CHAPTER THIRTEEN

Strays

Marisol escorted Damon from the police station's holding cells to the reception area. She had him by the bicep in a grip that surprised even Damon. Last night, Damon decided that he didn't feel like paying up after he lost a hand of poker over at Mother Leeds. When the table demanded payment, he answered by knocking the dealer on his ass. That single act could have gone overlooked. Emotions had been running high in town as the days wore on. Given the circumstances, even the most grounded among the denizens of Pepperbush weren't immune to letting frustration run its course. It's what Damon did next that was disturbing and landed him a night in jail. He dragged the dealer out into the streets in front of the bar and proceeded to beat him senseless. It took three other patrons plus Marisol, who was stopping by for a drink, to separate the men.

"You can take your friend with you, but he gets one warning and one warning only. If I pick him up for fighting again, I won't put him in a cell. I'll escort him past the gate personally." Marisol shoved Damon forward, almost daring him to give her a reason to exile him. The Baltimore native had a manner about him that Marisol couldn't stand. Everything about him set off alarm bells. If it wasn't for the fact that exile could mean certain death, she would have done it last night. She was a peacekeeper, not an executioner. Push anyone far enough, though...

Markus waved to Marisol as he guided Damon out of the police station. "Thank you, Sheriff. This won't happen again."

Marisol remained silent as she watched them leave.

Out in the streets, Markus followed Damon toward Mother Leeds. The hothead was moving at a pretty good clip. Markus wasn't sure if Damon just wanted to hurry back to their new home or if he had something else in mind.

"Come on, man. I thought we were going to make a go at this?"

"I never agreed to that. You can play with these hicks all you want."

"They're not hicks. They just don't live in the city. There's a difference."

"Whatever you say. When this shit blows over, we're going back to Baltimore."

"One of us is."

"What's that supposed to mean?"

"It means I'm done with this life. The crime, the violence, your father."

"So that's how you're gonna do me?"

"I'm not doing shit to you."

"Motherfucker, we raised you up from nothing. If it wasn't for us, you'd still be a corner boy."

"And you'll always have my respect for that, but when is it enough? When do I get to do *my* thing? When can I be my own man?"

"Your thing? Your thing is doing what you're told."

"After everything we've been through, you're going to talk to me like I'm one of your underlings? Like I'm some bitch?"

"You're acting like it. There's a way we do things. We look out for our own. Fuck everybody else. That's the way the world works."

"Yeah? Well, tell that to Miller and his crew. They went out of their way to help us."

"So?"

"So they're putting it all on the line to help a bunch of strangers when they could have left us here to die. You could learn something from that."

Damon picked up his pace, leaving Markus behind in the street to contemplate if it was even worth his time trying to reason with him.

8:40 am - Burke Residence

Tobias darted from one corner of the Burke residence to the other, checking and double-checking the windows and doors. Isabelle sat by the fireplace, smoking. She was trying her best to ignore her husband's latest overreaction to the latest bit of troubling news.

"Isabelle, I need to meet with Sam and our new guests as soon as possible. You should probably stay inside today, just to be safe. I'll be gone most of the day and tonight. Don't wait up. I'll have someone swing by to check on you after it gets dark. Oh, and make sure Tommy doesn't wander too far. Keep an eye on him. I love you." Tobias had a way about him when he was preoccupied. The way he talked at her was nauseating; he listed off demands like some overbearing boss saying what he needed to say with no regard for her feelings on the matter—or any matter of late.

Isabelle said nothing and didn't even raise an eye in his direction as Tobias hurried out. He slammed the door behind him. She hated that, slamming doors. How hard was it to close the door gently?

"Keep an eye on Tommy," she repeated. Like she needed to be told. "Don't leave the house? You mean my prison?" She balled her fists until her palms bled. She stood there staring at her empty living room. A rage was consuming her. She imagined smashing everything in the house, indiscriminately breaking all of it, her own belongings as well. She picked up a framed picture of her and Tobias on their wedding day. Just the two of them, happier times. The smile on his face in the photo only increased her ire. She slipped it into her purse just as Tommy entered the room.

"Where did Daddy go?"

Who the fuck cares? she desperately wanted to say, though she settled for a response more befitting a child. "He went to help his friends, Tommy. You remember Mister Sam?"

"Uh-huh."

"Well he's gone to help Mister Sam keep the whole town safe."

"The whole town?"

"That's right, the whole town."

"He's always going somewhere."

"That's because your daddy is a very important man."

"I don't want him to go."

"Aww, come here, sweetie. Hey, why don't we go somewhere, too? Just me and you. What do you say?"

"Okay. Where?"

"Hmm, let's see." She thought for a moment, and it dawned on her. "Let's go see your Aunt Nisha."

"Okay!" Tommy lit up. He loved Nisha.

Isabelle grabbed her purse and a bag of toys for Tommy. She made it a point to leave the front door open wide before they began their trek.

115

9:10 am - Bed-and-Breakfast

Jim lumbered through the streets, neck on a swivel when he wasn't mumbling to himself. He kept a watchful eye for Marisol and her police; he wasn't supposed to be here. He was a predator, refugees his prey. A man in his early thirties passed with his young daughter in tow; she couldn't have been older than five. Jim watched as they perused the offerings at Emily's Goods, the closest thing the town had to a general store. The little girl was all smiles as they continued their trek toward Grace's bed-and-breakfast, where a warm meal awaited. The child would eat while her father toiled away in the kitchen. He was one of Pepperbush's many refugees, taken in during the earliest days of the crisis before a ban on strangers was enforced. Grace was kind to the young man. She was kind to everyone, but she took an extra liking to the single father and his adorable daughter.

The young father pushed backward through the two-way kitchen door, out into the dining area, carrying two hot plates, one for himself and one for his daughter. Hot sausage and eggs, steaming beside a serving of jellied toast. The aroma wafting from the meal reminded him of home, a place he didn't want to think about anymore. His smile dropped. The plates nearly fell from his hands. His daughter was coloring on a child's placemat as she sat on Jim's lap.

"Have a seat, Dad," Jim sneered, his hand on the girl's leg.

"Daddy, Mister Jim is helping me color. Look." The girl kept her head in the placemat. Stick figures of her and her father surrounded by carriers were sloppily added to the artwork.

"Come to Daddy, sweetheart." The man knelt. The girl leaped from Jim's lap and ran to her father's extended arms. "There you are. Sit right there so Mister Jim can eat his breakfast."

Jim slid one of the plates of food to his side of the table, the meal that was intended for the father. "Thanks, Dad." He swiped the girl's toast for good measure.

"Can Mister Jim eat breakfast with us every day, Daddy? He says he keeps the monsters away from his friends. Can he be our friend, too?"

"I'm sure Mister Jim is very busy, sweetheart. He should probably be going." The anxious father monitored Jim through concerned eyes.

"Your daddy's right, little lady. I do have to be going, but don't you worry. You'll see me again real soon."

"Jim, please."

"I'll be back tomorrow. We can have breakfast again. Isn't that right, Daddy?"

"Of course, Jim," the man stammered as he lowered his eyes.

10:05 am - Carlyle Residence

Nisha was Isabelle's closest friend since high school. She always dressed nice, even when she wasn't expecting company. Black jeans and a purple top accented her dark features. Her thick curly hair was long, and it framed her face well when she wore it down. Lately, though, she had been keeping it pulled back with a few loose curls left dangling past her jawline to give the impression that she casually threw the look together. She didn't.

Tommy was spread out on Nisha's living room floor. An army of plastic soldiers surrounded him. He arranged the action figures in various poses. Today's event was his own re-creation of a tale he overheard his parents discussing that involved a shootout just beyond Pepperbush's gate.

Isabelle sat back in a chair at Nisha's dinner table while her host fixed the women drinks. She peered around Nisha's clean, immaculate home. A part of Isabelle envied the serenity of the single life. She would often comment about how they should switch up. Nisha could take Tobias and the kids; Isabelle would rough it alone. She was only partially joking.

Nisha joined Isabelle at the table. "So soldiers in our midst, huh? Who would have thought we'd live to see the day?"

"Tell me about it. I heard that Mayor Lancaster wants them gone. Says they're just scaring people for no reason."

"Donald Lancaster is only concerned about his reputation. If the soldiers put a little fear into the rest of us, it makes him look incompetent."

"Well that goes without saying. That guy's slimy as shit. I don't believe a word that comes out of his mouth."

"From your lips to God's ears." Nisha raised her glass in a toast.

"Can I ask you a favor?"

"Anything. What is it?" Nisha was concerned. It wasn't like Isabelle to ask for favors.

"Would you mind looking after Tommy for a couple hours? I haven't had a moment to myself in weeks. I just want to get out there, walk around. I want to see what's going on around town without people talking to me like all I am is a frightened mother. I'm not afraid, but nobody tells me anything."

"Oh, honey, of course. You scared me for a minute there. Take all the time you need. I've got board games, movies. I'll have Tommy so worn out by the time you get back he'll fall right to sleep tonight."

"Thank you, Nisha." Isabelle quickly finished her drink, gave Nisha a hug, and said goodbye to her son. "Two hours tops," she said as she gently closed the door behind her.

Nisha fixed herself a cup of coffee before making her way to the living room. "So what do you have here, Tommy? Who are all these little men?"

"They're Joes. They're my dad's."

"Oh neat. Do they have names?"

"That's classified."

"Oh, okay."

"Here, you can play with this one. He's a ninja, and this one's a firefighter and this one..." Tommy wouldn't tell Nisha the names of his toys, but he was more than happy to explain that each of them had a job and exactly what that job entailed.

1:20 pm - Mother Leeds

Mother Leeds had a decent turnout this afternoon, considering Takashi's briefing only let out a few hours prior. Lillian watched as Vanessa discussed Damon's growing instability with Markus. She liked Markus, but Damon she could do without. Markus would catch her staring. He would smile or wave. Lillian would usually turn away; she didn't want to lead him on. Her gaze often lingered on Vanessa, though. The way she smelled reminded her of when she was a child visiting the beach. The scent of cocoa butter hung in the air of her parents' rented villa. Vanessa reminded her of simpler times, peacefulness, security, and, most of all, warmth. When she thought of Vanessa, she imagined the sun and how it warmed her, enveloped her.

Lillian discovered while away in college that she liked girls. Vanessa was the only person she told. Sure, she knew that she could confide in her, but it was more than that. Lilian couldn't wait to move out of Pepperbush. The only thing holding her back anymore was Vanessa. Lillian didn't want to leave her, and she didn't have the nerve to ask Vanessa to abandon Mother Leeds. First things first, she needed to work up the courage to let Vanessa know how she truly felt. How would she even go about it? Should she just blurt it out at the top of her lungs? A part of her wanted to. She would lie awake nights, imagining herself standing atop the bar, mugs of beer at her feet, as she professed her love for Vanessa for all the world to see. Vanessa would come running across the bar, take Lillian in her arms, and the crowd would cheer. Happily ever after, right?

Of course, the crisis changed everything. A sadness hung over the place now, and an inescapable dread washed over everything. Every decision everybody made had the crisis in mind. If it wasn't on their lips, then it was certainly just behind their teeth. Impending doom was all around. Now, with the arrival of these soldiers, the doom was more real than ever. Danger wasn't some abstract possibility anymore; it was fact. Pepperbush was going to be attacked—soon. So yeah, there really wasn't a good time to talk to Vanessa, not anymore. So much could change in a day. Had Lillian known just yesterday what she knew today, she wouldn't have squandered the time.

Vanessa smiled when she talked with Markus. After all, he *was* from home. He reminded her of that. She had no real desire to return to Baltimore; he just offered some familiarity in a place that never really felt like home. She was the perpetual outsider. Except for Sam and Lillian, no one in town really paid her much mind. Of course, the people who lived here frequented her drinking establishment. What else was there to do?

Markus would drone on endlessly about how much he grew to despise life in the city, always careful not to reveal too much for fear of scaring away his new friends. Once again, Damon was up for discussion. Vanessa had heard it all before, but last night was different. Last night he scared her. Damon could have killed that man, and if not for Marisol's intervention, he might have.

The bell rang, alerting Lillian that another customer had arrived. To her surprise, it was her mother.

Isabelle took a spot at the bar in front of Lillian. "So what's good?" she asked with a smile.

"Mom, what are you doing here?"

"What, can't I get out for a drink like everyone else?"

"Of course you can. It's just... I don't think I've ever seen you in here before."

"Well now you have. I'll take a vodka tonic."

"Okay!" she said with a bounce of excitement. "Coming right up."

"So what's the word around town in light of our new guests?"

"Everybody's talking about it. Some want to leave now. Some already have."

"Oh, really?"

119

"Yeah, do you remember Dane Harris? He took his family and split. A few others went with. Can't say that I blame them."

"Interesting." Isabelle sipped her drink. She looked around the bar; it was busier than she expected. Truth be told, she didn't know what to expect; she probably hadn't set foot in the place in five years. A group of college-aged guys playing pool caught her attention. Maybe she would join them. Conversation with a complete stranger might be exactly what she needed.

Lilian leaned over the bar, scanning the floor with a sudden curiosity. "Mom, where's Tommy?"

"Nisha's watching him for a bit." Isabelle's face dropped, her smile faded, and her eyes had a sudden heaviness about them. She knew what came next.

"Are you sure he's safe? I mean, I love Nisha, but she's not exactly great with kids. I don't think Dad would be very happy if he knew you left Tommy with anybody."

Isabelle's attempt at serenity was over before it even began. "You really are your father's daughter. An hour Lillian. All I wanted was a fucking hour. Can't I get a break, too?"

"Mom, I'm sorry. I didn't mean—"

"Save it." Isabelle walked with purpose toward the back of the bar and the restroom area.

"Mom, wait." Lillian started to chase after her mother, but Vanessa stopped her.

"Let her be." Vanessa rubbed the small of Lillian's back. "She just needs to cool off. Everyone's on edge lately. It's only going to get worse now that the military is here."

"I suppose you're right. I just feel so bad for her locked up at home all day, every day. I didn't mean to drive her off."

"You didn't do anything wrong. I feel for her, too, but I wouldn't know what to say to her. I barely know the woman."

"That's kind of my point. If she got out of the house a little more, you would."

Isabelle barged into the men's room, where a tall, attractive man in a form-fitting red T-shirt stood in front of the urinal. He was one of the pool players. The man attempted to zip up as soon as he saw her, but she rushed over and spun him around. He was a good-looking guy, clean-cut, mid-twenties by the looks of him. She dropped to her knees and yanked his pants to around his ankles in one swift move. She looked up at his face and marveled at his tone physique. He smiled and gently began to run his fingers through her hair. She slapped his hand away and pushed him backward into the urinal, wetting the back of his shirt and exposed ass. "Don't fucking touch me," she said with authority. She wasn't here to be nice. She was going to treat him the same way she felt her husband treated her. *Do as you're told. Any thoughts you have on the matter mean less than shit.* She rummaged through her purse, spilling its contents about the dirty floor. "Here, hold this." She handed the man the framed photo of her and Tobias on their wedding day.

Isabelle said no more. She quickly set upon her task, not at all gently. An anger swelled as she thought of her husband. Instead of pushing him from her mind, she welcomed it. She imagined Tobias there, helpless to stop her. The man was finished in thirty seconds flat. Disappointing to be sure, but Isabelle wasn't fulfilled. The entire point of this exercise was to feel something, anything. It was over before she even had the time to process if she liked it or not. How it felt or how much further she would let this scenario play out was cut short by no fault of her own. Similar to her husband, this man was ruining a perfectly good fantasy. Isabelle wouldn't have it, not today. This man would have no say when it ended. She kept going until he finally pulled himself off of her.

"I need a minute, lady. What's the rush?"

It was as if a switch went off. Her face went red. She pushed him to the door. "Get the fuck out of here!"

The man was tangled in his bunched-up pants. He tripped and fell to his knees. She pushed him again. This time he hurried out of the bathroom, desperately trying to pull his pants up. He crashed against the wall opposite the restroom before scrambling out of the nearest exit at the back of the bar.

In the man's haste, he'd dropped the picture, and its glass frame shattered. The photo itself lay face-down in a puddle of piss. Isabelle smirked as she picked it up. With her finger, she guided droplets of urine around the surface of the photo, depositing them atop Tobias's smiling face. She tossed the broken frame into the garbage. The photo itself she held onto. Isabelle leaned into the sink. She stared at her reflection in the mirror, emotionless.

Another man entered. He was not nearly as appealing as the first, a little short and pudgy. She quickly turned to face him. "You, against the wall." She shoved the damp photo into his chest. "Here, hold this."

W.J. Hegarty

CHAPTER FOURTEEN

Apprehension

Evening had set on a troubled Pepperbush. Its citizens were home with loved ones. Refugees filled the various shelters, all preparing in their own way for the inevitable. Town Hall was empty this time of night, save for Mayor Lancaster and his inner circle gathered around a table far too large for the few men it hosted.

Mayor Lancaster sipped from a glass of Brandy, his leathery features illuminated by firelight. "It would be quite a shame if something tragic were to befall Mr. Burke sometime during the coming excitement, wouldn't you agree, Joshua?"

"I shudder to think about that, Donald. After all, the man *is* a pillar of the community."

Near on twenty-five years ago, Joshua fast-tracked a local bill that on the surface ensured every resident of Pepperbush, within or outside of town limits, received a lucrative tax incentive. The idea was that Pepperbush sat atop a newly discovered aquifer; the community literally had access to free clean water, virtually forever. It was decided that a percentage of the water would be pumped out and sold to local municipalities at a premium and that the profits would be shared with Pepperbush's residents in the form of waving state taxes. All well and good unless you scrutinized Joshua's paperwork with a fine-tooth comb, which no one did.

Essentially, by agreeing to this proposal, the citizens of Pepperbush not only signed away any rights to a natural resource below the very land they owned, but they would now be taxed in perpetuity for its usage. The people of Pepperbush would also pay for the inconvenience of Donald Lancaster's new water-bottling company, which set up operations a county away from Pepperbush's prime location directly above the source. Joshua hid the bill's intent under layers of technical jargon and legalese that your average citizen couldn't decipher even if they could keep awake long enough to read the document in the first place.

Mayor Lancaster received a phone call from a furious Jim soon after Takashi and his men arrived. Phone service was still spotty at best. Like the Internet, it would be available one day and gone the next. Jim was a town over, at an abandoned convenience store twenty miles away. Apparently, the sheriff had taken it upon herself to exile the mayor's muscle without bothering to speak with him first. That simply would not do. Lancaster promptly sent Phillip on an impromptu road trip to fetch his attack dog. Phillip was uneasy. Like everyone else in the room, he hadn't set foot outside of town limits since before the crisis. Driving past the gate guards unmolested was of no consequence for Mayor Lancaster's men. Though someone like Phillip leaving the safety of the berm raised eyebrows, it wasn't uncommon for Jim to come and go at all hours. So when Phillip returned an hour later with a battered passenger, no questions were asked.

At a glance, Jim looked out of place with these men, and he was. The man was crude, cruel, and unkempt before the world turned to shit. Now he was nearly off his leash, if anyone ever really had any control over him to begin with. Mayor Lancaster never asked Jim directly to see to the more unsavory tasks that needed doing. Implications were all that were necessary to send the brute on his way. Lancaster hinted that Tobias was stirring things up, things that the Mayor would prefer to be left alone. An eye towards Jim was all that was required to set him to task.

Jim nodded. "I got something in mind for the Burkes, no problem. They were on my radar, anyway. Fucking loudmouth is all Tobias is. I'll take care of it. There's something I need to see to first, though."

"Care to elaborate, James?" Mayor Lancaster raised his eyes from thought. He took in Jim's large shape, outlined by the firelight. The brute's eyes stared off blankly into the flames.

"Not particularly, no," Jim said plainly.

"Well then, it's probably for the best that we leave it at that." Mayor Lancaster chuckled with an overly long pull from a large cigar.

"What about his family? Little chance he'll be very far away from them." Phillip had grown convincing at hiding his displeasure with his master's more nefarious schemes.

"Well if the man was foolish enough to leave his back door unlocked, one wouldn't be very surprised to find that a few of those things had managed to have their way with his loved ones. All the more tragic if you ask me." Lancaster spit a mouthful of Brandy into the fire. Its sizzle echoed throughout the chamber, and his familiar grin finally returned.

Jim chuckled, more of a snort than a true laugh. His belly fat and large man-boobs jiggled up and down with each heave of his stout frame.

Lancaster and his lapdogs were pleased with themselves, and the laughter echoed throughout Town Hall.

"Heartbreaking, really," Joshua added with a nudge to Phillip, who remained mostly silent throughout the proceedings.

Phillip was apprehensive over his colleague's implications. Murder over a public disagreement was inconceivable. His mind raced. *Is this really happening? Am I hearing this right? They're talking about murdering a man and possibly his entire family to boot.* He didn't dare express his reservations aloud. Phillip was on the wrong side of the angels to be sure— more than twenty years at Lancaster's side ensured it—but this was something else entirely. Rigging ballots and swaying local opinion through less than savory means was bad enough, but he grew accustomed to it over the years. The knots in the pit of his stomach after breaking the law or intimidating people for Lancaster faded years ago. In their place, a sort of callus grew. Scar tissue covered up the old feelings, but they were still there, deep down as they were. There *was* a good man in Phillip still. Once this impending danger had passed, Phillip had every intention of joining Tobias on his journey. His days as Mayor Lancaster's lapdog were at an end. Colonel Takashi's revelation this afternoon put all of that into jeopardy.

11:40 pm - Shearburn Residence

Mother Leeds closed early. Everyone needed time to prepare for the coming turmoil, including the owner of the town's bar. Vanessa toiled away at her computer for a sizable portion of her time off, Since the power returned, she had been unable to reach the Internet. Miraculously, after a few hours of frustration, she was finally able to bring up the web. Relief really took hold when she found her game was still up and running. "Where the hell was this server anyway? On the moon? How the hell was it still operating?" Only two of her friends were logged in. The ghost town for a chat didn't bode well for the other users she had hoped were simply busy during their absence when she was last online.

69kilr69: don u get it girl he's not coming back he is fucking dead
spArkLe: bullshit 69 he just lost power he'll be back soon watch
69kilr69: yeah whatever
PprBsh84: hey guys im back power was only down for a few hours last night into this morning
69kilr69: we were worried
spArkLe: glad to see you r still with us
PprBsh84: they say if, when the power goes again might be for good
spArkLe: keep ur chin up
PprBsh84: Look guys I might not be on for awhile, something happened
69kilr69: wats up
spArkLe: is everything ok?
PprBsh84: a group of soldiers showed up last night, looks like they've been through hell, said there was an army of those things chasing them from Philly heading right for us
69kilr69: ....
spArkLe: OMG Ppr! I'll be praying for you tonight
PprBsh84: It's Vanessa, my name is Vanessa and I live in a little town called Pepperbush north east of Philadelphia on the outskirts of the New Jersey Pine Barrens, if anyone in the area is reading this be prepared, we r not
spArkLe: Good luck Vanessa be safe tonight God bless u
69kilr69: don't b a hero if you have to run run
PprBsh84: thanks u 2 really enough about me what else is going on today?
69kilr69: MandyLove was logged in earlier said shit was bad over there
spArkLe: I was just telling her she should
69kilr69: quit playin spArkLe
PprBsh84: you still there sweetie?
spArkLe: has logged off
69kilr69: fuck
PprBsh84: Jesus I never imagined it would come down to just the two of us
69kilr69: i hear that
PprBsh84: hey while were still here
69kilr69: yeah
PprBsh84: no hard feelings for all the fights we use to have ok?
69kilr69: i feel ya, me too

CHAPTER FIFTEEN

Mobilize

Sam offered Takashi and his unit room to spread out in the security headquarters. Although it was cramped for space, the effort was appreciated. Sam was also in attendance. His men were spread out around Pepperbush, helping with various aspects of preparing for the coming conflict. Garrett and Soraya displayed what little remained of their weapons and ammunition in preparation for the long night that lay ahead. Strategies were drawn up, and plans of attack and defense were suggested, shot down, or agreed upon. They had been at it since before dawn.

Garrett tossed one of their few remaining boxes of ammunition onto the table. "We're not looking good, Colonel."

"That's not what I asked, Garrett. Inventory, what are we working with?" Takashi furrowed his brow. His tense posture wasn't lost on those in attendance.

"Soraya and I policed up everything we dragged along here with us. Roughly four thousand rounds of rifle ammo. That's about five hundred rounds each, give or take. About one hundred rounds each for our sidearms and no explosives to speak of, sir."

"You're right. That's not good."

"Honestly, sir, if the infected number even a fraction of what we faced in Philadelphia, from a purely mathematical standpoint, we can't possibly put them all down."

"Not by ourselves, anyway," Miller added. "These people are well-armed and are willing to help."

"Oh, that's just great." Radzinski was frustrated. "We're not shooting at birds and squirrels here. These backwoods motherfuckers don't have one clue as to what's going on."

"They volunteered to help, Radzinski," Miller said. "That's good enough for me."

"Yeah well, then they better know what they're doing because it's *our* asses on the line." Radzinski disregarded Miller and the others in attendance as he moved in closer to Takashi than either man was comfortable with. "I mean, what are we still doing here anyway, sir? We warned them. Conscience clear, let's bug out."

Miller stepped between Takashi and Radzinski before his commanding officer could answer. "Where do you think these people are supposed to go, huh? Or us for that matter? You got an answer for that? Holding out here is just as good as anywhere else. Hell, this town is probably safer than most, being out here in the middle of nowhere."

"Tell that to those rotten fuckers following us." Radzinski pushed away from Miller's proximity. He needed Takashi to see reason. "Colonel, this shithole is going to be overrun and we're going to burn through our ammo, and for what? Just to hit the road again? Only difference is we'll be even more beat up than when we got here in the first place. I vote we pack our shit and go, right fucking now."

"Well, I guess it's a good thing this decision isn't up for a vote, then." Again, Miller intervened. "We're not going to leave these people to die. Besides, there's too many of them to transport, anyway. There *is* no other option. We make our stand here."

"We're no good to anyone if we're all dead."

"Miller's right, Radzinski." Takashi at least heard the man out. "We're not leaving these people to face a conflict of our own making. But I won't force any of you to stay. There's the door. Use it if you have to."

"We *could* attempt to evacuate," Aiko offered.

"Evacuation *is* a viable option, sir," Jeremiah said. "But we would have to act now."

"See!" Radzinski was thrilled with the apparent acknowledgment. "This town's a fucking death trap. The medics get it. We shouldn't stay here."

"That is not what I said, John." Jeremiah was quick to dispel any misinterpretation of his statement. "I suggested an evacuation, *not* abandonment."

Radzinski relented, though he continued to pace the room.

"I don't see that we have any other choice *but* to stay." Takashi declared the matter final. "We have no set destination, no unit to meet up with or base of operations to fall back to. The logistics of evacuating all of these people in the next twelve hours makes it impossible to do anything other than to try to ride this out. However this plays out, people, we're in it for the duration."

Sam laid out a map of Pepperbush for Takashi and his unit to better familiarize themselves with the town's layout and terrain. Each soldier's designated location was marked in red, as well as the expected direction of the attack.

"Garrett, you've done this before, I assume?" Takashi asked.

"I have, sir. Only we were up against hundreds, not thousands." Garrett pointed out his location on the map. "My nest is ready for the long haul, and I'll have support from the bar below. A few of the locals or refugees offered to help. Hell, I don't know who's who, sir. I can't tell them apart."

"Does it matter?"

"They're breathing. That's all that matters. From my vantage point, I should see those things coming over the berm before anyone else does. More importantly, I've got the gate covered. Anything moves half a klick from our exit gets put down."

"Good." Takashi turned to the youngest of his unit. "Broderick?"

"The church looks good, sir. Once the last of the refugees is inside, I'll secure it for the night. Nothing is getting in there. I can promise you that." Broderick was brimming with confidence. His emotional state stirred a tinge of hope in the colonel as well as the townsfolk who were under his care.

"And I'll be here, coordinating the defense with Sam." Takashi pivoted from his busted leg. He would be useless in the coming fight. He knew it, but more importantly, his unit knew. If he was out in the field with the rest of them, their concern for him would be a distraction. "Miller, Radzinski, Rachel, and Soraya will be spread out along the southern edge of the berm with their designated groups of volunteers. And for God's sake, let the locals know to conserve their ammo. You cannot stress that enough tonight. Remember, people, keep these civilians in line. No cowboys out there, understood?" Takashi put much-needed emphasis on the term "cowboys." He'd seen it many times before with local populations offering assistance. They always meant well, but oftentimes, they merely got in the way. Most recently, only a few weeks ago, back in Philadelphia before things got really bad, groups of armed citizens would periodically show up, insisting on giving support. Although their intentions were good, their undisciplined style became more of a hindrance than anything else. In more than one instance, they cost more lives than they saved. "Jeremiah and Aiko will dig in with the displaced residents in the north. In the event that we become overrun, it will be up to you to mobilize their evacuation. Keep them ready but try to prevent panic." He shot a glance in Radzinski's direction. "If anyone has any questions or *constructive* input, now is the time."

"Nothing to add, sir," Jeremiah responded, monotone and as devoid of emotion as ever.

No one else said a word.

"Okay, people, fall out," Takashi said. "Broderick, you're with me. I want to make sure the relocation is continuing smoothly before we take our positions."

No more words were spoken as the unit filed out of the small security shack. The next few uncertain hours weighed heavily on their minds.

11:55 am - Mother Leeds

Mother Leeds was nearly empty, save for those who lived there, and Garrett, who was preparing for the inevitable.

Damon sent a barstool spinning across the hardwood. The stool tumbled into a table, sending a stack of neatly arranged chairs to the floor. "Wonderful, now there's an army of those fuckers on the way? I told you the day we found this dump we should steal a car and get the fuck out of here. Now we can't leave!"

"Where the hell would we have gone? Back to Baltimore? That place is fucked. You saw it yourself on the news." Markus stacked the chairs for a second time. "Don't put this shit on me, man."

"Let's just go, dude. Fuck these people. We can be a hundred miles out before those fucking things even get here. These hicks don't know shit. Fuck them. The soldiers will deal with this mess, man. Let's just go." Damon stood at the front door, gripping its handle tight. "Come on, man," he pleaded.

Markus walked across the room and pushed the door closed. "No," was all he offered Damon before returning to securing the bar.

"Fuck these hillbillies!"

"I wish you wouldn't say shit like that, Damon." Markus finished nailing a board to a window frame, then turned back to his friend. "These people have been good to us, and Vanessa's giving us work *and* letting us crash at the bar? Come on, man, you're too fucking stubborn."

"You know, you're turning into a real bitch out here in the country, bro. What the fuck's up with you lately?"

"You name one motherfucker back home who would let strangers live in their place and I'll shut up."

"Fine, but if we have to bolt and these *friends* of yours slow you down, you're on your own. Besides, we need to be boarding these windows up, anyway." Damon deflected, he continued the work as if that was his intent all along. Though he kept a watchful eye on the street through cracks in the boards.

The bell attached to the front door rang, alerting the men to visitors at the entrance of Mother Leeds. An unfamiliar trio entered, led by a tall, beautiful redhead. "Hello, is anyone in here?" She peeked in slowly at first, then made her presence known.

"I'm sorry, but we're closed." Markus hurried to greet them before they wandered too deeply into the bar. "We're really not set up to take in any more bodies tonight, just the staff." He blocked their way from going any farther. "Grace is looking over anyone without a place to stay. She's in the church at the other end of town. If you hurry, you can make it before they lock down for the night." Markus reached around the group and held the door open.

"In case you haven't heard, there's a shitstorm headed our way." Damon approached the group, arms outstretched and waving inches from their faces, attempting to shoo them away.

The redhead ignored Damon, determined to focus her attention on Markus. "Where are my manners? Let's try this again. Hello, I'm Samantha. This is Ayn and Ryan." She gestured to her companions, a fresh from the dorm—looking young man with a pronounced limp and a slender blonde who looked like she hadn't eaten in weeks. "We came in with a group of refugees a few weeks ago. Until today, we'd been staying at the bed-and-breakfast, but it looks like they're closing the place until this blows over." Samantha pulled a barstool close but didn't sit.

"Nice to meet you, Samantha. I'm Markus." While he reached out to shake her hand, his eyes met hers. He stammered for a moment before composing himself. "Vanessa's not here right now. She owns the place. I guess that leaves me in charge, so what can I do for you guys?"

"Well, we were sort of wondering..." Ryan spoke up but was hesitant, so Samantha continued for him.

"I know that they want the refugees to ride this out over in the church. I just don't like that place. It's too far away from the gate, and well, you guys are right here, so..." Samantha finally took a seat, maybe a little closer than Markus was prepared for.

Markus pulled up a stool beside her. "From what I hear, the church might be the safest place in town, Samantha. They're going to be well-armed in there, not to mention one of the soldiers is camping out with them for the duration."

"If it's all the same, I'd like the option of leaving this town entirely if I need to. Seeing as the bar is right at the edge of town, I thought we could stay here... if that's okay, I mean." Samantha placed a hand on Markus's. She looked into his eyes for a brief moment before he stood up.

"All you had to do was ask." Markus smiled.

Damon sighed.

Everyone went quiet as Garrett entered the room. He saw the newcomers' arrival from his vantage point on the roof. As far as he was concerned, the extra support was a relief.

Garrett spent more than half his life in the Army. Having been stationed in dozens of hotspots in his nearly thirty-year career, he had seen more than his share of combat. Most importantly, in that time, he'd interacted with people from many cultures and all walks of life. That experience trained him to read people very well. He could look at a crowd of complete strangers and pick out who needed direct oversight and who could be trusted to follow orders without supervision.

With so many years in service, he was a lifer in every sense of the word. The last seven of those years were spent as an instructor at sniper school, his days of touring the world long behind him. Among his students he had a reputation of being a hard-ass. Tough but fair. More than fifty percent of his students washed out due to the rigors of his advanced form of training, but the ones that graduated were loyal for life. They shared a sense of mutual respect most of the washouts could never understand. When he was ordered to leave his newest class for immediate deployment to Philadelphia, he knew the situation was something to be concerned about. Whatever lay ahead was certainly not the training exercise rumor some green officers were spreading around. "I need hands and eyes. You and you are with me on the roof." He singled out Damon and the newly arrived Ryan.

"But I just got here." Ryan held his arms up as if to ask, *Why me?*

"And I appreciate that, son, but right now, we need all the help we can get. I'll thank you when this is over." Garrett gave the kid a firm pat on the shoulder on his way over to converse with Markus.

"What can I do?"

"I need you down here, Markus. You and the ladies keep your eyes on the street. If anything shows itself, do not engage, but let me know immediately. Are we clear?" Garrett made sure he held eye contact with Markus. He felt the young man's trepidation but needed one last sign of reassurance. He knew he could count on the young man to see the others through if it came to it. It was vital Markus knew that as well.

"Yeah, we're good." Markus left the barstool and Samantha behind, following Garrett on his trek through the bar.

"Excellent, while you're at it, I'm going to need the three of you to start boxing up some of this alcohol and any nonperishables you can find. Canned goods, dry goods, nothing that can go bad if we have to bug out." Garrett casually flipped through a half-full box of cleaning supplies left on the bar top.

"What's that all about? Are you planning on taking off if shit gets too heavy?" Markus asked.

"With any luck, no, but *if* we have to leave in a hurry, it's best to have what we need ready to go. You follow me?"

"Yeah, I got it. Be prepared," Markus answered with the confidence Garrett expected from the young man. "We'll just stack the supplies by the front door for now."

"Good. Look, I'll be honest with you here, Markus. There is without a doubt a shitstorm of epic proportions headed our way. Possibly thousands of infected have been following us since Philadelphia."

"Thousands?" Samantha stood. Her carefree demeanor faded, if only just a little.

"Yes, girl, thousands." Garrett tapped Samantha on the head like a child.

Markus turned away, already fully engulfed in his task. Samantha and her companions drew close and eyed the spacious room as Garrett continued.

"One way or another, we're in for a long night, boys and girls. Do as I say, when I say, and every one of you will live through this. I promise."

1:30 pm - Southern Perimeter

The last of a caravan of vehicles out of the southernmost cluster of homes meandered out of sight toward the northern edge of Pepperbush.

Broderick ran past the procession to meet up with Takashi and stood at attention. "That's the last of them, sir. Everyone south of Main Street has

133

been relocated to the north. The ones who couldn't find a place to go are on their way to the church, where I'm heading now."

"Well done, Broderick. When you've got the church locked down, radio in."

"Yes, sir." Broderick saluted before boarding one of the few remaining vehicles and disappearing into the night.

"How many volunteers did we manage?" Takashi turned his attention back to Miller.

"Almost seventy, sir. They're divided into three groups spread out along the southern edge of the berm."

"That's a better turnout than I expected." Takashi allowed himself a near smile before he was interrupted.

"As long as these yokels don't shoot me in the back of the head, we might just pull this off," Radzinski sneered.

Takashi ignored the comment. Either Radzinski would make use of the volunteers or he wouldn't. The time for engaging the man in futile arguments had passed. "If you have everything you need, fall out to your position, Marine."

Radzinski didn't respond as he mounted the running boards of his waiting transport. He banged on the truck's roof, signaling the driver to go.

"Discipline's a running issue with that guy, huh, Colonel?"

"I've noticed it, too, Miller, believe me. The outbursts and increasing lack of discipline have only gotten worse since we've been on the road. The thing is, he wasn't like this before Philadelphia. At least that's the way I understand it. To be perfectly honest with you, talk from his commanding officer was that he was ready to recommend Radzinski for a promotion before all this began."

"They say war changes a man, sir."

"That it does. War is one thing, Captain. I don't know what to call this." Takashi managed a brief sigh as he signaled Ron, who was waiting by a tree. "Ron, time to go. Miller, I'll be at command with Sam and this useless leg of mine," Takashi said while knocking against the hard-plastic brace covering his knee.

"Don't let it get to you, sir. You'll be back in the shit with the rest of us in no time." Miller's words of encouragement fell on deaf ears as for the first time in Takashi's thirty years of active duty, he would be sitting this one out.

"Remember, if it gets too bad down here, don't wait for my orders. Just fall back. You're in charge, Captain."

"Understood, sir. Be safe tonight." Miller extended his hand. Takashi shook it before heading off toward Ron's truck.

2:05 pm - The Church

Broderick was a wet-behind-the-ears country boy from Arkansas before enlisting in the Army at eighteen. While most of his friends were having the time of their lives putting high school behind them with a near endless stream of parties, Broderick spent his days and weeks after graduation meeting with his recruiter and volunteering for community projects. Serving his country was a family tradition stretching back generations, and who was he to question it, much less be the one who broke that long line of proud family service? Before that summer was over, he was off to boot camp. His friends would figure it out eventually. After all, not everyone had what it took to serve their country; he was sure of it. Following boot camp, he crisscrossed the world. Each stop at a major city during his short time in the Army seemed like landing on an alien world for the young man. For a time, he lived in perpetual amazement at the beauty of these strange and wonderful new places he had only seen on TV.

A mere eighteen months out of boot camp, just six weeks away from his twenty-first birthday, Broderick was in for quite the treat. His friends in his unit had decided on a surprise for his birthday. Deployed or not, such a landmark occasion shouldn't go unrecognized, they felt. His buddies had it all planned out. They would have seventy-two hours of leave, plenty of time for the boys to show Broderick the time of his life in Thailand. Debauched though it might be, the things they had in mind would stay with the kid for a lifetime. With only a few weeks left to go, the anticipation was palpable within his unit. His friends could barely contain their excitement, almost ruining any chance at a genuine surprise, as some were quick to point out.

Orders would be rescinded a few days before their unit was scheduled to be deployed somewhere in Southeast Asia. Strange, why would they suddenly be sent to Philadelphia? It didn't make any sense. Since when did American soldiers get deployed, combat-ready, within their own borders? They didn't. The consensus going around his unit was that this was most likely a last-minute training OP before heading out. No matter, they would still show Broderick a good time, wherever they happened to touch down. The joyous atmosphere of their unit quickly diminished once they put boots down in Philadelphia. The idea of celebrating Broderick's birthday faded in the face of an unimaginable crisis.

Several dozen people decided to ride out the coming attack in Pepperbush's sole church. Sitting up on a small hill in the northwestern side of town, it was located in one of the more naturally protected plots of land within city limits. The church was deemed by Colonel Takashi as the largest structure farthest from the projected attack points. It was decided then that this would be the best location to hide those with no place to go, as well as the frail or those unable to fight.

Over the last few hours, Grace kept herself busy by welcoming people to the church and showing them around. The task was exhausting for the old woman, though she did an admirable job keeping it nonapparent for the already frightened people. "Everyone, go ahead and make yourselves at home. There's plenty of room for you all. Beds are in the back room for those of you having trouble walking. Drinks and sandwiches are by the alter if anyone is hungry. And please, if you see someone in need, give them a hand." She announced a variation on that greeting as people trickled in.

"There must be fifty people in here, Grace. Quite a turnout, huh?" Don commented, a nervous smile hiding behind his thick black beard.

"Forty-seven to be exact. I've been keeping count. Including one of those brave soldiers. Broderick, I believe the young man's name is."

"That's me, ma'am," Broderick said while carefully making his way through the growing crowd to stand at the elderly woman's side. Together, they surveyed the growing numbers. "All the doors and windows are secure, ma'am. We don't expect to see any infected this far north. However, I think it's pertinent that we push some of these pews against the doors," Broderick suggested. "Just as a precaution."

"Certainly, my dear. I'll have some of the younger men help you." Grace hobbled her way to the back of the church, toward a group of men she noticed chatting in a corner.

"Thank you, ma'am."

Broderick, Don, and a few others continued the finishing touches of securing the church. Dozens of people meandered around the large open room, some lying down to rest weary limbs, others taking up positions in pews, praying. Broderick scanned the crowd. His stomach twisted in knots at the realization that three-quarters of these people under his care were elderly or crippled. He watched a pair of old women who must have been in their nineties wheel another elderly man who barely looked conscious to the front of the altar. The women made the sign of the cross in near unison, bowed their heads, and began to pray. He looked to another side of the room where Emily sat alone in a pew, happily doing a crossword puzzle. If Takashi was wrong about tonight and the horde of infected following them from Philadelphia showed up anywhere other than the south, things were going to get real bad, real fast.

3:50 pm - Burke Residence

Tobias was at home, seeing to last-minute security of his own. Even at the northernmost homes, where it was deemed relatively safe, at the very least making sure all the windows and doors were locked was a priority, even with the outsides boarded up. First the living room, followed by the foyer and the kitchen, each room he checked, Tobias found the windows unlocked. *What was going on?* he thought. Now was not the time to overlook the most basic safety measures. "Why are all of these windows unlocked, Isabelle?"

Isabelle barely registered Tobias with a glance. "Oh, I cleaned those yesterday." She shrugged. "I must have forgotten to lock a few of them."

"Jesus, Izzy, every window in the house is unlocked! You know what the soldiers said." Tobias rushed to the other end of the kitchen only to find the back door unlocked as well. He slammed the door shut and promptly locked it. "Dammit Isabelle, you have to be more careful. I don't want to think about what would happen if just one of those things got in here, especially if I wasn't home."

"It must have slipped my mind, Tobias. I'm sorry." Isabelle still refused eye contact.

"Are you okay? I'm mean, is everything alright, honey?" Tobias took her hand in his.

"I... I've just had a lot on my mind lately, you know?"

"I know. We both have. This is just not the time to let our guard down. That's all."

Isabelle yanked her arm away and wiped her hands on her dress. His mere touch sickened her of late. She had grown to detest Tobias's lectures, but more so his attempts at amiability that immediately followed. One moment, he was the overprotective husband with all the right answers and apathy toward her feelings. The next, once his point was sufficiently made, he was compassionate and warm. Like she didn't see right through him.

"Okay, I get it. If I forgot to lock the fucking door, big deal. It's locked now. Jesus Christ, Tobias, you're relentless with this shit." Isabelle pushed a box aside. Its contents spilled to the floor.

"Relentless? Excuse me if I'm out of line, but you've never even seen one of those things outside of the news, and trust me, you don't want to. I know

Takashi said the infected won't make it this far north, but we still need to take precautions, which begin with keeping the house locked."

"Precautions, yeah I get it. And priorities, right? The outside of the fucking windows are boarded up! If they can get through that, a locked window won't mean shit. Just leave me alone, Tobias." Isabelle stormed out of the front door, leaving it wide open behind her as Lillian rounded the corner into the kitchen.

Tobias leaned against the refrigerator, his hands pressed to his forehead. He heard his daughter coming and quickly composed himself for her benefit.

"What's going on, Dad? What's Mom so upset about?"

"I wish I knew, Lily." Tobias led his daughter off into the garage. "Come on, let's go pack a few things into the SUV just in case."

5:55 pm - Police Station

Marisol and her modest seven police-officer force were joined by just over a dozen volunteers, mostly armed with shotguns and hunting rifles. The police station, though small, was well-fortified. The sheriff was wrapping up the assigning of tasks while Seth handed out extra ammunition and sidearms. More than a few of the volunteers had their own, though no one would turn down the extra bullets.

"Isaac, you're staying here with Corey and any officers who aren't already on patrol. This building absolutely must stay secure in case we have to come back here in a hurry. Is that clear?"

"Yes, ma'am. When you get back, you'll find this place better than you left it."

"That's what I want to hear, Isaac. Seth, myself, and the remaining police will be out with Takashi's unit, patrolling the perimeter. They're expecting a few hundred of those things *at least*, so we've got our work cut out for us tonight. If anyone comes looking for help, let them in, but keep an eye on them. Don't take any chances. If someone is acting suspicious or snooping around where they don't belong, put them in a cell. We can apologize later. If things get bad tonight, we cannot afford to lose the station, no matter what. Is that understood?" Marisol didn't have to wait long for her men to respond in unison. Preparations were going much smoother than she anticipated, at least for now.

Behind the police station, Soraya was giving some volunteers a quick lesson on proper covering fire and successfully engaging the enemy when outnumbered. For most of the volunteers, their only experience with firearms was the occasional hunting trip or shooting at static targets. A scant few had served in various branches of the military, decades ago. That, at least, was a small comfort.

"I'll be honest, lady, I ain't ever shot at nothing coming at me before, except that old black bear that one time. He might've been running away. I'm not sure now. Scared the shit out of me, though."

"Do not worry. Same principle as the bear. You take your time, aim for head, okay? It will kill them." Soraya knew it would be a very long night.

Under different circumstances, she would have loved to explore the surrounding forest, see the vibrant new colors of spring emerging from a long winter, take in the local wildlife, and maybe even spot a deer or two. If she was really lucky, she might have even stumbled upon a tranquil creek to swim in. Now the only thing on her mind was survival. If she saw the sunrise, she would count it a blessing.

9:20 pm - Southern Perimeter

All around Rachel, volunteers were spread out among the trees, a few dozen rifles aimed into the darkness at invisible enemies. A good number of those rifles trembled. The night's dew slid down their barrels and stocks, wetting the volunteers' hands. Rachel watched as some of them shook their hands or fumbled around trying to dry themselves. Mostly these people were simply nervous. She couldn't fault them for that, but when the time came, would these little distractions cost everyone she was assigned to their lives? Those in her charge could only guess what lay ahead. A few were brimming with confidence, though it was more than clear to her that most couldn't hide an overwhelming sense of dread. They were right to be afraid, as far as she was concerned. After all, it was less than two weeks ago when she and the rest of her hodgepodge of a unit barely made it out of Philadelphia alive. Rachel knew what these people had coming their way, and if not for a sense of pity over her and her unit leading scores of infected to their doorstep, she would have left first thing in the morning.

The leaves hanging by Rachel's face popped and jumped under the first raindrops of the evening. "Wonderful." She sighed.

Springtime always brought an excess of rain to Pepperbush. How the downpour would affect the town's chances of surviving the coming onslaught remained unknown. Rachel's already low spirits sunk even further. It was one thing to fight an enemy who was shooting back at you in bad weather—they had to deal with it, too—but no one knew how inclement weather would affect these things, if at all. Rachel tried not to show it, but she was scared. Terrified was more like it. Her eyes darted from one man to the next. It was unmistakable; uncertainty was spreading through her ranks with the rain and there was shit she could do about it.

Water trickled down Rachel's weapon, collecting at her grip. She had seen combat over the years in Afghanistan and Iraq. She was nervous then, too, but this was different. There were no grizzled old soldiers to ease her fears with tales of past glory or buddies she'd served with to help cut the tension. No, it was very simple for her. As far as Rachel was concerned, this new unknown enemy was terrifying. There was something very unsettling about an enemy who didn't fall from repeated rounds to the chest. The rain's intensity turned to a steady downpour, blurring her vision, but maybe, just maybe, the weather would keep these things away, she hoped.

CHAPTER SIXTEEN

The Calm Before

Takashi stood on the porch of Sam's makeshift command center. Steam rose from his coffee as he peered into the darkness. The wind began whipping up, pushing the rain like so many tiny hammers pounding the sheet-metal roof of the overhang. Sam joined him, peering out into the rainy darkness.

"I appreciate the coffee, Sam. I love the stuff. Can't remember a time when I didn't." He closed his eyes, enjoying another long, slow sip.

"So how bad is it out there, Colonel? The cities, that is."

"It's a war zone out there. The whole damned country. Baltimore was the first of the major East Coast cities to fall. People, ordinary citizens, fled in all directions, leaving armies of infected in their wake. Once turned, the infected just roam on a journey to God knows where. Some carriers become distracted and just wander off on their own. The remainder press on, merging with and wandering away from other groups. Something still active in their brains compels them to keep moving. That's all they do until eventually they join with other large groups wandering themselves. There's no science to it, not yet anyway. It wasn't long before the Eastern Seaboard was pockmarked with thousands-strong hordes of infected. This country— the whole world, for that matter—after this is over with will never be the same again. It can never go back to the way it was, not after something like this." Takashi took another sip from his coffee. "Little pockets of humanity like you have here, tucked away in the middle of nowhere, are most likely the only spots left that have any chance of surviving this." Takashi never took his eyes from the darkness as he continued. "It was obvious, early on, that my superiors and theirs weren't giving up the whole story. And not just for the civilians, either. My unit, and I assume many others just like us, were as equally in the dark as you. We were woefully unprepared for this."

"Even if you *were* ready for the unthinkable, what are you supposed to do with millions of folks living in apathy? The problem here in Pepperbush, leastwise, was that most people were content to know that whatever was going on out there wasn't happening to them, at least not on the same scale as we saw on TV. Weeks of that mindset led us right here. We're just not ready for this."

"I don't know if anybody is. We ran into quite a bit of that ourselves. Civilians refusing to listen when ordered to leave their homes only compounded the problem. But what can you do? Short of nuclear fallout, I don't think I'd abandon my home, either, no matter what I was told. Honestly, I don't know much more than you. Like I said, we were on the ground as things escalated. I'm sure you're aware that in the first days of the outbreak, all private and commercial aircraft were grounded. Military and official government craft still had unrestricted access to the airways, of course. The occasional private jet would be spotted from time to time, certainly not military, but the super-rich and powerful elite don't answer to the same rules as you and I." Takashi slowly shook his head.

"They never have."

"Even when you're trying your best to keep people safe and contain a situation, you are *always* going to have those hotshots who refuse to listen. And you know what? I get it. I really do. No one wants to be told they can't do something, especially in their own back yard. Anyway, a few days after the flight ban went into effect, we watched an F/A-18 shoot down some poor bastard's Cessna. Who can say what was said to the pilot over the radio, if anything at all? By that point, preventing the virus from spreading was all that mattered. No warning shots were given. Apologies could come later—or never. It didn't matter. No one seemed to care, really. The neighborhood it crashed into was already overrun by infected. Besides, there were more important things to worry about than some guy getting blown-up for breaking the no-fly rule. He could have been a terrorist, for all they knew. After all, that's what command was saying then. This had to be the work of terrorists, a chemical weapons attack of some kind. They were sure of it."

"But you don't believe that, do you?"

"Who can say for sure? I don't know. It could be, I suppose. I've certainly never witnessed anything like this before, though, and I've seen black-project stuff that would blow your mind. But a weaponized virus like this, on this scale? No, this is something else entirely. Shit, by that point the country was largely under martial law, anyway. The cities that hadn't had an outbreak yet were heavily policed to the point where they may as well have been Cold War Eastern Bloc states. How long has it been? Four weeks? Six? Doesn't matter, I guess. Sometime during week three or four, they had a radical idea to stop the spread of the virus. It was thought that spraying a region with a sleeping agent from planes would knock everyone out, making it easier for the CDC to move in and quarantine an area. Unbeknownst to them at the time, unfortunately the infected were immune. In essence, all they achieved that day was spreading the infection to the remainder of the city, who while unconscious became helpless victims. The dead's numbers multiplied tenfold in a matter of hours."

"Goddamned fools."

"You'll get no argument on that front here. But they had to try *something*. The days of endless debate are over. If we don't act fast, we'll lose everything. If they didn't know it then, they damn sure know it now."

11:45 pm - Shearburn Residence

Vanessa was nearly finished securing her home for the long night. She was done boarding up the first-floor windows and arranging furniture as makeshift blockades against the doorways. The furniture's additional weight was merely a precaution for fear of the door frames themselves collapsing under the strain of dozens of infected piling up. This would go much quicker if she had some help, she thought, but seeing that the entirety of town was currently doing the same thing, she was alone, as usual. Markus would have gladly helped, but she thought it best to leave Mother Leeds in the hands of someone she could trust. Lillian had every intention of riding the night out here, but her father balked at the idea. Rather than arguing, she relented. Vanessa's thoughts momentarily drifted back to a better time when she and Clint first moved to Pepperbush. She smiled at the thought of him clumsily tipping over the china cabinet while trying to move it. At the time, she was pretty upset, as the porcelain heirlooms came from her late grandmother, herself coincidently widowed at a young age.

Most of the windows were high enough off the ground that they should be safe. If any of those things broke the glass, they probably couldn't climb in anyway. Her main concern was the front and back doors. To help with the issue, Sam suggested pulling her car up right next to the front door. The vehicle's weight, along with the front door opening out, should be sufficient to keep any unwanted guests from getting in, he told her. With any luck, when the night was over, she would be able to return home and find her house the same as she had left it, more or less.

She was nearly done securing the first floor and only had a few more things she wanted to do before heading off for the church. She promised Grace she would ride out the night with her and Broderick for the duration to help them look after the elderly and those unable or unwilling to help fight off the impending attack. When the house was secured, she would climb out of a second-story window onto her patio's roof, then lower herself down the ten-foot drop to the ground. She was confident that she would be able to get back up when the night passed. If not, someone had to have a ladder she could borrow. All that remained was to tip over her refrigerator, wedging it in between an adjacent wall and the back door in hopes of blocking that entranceway.

Vanessa allowed herself a moment's rest, wanting a little peace before her world got a little closer to hell than it already was. She took a seat on the stairs, opened a beer, and lit a cigarette. *Ten minutes won't kill anybody*, she imagined while enjoying a momentary respite.

Vanessa stubbed out her cigarette and went upstairs to retrieve her shoes. Before his passing, Clint continually told her it was unsafe to rearrange the furniture or do yard work barefoot, but she always laughed it off.

"Have you ever met anyone that actually dropped a sofa on their foot? I haven't," she would reply. "That's stuff you see in movies." Her logic on such things was forever lost on him, but that was part of her appeal. Vanessa's carefree nature always intrigued him.

A knock on the back door pulled her from thought before she reached the top of the stairs. Maybe it was Sam or Markus coming to give her a hand.

Typical, now that I'm almost done, she thought with a smile. The effort was appreciated nonetheless. Whoever it was could at least help her climb off the roof. "You're late, slacker. I'm already finished," she yelled as she ran to answer the back door.

"Matter a fact, I'm just in time, sweetness," an intoxicated Jim slurred as he pushed his way into her home. His other hand carried a half-empty bottle of whiskey.

The door slammed open, hard, breaking a pane of glass and embedding the doorknob in the wall.

Vanessa gently approached the staggering brute. "Jim, get out of here. I'm trying to lock up. I have to leave. I promised Grace I'd help out at the church tonight," Vanessa said while gently guiding him back the way he came.

"You ain't going nowhere, bitch." Jim slapped her in the face, sending her spinning to the floor.

Vanessa was quickly to her feet and dashing for the living room. She crashed hard into the front door and unlocked it in one quick motion. It didn't open. In her panic, Vanessa overlooked her car, pinning the door shut from the other side. Sam's idea to keep the infected out had her trapped with a monster just as deadly as the throngs descending upon Pepperbush.

Jim was on her fast for a big man. His arm came down like a sledge.

Vanessa's head was spinning. She was dazed from the blow Jim landed squarely on the back of her skull. She struggled to keep control of her body as her legs buckled.

Jim lunged. He pushed her hard, snapping her neck back and sending her crashing into the wall. The impact collapsed her to the floor. "You always thought you was better than me, ya little whore. Who the hell you think you is, coming to my town, flaunting that ass in my face like you laughing at me or something?" Jim yanked her up onto her knees by her shirt.

"I've never done anything to you, Jim," Vanessa choked as she tried to rise.

"Where you think you're going?" Jim said as he clubbed her in the head again with his huge bear-like fist.

Vanessa crumbled to the floor, unconscious.

Jim leaned over his prey, ripped open her shirt, and knelt down astride her, his mouth agape, drool falling onto her breasts. Jim fondled Vanessa's chest while putting his other hand down his pants. "Whore." He spit on her face. "Come to my town?" Jim struggled against his own large bulk to return to his feet. He unfastened his belt and dropped his pants. "I got something for you." More drool fell from his mouth as he slurred. He shook his limp manhood furiously, cursing its uselessness while releasing his prey in exchange for the whiskey bottle.

Vanessa was up in a flash. She lunged at Jim's exposed genitals, latching onto as much flesh as she could grab with both hands. She was sure to dig in deep with her fingernails. Jim screamed for help as he pulled her hair and flailed about, trying to wrestle her hands away. His manhood was ripping and tearing with each passing second. Vanessa's hands and arms quickly soaked with his blood as her fingertips finally penetrated his soft flesh and began migrating beneath the surface.

Jim's pants and underwear remained tangled around his ankles as he tried in vain to stumble away. Off-balance, Jim crashed through the coffee table to the floor. The furniture exploded on impact. Glass and wood shards littered the room. The impact sent Vanessa's laptop skidding across the floor. She stayed with him for the duration of the fall, digging deeper and deeper into his skin. Jim's screams changed octaves as Vanessa succeeded in tearing his dick and balls completely from his body. Ripped, jagged flesh lined a bloody, oozing cavity.

Vanessa's living room walls dripped with blood. The carpet, the furniture, and her, all hopelessly drenched. Jim's wound gushed. He stumbled and tripped, clawing at the damage, trying desperately to hold back the crimson from leaving his body. His flaccid, severed genitals lay in a puddle at his feet. He smashed them beneath his boot in his panic.

As Jim's agonizing wails grew, Vanessa tried to cover his mouth, attempting to muffle the sound, to no avail. His screams were booming, and if not for the abandoned street, they would have most certainly attracted attention. She leaned hard against Jim's throat with her elbow. His screams gradually turned to loud gurgles, though she begged the universe for him to go silent. "You like that, motherfucker? Can you breathe? You like how that feels?" Vanessa screamed at the man, nose to nose with her would-be killer.

She applied more pressure, the full weight of her body against his throat. One by one, as they succumbed to the weight of her sharp elbow, the tiny bones in his neck began to pop. Jim's naked, blood-drenched body was slippery. Vanessa could barely hold on as the dying man struggled. He tried to grab her hair and momentarily pulled her head to the side, but she fought against it. Ultimately his struggling did no good as Vanessa put all of her weight onto her elbow, crushing Jim's neck and cutting off his air supply completely. He began to cough up blood as the gurgles grew slower and much quieter. Eventually, after what seemed like far too long and when Vanessa was on the verge of exhaustion herself, Jim finally stopped fighting. Spent, Vanessa slid off of Jim's mass, coming to rest on the floor beside him, panting for breath.

Vanessa's living room was silent, save for a low hum and a quiet gurgle spewing from Jim's crushed throat. Spittle erupted from his mouth as tiny geysers of blood sprayed into the air in sync with the dying man's futile gasps for breath. Otherwise, Jim wasn't moving. Fine mists of red landed on Vanessa's face, fast becoming trickles of blood dripping down onto what was left of her torn, blood-soaked shirt.

"You son of a bitch, you son of a bitch!" Vanessa screamed. She reached for her laptop and slammed it down on Jim's chest and face over and over again. The device shattered. Jim's nose and teeth did the same. She ceased her pummeling after his jagged broken teeth and her ruined computer began tearing into her hands.

Vanessa dropped the broken machine in a heap next to Jim and leaned back against the twisted remains of her coffee table, panting like a dog. The room before her was ravaged. Broken furniture littered the place, and blood spray covered the walls, culminating at Jim's dying mass at her feet. His face was near unrecognizable. An occasional twitch from his hands or a leg kept her mind on the situation. She inched closer to the bloodied behemoth and put an ear to his chest. A slight wheezing was just audible. Jim still lived.

Vanessa slowly rose and made her way to the kitchen. Her hands shook nearly uncontrollably as she opened the refrigerator and fumbled for a beer. Her back was already tightening as she wearily sat at the kitchen table and lit a blood-soaked cigarette with trembling hands. Outside, the rain continued to pour as thunder and lightning set in, some of if deafening. Between bursts of thunder, Jim's gurgling was clearly unmistakable and seemed to grow louder with each passing barrage.

Over on the countertop, near where she always left her keys, the knife rack had spilled over in the struggle. Shiny blades glistened, twinkling along the walls with each flash of lightning. Vanessa wasn't about to leave Jim like that, even if he was a piece of shit. Did he deserve it? Absolutely, but she wouldn't—she couldn't. She knew what needed to be done.

Sobbing, Vanessa held the tip of the knife near Jim's eye. Tears ran down her cheeks, falling to mix with the blood on her shredded hands. She knew she shouldn't be upset. This monster would have done a hell of a lot worse to her had he kept the upper hand. The thunder roared again, followed by a quick spasm from Jim. Startled, she drove the knife deep into his eye socket. Vanessa pierced him in the eyes repeatedly. As she continued her assault, Jim's head rolled to the side. The blows continued but were no longer penetrating as the knife scraped his skull. Glancing blows sliced off pieces of his cheek and jaw. She continued thrusting long after what remained of Jim's face was scattered in front of her, until ultimately the knife broke. Vanessa collapsed atop the wet mess that was Jim. She slid off his slippery bulk and onto the floor beside him, exhausted from the effort and panting for breath.

1:07 am - The Berm

Charles and Beth had married just weeks before the outbreak. Neither had much in the way of savings to speak of, so even the most modest of honeymoons remained a pipe dream. They were more than content with each other, so a vacation as far as they were concerned didn't mean a thing. They were in love, and that was all that mattered. It was amusing for them to listen to their friends and family bicker over their lack of a honeymoon. The arguments that sometimes ensued and the entertainment they offered were well worth missing a trip to some stuffy resort.

They were the only legitimate couple working berm duty. It was completely Beth's idea, as Charles wouldn't hesitate to let people know. Everyone had to contribute in light of current circumstances, and she thought it much wiser to walk for a few hours at a time rather than do any number of the other boring, sometimes downright awful tasks that needed tending to around town. Charles wouldn't argue her logic, but nights like this gave him pause.

Conditions made it nearly impossible to see more than a few feet in front of them as they came upon a ladder to a watch post near the southern edge of the berm. The pouring rain and near-constant thunder became disorienting as Charles helped his wife reach the top of the rickety platform.

"Want to mess around?" he said, only partially joking.

"Very funny. This is ridiculous." Beth pulled her hood tight. She could barely keep her eyes open as the cold rain ran down her face and into her coat. Any attempt at keeping out the weather failed miserably for her. "*We* can barely even manage in this shit. There's no way those things can find us in a tsunami."

"I don't think you know what a tsunami is, babe, but I hear you. Let's just take a look and move on," Charles suggested. He shone his flashlight down the outer edge of the berm. The light illuminated thousands of infected clinging to the slick, muddy wall. The mass stretched the length of the berm and back out into the forest as far as his light would allow.

The closest of the infected were already atop the berm on either side of them. The downpour masked any noises the creatures made. The infected lunged, forcing the couple over the edge and away from the safety of their perch, down into the sea of flailing limbs below. Charles and Beth were swallowed up by the horde with no time for even a whimper as their bodies were torn limb from limb. Crunching, tearing, and a cacophony of excited moans were all drowned out by the growing storm. Any trace the newlyweds ever existed disappeared in seconds beneath a mass of rotten flesh.

Just beyond the southern edge of the berm, carriers clawed and dug at the town's only defense. The undead masses piled atop each other like so many army ants. The first to reach the berm were trampled into the soft mud by the sheer weight of numbers forcing their way in from behind. As far as the eye could see along the southern defenses, a massive wall of infected numbering in the thousands bore down on the unsuspecting town. Inch by inch, they crawled up the berm. The slower, heavier ones were buried in the mud and acted as footholds for lighter, more agile carriers. First by the dozens, then in the hundreds, infected began pouring over the top of the berm, their moans and shuffling drowned out by the fury of a late-spring thunderstorm. Pepperbush had been taken unawares.

W.J. Hegarty

CHAPTER SEVENTEEN

Onslaught

The engagement was underway at the front line. A shot rang out, followed by another, then another. Within moments, a barrage of gunfire erupted in the formerly peaceful forest surrounding Pepperbush. Once it began, there was no stopping it. The soldiers and a handful of the volunteers remained calm, picked their targets, and didn't waste any ammunition. The remainder of the would-be marksmen, however, were consumed by fear, firing at anything that moved. Not far from Miller, three men targeted the same infected. By the time they put it down permanently and moved on to other targets, the thing's chest looked like a cannonball had hit it.

What a waste, Miller thought. If that was the best he could expect from these volunteers, every one of them might as well retreat now, including his unit. Maybe he didn't make himself clear, he wondered. These people had to understand that their ammo was finite, right? He couldn't dwell on that any longer. An unending wave of infected was pouring over their defenses. It was as if some conveyor belt from hell was depositing them by the truckload over the top of the berm. Did Philadelphia's entire populace follow them here?

Radzinski wasn't faring much better at his end of the conflict. Lightning and automatic rifle fire lit up the night, revealing legions of infected. Each minute that passed, hundreds more undead tumbled down the berm into Pepperbush, crashing down into this once safe town. Radzinski and his men held their ground firm while unleashing a torrent of bullets upon the putrid flesh of the enemy.

"Choose your shots, boys. Controlled bursts only!" Radzinski cried out to his untrained volunteers.

In the distance, a carrier's arm was blown off, much to the Marine's dismay as the shot was a clear waste of ammo.

"Fuck!" Radzinski shouted just before a second shot from his rifle took off the top of the creature's head.

Three more infected fell to his rifle in a matter of seconds. A few dozen more fell to his group's barrage every minute. Limbs detached from bodies, and heads exploded in the hail of gunfire they unleashed upon the horde. Forty yards in front of the men, bodies of the infected began to pile up, forming a wall of sorts. Another obstacle for these things to maneuver around.

On either side of Rachel, a long line of muzzle flashes disappearing off into the distance illuminated the darkened tree line. The sound was deafening. An almost constant barrage of gunfire from nearly a half-mile of townsfolk, refugees, and a handful of soldiers pressed the horde, nearly keeping them at a standstill. For every infected that fell, it seemed that three took its place.

Soraya ran from man to man, keeping them aware of ammo consumption. She stopped at a volunteer who was firing wildly into the darkness, grabbed his rifle's barrel, and pointed it at the ground. Another shot rang out, exploding a small crater of dirt at their feet.

"What are you doing?" the man yelled, on the verge of panic.

Soraya kept the gun pointed at their feet while getting in the man's face. "Shooting at nothing is no different from shooting the ground!" she shouted. Soraya depressed the trigger for him this time. A second shot rang out, and the man nearly dropped his weapon. Soraya slapped the man's hand and grabbed him by the chin, pointing his face toward the oncoming horde. "If you do not aim, you do not kill. Wasteful." She yanked his rifle away and aimed it at the approaching infected. Soraya pulled back the single-bolt action, took a second to aim, and fired. An infected fell nearly one hundred yards away from them. She repeated the process again for the man's benefit. "You see?" Soraya directed his head toward the fallen beast. "You can do this." She handed the man back his rifle before moving on.

Marisol, Seth, and a few of the other police officers who were a part of Soraya's group began to spread themselves out amongst the more unseasoned volunteers.

"I've got this end covered, Soraya. Head down toward the other side. We'll meet up in the middle when we start to thin these numbers," Marisol offered, continuously firing on the encroaching mass.

"Thank you, Marisol. I am on my way." Soraya made her way down the line, helping where she could as she continued firing on the carriers as often as she was able to while also attempting to keep her people focused.

The infected began tripping over their fallen brethren. The ones that fell were quickly trampled into the soft mud whether dead or not, slowing the progress of the ones behind.

Soraya shot another and watched as three more stumbled to clear its corpse, one of which fell over. "Do not bunch up!" she yelled while pointing to the stumbling infected. "Make them fall." Soraya ran back down the line, pointing out her revelation. Most volunteers under her charge had already begun firing wildly at anything that moved in the distance. The time she spent pointing out one man's mistakes was long enough for three others to lose their composure. Everyone around her was firing as fast as they were able. Her shouts became drowned out by gunfire and the storm. She pulled on a man's arm, trying desperately to make him listen. He couldn't hear her over the onslaught of gunfire and pushed her away to better aim his rifle. Soraya looked up and down the line. Bright flashes illuminated her people's positions. Every second another shot lit up the night. Soraya knew her men were out of control and would keep firing until they were completely out of ammo. Apprehensively, she too raised her rifle and fired into the horde.

2:40 am - Mother Leeds

Far in the distance, a carrier's head exploded. Its traveling companion barely registered the thing's fate as it too fell. Behind it, more continued to drop. On the roof of Mother Leeds, Garrett breathed in slowly. A quarter of a mile away, another infected fell. He couldn't keep up this pace all night. No matter, though. His ammunition wouldn't last, anyway. Behind him, Damon stayed at the ready with a second fully loaded magazine at all times. Working in tandem with Damon's constant supply of fresh ammo, Garrett was putting down nearly two dozen infected per minute. Joining them, Ryan patrolled the rooftop, looking for any carriers who might have snuck their way into the town's interior.

Below in the bar, Markus, Samantha, and Ayn could clearly hear the gunfire over the storm. The girls jumped with each gunshot or volley of thunder. A few roars from the clouds startled Markus as well, though he did his best to conceal it.

"I guess those things really made it over the berm after all," Samantha muttered with an air of surprise as if Garrett's warnings were merely an exaggeration. "I can't believe this is actually happening. It seems like just yesterday I found this place." She grew sullen. "I was lost, you know, heading for New York, a modeling gig. It was going to be the one to finally get me noticed. Then I took a wrong turn off the interstate, and, well, here I am." Samantha twirled her long red curls as she paced the bar. Back and forth she trod as if waiting for customers who would never show.

"Well, it *is* happening, Samantha, and I need you here with me. This is as real as it gets." Markus attempted to keep the woman focused. "If these things are half as bad as the one me and Damon ran into, then we're in for a long night."

"Do you think they'll make it this far? Into town, I mean?" Ayn leaned against the opposite wall, peeking through the cracks of a boarded-up window. She was rail-thin, and her clothes hung off her bony body. In the dim light, leaning forward like she was, she could have easily been mistaken for one of those things. Candlelight flickered, keeping her face mostly in shadow, though a slight stream of tears was unmistakable to Markus. He joined her at the street-side end of the bar, peered through the hodgepodge of boards covering the front windows, and squinted for a glimpse of any familiar shapes in the darkness. "Let's hope not," he said. "Because if they hit Main Street, we're all fucked."

3:15 am - Security Headquarters

Takashi paced the small security building, waiting for news from his unit. Thunder and pouring rain made it impossible to accurately judge how much gunfire was coming from the south. His radio sat upon Sam's desk as he desperately awaited a status report from his unit. He trusted each of them to get their jobs done, but he needed an update. It was useless for him to be so far from the front line, giving orders if there was no intel to analyze, and he knew it. As if in response to his worries, the radio suddenly came to life.

"Colonel, Garrett here. Do you have ears on? Over." The radio buzzed for a moment, then went silent.

Takashi snatched the device from Sam's desk. "Garrett, I need a sitrep from your vantage point now. Over."

Sam and Ron eyed each other, daring not to move for fear of interrupting the radio's increasingly delicate signal.

"Infected have breached the southern wall, sir. All squads are engaging the enemy. Over."

"Goddammit, how many casualties?"

"Hard to tell from here, sir. I haven't seen or heard anything yet, but that doesn't mean no one's gone down, though."

"How many carriers are we dealing with, Lieutenant?"

"Impossible to say. I'm guessing thousands. I'm going to need a second, Colonel." Garrett cut off communication.

Takashi would have to have been blind to miss Sam's stern demeanor. Pepperbush's head of security would stay at the colonel's side for the duration. For a moment, Takashi made eye contact with Sam and thought that under better circumstances the man could have made himself an honorable career as a leader of men. Why he chose the life he did was lost on Takashi. A conversation for another day, perhaps.

From Takashi's location, he could clearly make out the distinctive crack of a high-powered sniper rifle. Over the next twelve seconds, three more bursts pierced the storm.

Sam peered into the darkness with a pair of binoculars. "I can't see a damned thing, Colonel."

The radio buzzed to life again. "Sir, from what I can tell, carriers have taken the southernmost sector." Garrett was urgent but calm. "I could be wrong, but it's damn hard to know for sure in this weather."

"Understood, Garrett. What does your position look like?"

"No movement on this end of Main Street and the gate is clear for now. Will continue support from my location. Over."

"Keep me posted." Takashi broke contact before throwing his radio onto the desk and kicking a small wastebasket out into the storm.

No sooner had Garrett signed off than Takashi's radio crackled to life again. This time it was Miller on the line.

"They're everywhere, sir. Hundreds of them. Southern wall completely compromised. Falling back to the neighborhood," he shouted, gunshots and screams clearly audible through the static.

"Miller. Miller, say again. Everything after southern wall," Takashi responded with urgency.

"Don't know how much longer we can—" The radio went dead.

"Miller, fall back. Do you hear me? Fall back dammit," Takashi ordered, but it was no use; the transmission had ceased.

155

Takashi leaned into the front door as the wind whipped into the small structure. A frail screen door repeatedly banged against the front of the building. He turned from the storm and shut the interior door.

Sam could see that Colonel Takashi was losing hope as the man pulled him aside, out of earshot of the others in the room. "What are your thoughts, Colonel?"

"It may be too early to tell, but keep your people apprised of what you just heard. I'll do the same, at least for the ones I'm still in contact with." Takashi looked Sam in the eye. "Start processing the idea of abandoning town."

3:33 am - The Farm

After starting a cozy fire in his living room fireplace, Thomas went from room to room, opening the windows and unlocking the doors. He was a very old man, and without his farm, he would be a burden on the good people in town. That was what *he* thought, anyway. The citizens of Pepperbush would have had a few things to say about it had they known how he felt. Whatever fate had in store for the town he loved so this evening, he realized that in all likelihood his farm wouldn't survive the night.

He'd lived a good life, and it was better this way, really. One less mouth to feed was how the old man justified his sacrifice. His motives were not entirely altruistic, though, as Thomas yearned to see his wife again. Soon, he imagined. Jefferson, his oldest son, would be angry with him, wondering why he was giving up after fighting so hard his entire life. The thought made the old man chuckle. Jefferson had always been headstrong, sometimes missing the point of an entire conversation as a result. Tonight would have been no exception.

Thomas sat by the fireplace in his old rocking chair, flipping through a dusty photo album. His eyes teared up at a picture of his whole family together in happier times: his wife, three boys, and daughter. He touched the photo and smiled; they were celebrating his seventy-first birthday, eighteen months before his wife took ill.

"At least you went fast." He sighed contentedly. "And thank God you didn't live to see what this world you loved so much has become."

His attention moved to his children, and he drifted back to the days each were born. Again, his mind soared as he pictured vividly the day each of them moved out. Off to the big city to make a life for themselves. A tiny piece of his heart went along with them. Ever the optimist, Thomas was confident that his children were safe, wherever they might be.

Glass broke in the kitchen, and dishes crashed to the floor. It was time; the infected were in his home. Thomas removed the old family photo from the book, kissed it, and tucked it away in his left breast pocket. He closed his eyes, rocked his chair forward and back ever so slightly, smiled, and whispered, "God, I love you, Margaret. I'm coming home, darling."

3:50 am - Burke Residence

Tobias paced the living room. He kept his rifle propped up against the front door; he was ready to drop everything at a moment's notice should he receive the call. With each stray noise he would dart to the entranceway and equip his readied weapon.

Isabelle sat by the fireplace, smoke from a freshly lit cigarette wafting around her face, her previous butt still smoldering in the ashtray. In the dimly lit room, the fire danced in her contempt-filled eyes.

"Do you really need to smoke so much? The kids are right here," Tobias asked. His way of telling her to put it out.

"The kids are *not* right here. They're upstairs in their rooms," Isabelle answered with a long drag of her cigarette. "If you pulled your head away from the window for more than thirty seconds, you'd know that."

"It's just too much with the windows locked and the air off. The smoke bothers me," he replied, returning to the window.

"Do you ever stop and consider what *I* want? What *I* need?" she returned unapologetically.

"Izzy," Tobias tried.

"I'm serious, and if you call me 'Izzy' one more time, I'll beat your fucking head in with this ashtray. You know I hate that name," she said calmly. "Tell me, Tobias, when was the last time you even considered my needs? Was it last week? A month ago? And don't give me this the-town-needs-me bullshit. *I* needed you."

"You *needed* me?" Tobias turned to face his wife, who was glaring intently into the flames.

"I stopped needing you the day you left me barefoot in the kitchen to go play messiah of the people." Isabelle lit another cigarette.

4:05 am - Shearburn Residence

Vanessa stirred. She slowly rose to a seated position beside Jim's battered corpse. Drying blood was sticky. Her hair, she found, trying to run her fingers through it, was matted into clumps with the stuff. She stretched her fingers, releasing them from the grip of drying blood gluing them in place. Her arms, chest, and face were covered in crimson. What remained of her white tank top resembled a butcher's smock.

She sat on the floor beside Jim, staring at his lifeless corpse, then back to her own bloodied body. She killed this man with her bare hands. The thought yanked her from contemplation. Vanessa struggled in vain to move the body outdoors. If she could just get him outside, maybe, with any luck, those things would dispose of this garbage for her and she could avoid having to explain any of this. She slipped and fell in the blood puddle; it was no use. Even in death, Jim proved to be just as stubborn as ever.

"Fuck this," she panted. Vanessa kicked herself away from the corpse and slid a few feet from it. She was finished trying to move the brute.

The unmistakable sound of breaking glass could be heard from the direction of the kitchen. Vanessa was on her feet and pressed against the wall before the commotion stopped. A framed picture's reflection, adjacent to the kitchen, allowed her a distorted view of the cause of the racket. An infected was fumbling around the doorway, one foot in and the other, twisted and broken, dragging behind it in the rain. The carrier looked to the cabinets, down to the floor, and back to the broken windowpane its shirt was stuck on.

The beast paused and for a moment. Vanessa could swear the thing looked confused. Maybe it recognized the sight of a kitchen, or maybe somewhere deep in its rotting mind it could sense her. The thing focused its gaze at the misplaced appliance, almost as if it knew the refrigerator shouldn't be slid halfway to the door like that. Behind it, a second crept into the doorway, slipped on the pile of broken glass, and crashed to the floor. The impact freed the first from its bonds as the second remained on its back, staring at the rotating ceiling fan, its mouth opening and closing slowly, almost in rhythm with the fan blades.

Vanessa had seen enough. She inched away from the wall and tiptoed back toward the stairs. She was nearly halfway up as the first carrier came into full view. The thing was a mess. Rotten bite marks and deep gashes littered its body. Its left arm was missing at the elbow, and the left breast was mangled. What remained swung from ruined flesh. One of its feet was barely attached by a string of impossibly stretched skin and tendons. Vanessa laughed to herself for a moment, and just as fast as it happened, she covered her mouth, holding back a retch. After what she had just done to Jim, seeing this thing in her living room, torn to pieces but still upright and moving, shouldn't have bothered her, but there she was, contemplating the absurdity of what she was witnessing.

The carrier crossed into the living room. Its head twitched slightly and its one good eye, milky as it was, made contact with Vanessa. She began to breathe heavy but stayed calm as she slowly climbed the stairs one at a time, never breaking eye contact with the carrier. The duo moved in unison. For every step the infected made forward, she took one back, up one step, up another, and the next. The beast followed suit, tracking her across the room, its milky eye fixed on Vanessa. Oblivious to Jim's body, the carrier tripped over it, falling to the floor and shattering every bone in the left side of its face.

The carrier attempted to stand and inadvertently placed a rotting hand on Jim's body. It slipped off, crashing face-first into Jim's wet neck. Distracted by an unexpected feast, the carrier lost interest in Vanessa and proceeded to tear at the still-warm flesh. Jim's damaged groin seemed to be of particular interest to the thing, as it tore and bit at the wound, enlarging it to fit a good portion of its mouth and jaw inside the cavity. Jim's intestines were pulled from the hole and promptly devoured by the hungry beast. Foot by foot, the creature pulled Jim's insides out. Whenever it dropped a piece, it simply reached back inside to pull out more.

Vanessa held a hand over her mouth, desperately hoping not to puke. She reached the top of the stairs and disappeared around the corner. The carrier was finally out of sight. Mindful of every footfall, she crept as lightly as she was able toward the window above her back porch, which led to a small overhang and escape. She put one foot out of the window, followed by the other and finally the rest of her body. Vanessa was on the small patio roof. The cold downpour drenched her in seconds. Caked blood melted from her hair and slid down into her eyes as she struggled to see, searching desperately for more infected below.

W.J. Hegarty

CHAPTER EIGHTEEN

Incursion

Desperation had set in for those charged with helping Takashi's unit defend the front line.

"There's too many of them!" one of the volunteers yelled while taking a few steps back.

"Keep your shit straight and we can do this. Hold your goddamn ground until I say otherwise!" Radzinski ordered the woman, himself never taking too much attention from the encroaching mass.

An ever-increasing number of undead fell as Miller and his group continued to fire upon the horde of infected. Hundreds of bodies littered the forest floor at the southern defenses. Infected tripped and fell over each other in a furious attempt to reach the group. Three carriers lunged at a man. One of them bit down on his chest and face. A second woman opened fire at the group and was quickly swallowed up as well. More of the inexperienced men shot randomly. Ignoring what Miller had said about choosing their shots, they went full automatic, spraying the oncoming horde with dozens of bullets. Chunks of rotting flesh and limbs torn from bodies flew in all directions. As a testament to the men's ignorance, few infected stayed down.

"Oh, fuck this!" one of the volunteers yelled. A kid, no more than twenty years old, Miller guessed. The sustained battle was too much for the young man, and panic sent him running down the front of the line, oblivious to the deadly rain of gunfire. A stray bullet caught him center mass. Another sent him spinning. The third bullet finally buckled his legs from under him. The boy was dead before he hit the ground. Farther down the line, others took notice of the friendly fire. Uncertainty spread throughout their ranks. Concentration was lost, targets were missed, and the line fell apart. The mass of infected pressed forward, gaining ground with each failed shot as the other volunteers began firing wildly, rarely hitting their targets, much less putting them down.

Each depression of Miller's trigger dropped another infected. Most stayed down. The others, though, were merely a waste of ammo. They should have evacuated. Not leaving when they had the chance clouded Miller's mind. "This is suicide." Doubt was creeping in.

Volleys of lightning illuminated thousands of infected pouring over the entirety of the berm's southern perimeter. Lines were quickly overrun; the volunteers fled in every direction. Some disappeared into the darkened forest. Most were swallowed up in waves, unprepared for the sheer numbers descending upon them.

Soraya spun around with her kukri extended. She cleaved a carrier's head in two and kicked a second to the ground before pouncing on it and burying her blade in its skull. Marisol helped the young Israeli to her feet. The pair of them and a handful of others desperately raced for the police station.

Another flash of lightning lit up the berm for a brief second, long enough for Radzinski to gather the full scope of what they faced. As far as he could see, stretching the length of the berm, thousands of undead clawed at the ground, desperately trying to get to their feet. Heavy, deep mud was the only thing preventing a full-scale slaughter. "Holy shit! We're out of here. Come on." Radzinski yanked Rachel by the back of her tactical vest and flung her toward the nearest homes.

Rachel swung her empty rifle like a bludgeon, smashing in heads and trying her best to keep the oncoming swarm at arm's reach as she stumbled into the path of her fellow soldier. Three carriers were tangled up in a bush between them and Radzinski. Two of them yanked his gun from his grasp. He let the weapon go. As he fell backward, he used the momentum to roll away from the bush, tripping up two more carriers in the process. Radzinski rose to his feet, sidearm in hand, and dashed for a cluster of homes in the distance. He used the weapon as a club, bashing in approaching carriers' faces or swatting away arms. Radzinski would conserve what little ammo remained for as long as he was able. Rachel joined him in the fracas, the pair of them clearing a path for any survivors as best as they could.

"Conserve your ammo goddammit!" Miller barked at the panicking volunteers with no effect.

More and more infected filled the spaces between the trees and buildings. The southernmost homes had been engulfed in a sea of undead. Low on ammo, most of the men who hadn't already fled were quickly overwhelmed and ripped apart, sharp teeth easily rending flesh from bone.

One of the volunteers heaved a propane tank from an overturned barbecue grill above the heads of the oncoming horde. Another man's weapon tracked the projectile. He fired, and the container exploded over the carriers' heads. A shower of shrapnel followed by a fireball engulfed the crowd. Dozens of burning infected, unresponsive to the searing heat, continued their march toward the houses.

"Fall back!" Miller yelled, though his cries landed on deaf ears.

Raging winds and pounding rain compounded with the moans from thousands of infected drowned out any chance at communication. A group of volunteers scrambled between the houses. Others forced their way into one of the homes in an attempt to barricade themselves away from the horde. The weight of the infected piling up at the back door ripped it from its hinges. A wall of undead spilled into the house. Some still in flames ignited curtains and furniture. Within minutes, despite the storm's intensity, a half dozen of the southern homes were engulfed in flame. High winds threatened to spread the fire.

Miller and three volunteers were all that remained of his segment of the southern defense. The group of four fell back, hoping to gain a little ground on their retreat to Main Street.

Beyond the western wall on the outskirts of Pepperbush, Thomas's farmhouse and fields were brimming with infected. Thousands of them made their way to the berm. Carriers climbed up and over each other, eventually sliding down the other side into the unprotected western portion of town. Scores of infected penetrated the defense's overlooked weak point en route to the already overwhelmed and unsuspecting populace. They crept through the trees and fields, instinctively wandering down dirt paths. A second wave of infected quickly spread to all corners of Pepperbush.

4:15 am - The Church

As the night wore on, the storm's intensity increased. Outside of the church, shutters banged against the building. Shingles flew from the roof, becoming deadly projectiles. The branches from a 120-year-old oak crashed against the building, slapping the worn wooden siding, scraping the windows and threatening to burst through the side of the church. Inside, the clattering echoed throughout the large open room. The banging seemed to follow the structure's skeleton, down the old framing to ground level, rattling the dozens of stained glass windows and threatening to tear the doors from their hinges.

"That's not the wind. Someone's out there." Don pulled aside a curtain to see who was trying to gain entrance to their sanctuary.

Through the stained glass windows, it was clear: the silhouettes of dozens of infected shambling about the church grounds were unmistakable. They had been overrun. The idea of safety at only a stone's throw from combat was wrong. Takashi was wrong; they were surrounded.

"Holy shit, they're all over the goddamned parking lot! Everybody, out the back. Hurry! We got to get the fuck out of here!" Don sprinted to the rear of the church.

In his haste, he knocked Emily to the floor. On her way down, she hit her head on a pew. Blood trickled from a cut above her eye as she tried to right herself. A second older woman helped her up into the nearest pew. This woman produced a dirty handkerchief from her pocket and dabbed some blood from Emily's eye.

"No, Don, wait!" Broderick lunged at the man. He found a handful of Don's shirt, but Don yanked himself free.

Don threw aside the cabinet, blocking the back door, forced it open, and darted for safety. He was free from the prison of the church. The other side of the building was swarming with infected as well. In a desperate bid for freedom, Don ran straight into the mass before he could realize his error. He was tackled to the ground almost instantly. The sheer weight of the mass pinned him to the earth while countless mouths and fingers ripped his clothes off and chewed and tore at any piece of exposed flesh they could find. Don was swallowed up, completely out of sight in a matter of seconds as hundreds more crawled over or around the mound of bodies in a bid for the narrow doorway.

The mass of carriers tumbled over each other in a mad dash to reach the trapped people inside. The front and back of the church became mirror images of each other as infected swarmed into the building, trapping the huddled people inside thanks to Don's irrationality. At the front of the church, windows broke under the sheer weight of undead piling up outside.

The dozen or so who were capable opened fire on the horde. Bullets sprayed the infected with little effect. A lucky shot caught a carrier in the face, sending the ghoul spinning into altar candles. The fallen torches rolled in all directions, igniting the altar's tapestry.

Amidst the chaos, Grace along with several other people succumb to their fear. Kneeling in their pews, they prayed for a quick end. Off to the side of the altar in a back room, the crippled and wounded were easy prey for the voracious attackers.

Broderick's shotgun blasts tore limbs and chunks of flesh from the encroaching infected. "Stay together. Don't let them get between us!" he shouted, though most ignored him as they ran haphazardly about the room and fired randomly into the attackers.

A few, though, listened to the young soldier's advice and stayed grouped tightly with Broderick. Gunfire echoed throughout the church. A carrier's knee was blown out mid-stride, sending the creature sliding headfirst into a table leg, crushing its face. Its mangled jaw and broken cheekbones didn't slow it down as the ghoul used its momentum to crawl toward a group of panicked parishioners in their pews. Another carrier's head exploded in a shower of gore, spraying a woman who was standing too close. Chunks of skull and cold torn meat flew into her eyes and mouth.

"Oh God, get it off me!" the woman screamed, wiping at her brain- and blood-drenched face. "It's burning my eyes!" The woman flailed about, tearing into her own skin and trying desperately to wipe the filth from her face. Blinded, she ran headlong into a group of infected that promptly shredded her clothes, exposing the warm flesh beneath. The horde wasted no time rending her to pieces, ripping and chewing at any hint of meat.

Three of the more able survivors worked desperately to extinguish the fires. Trying to smother it with coats and blankets, they were transfixed by their task and were taken unawares, the lot of them tackled to the ground and savaged by yet another wave of infected. Chunks of flesh were torn from their faces, and fingers were bitten off. One woman squirming to escape rolled into the fire, igniting herself and a few nearby infected. She howled in agony, desperately searching for a way out into the cold rain. The infected took no heed of the tormenting fire; they chewed and scratched at the woman. Blackened, charred meat was no different from raw.

Fire spread up the walls to the ceiling, rapidly filling the church with thick black smoke. The lack of air caused some trapped people to panic and bang fruitlessly at the windows. The infected outside took notice. Mimicking the people's actions from outside, they rattled the windows as well. Glass shattered as dead arms reached inside to pull desperate people out through the razor-sharp glass. A myriad of carriers were worked up into a frenzy over fresh-spilled blood that poured from dozens of deep wounds.

The carriers' numbers grew by the second. The survivors shrank in number as they were forced farther back into the church. Another infected lunged at Broderick and grabbed hold of his shotgun. The young soldier booted the creature in the chest, sending it back a few feet and giving him time to pull his sidearm. Two shots to the head put the thing down.

"Come on, Grace! Don't just sit there. Get up!" Broderick tried to pull Grace from her pew with no effect. He could only watch as greedy hands and hungry mouths pulled her and a few others beneath the pews.

In its haste to grab Grace, one of the infected tumbled over a pew headfirst onto the floor. Now under the pew and undaunted by the impact or its cracked skull, the undead fiend continued its pursuit across the floor to Grace's exposed legs. The creature wasted no time clamping its jaw down tight upon her limb. She screamed for the Lord to help. Her only reply was hundreds more teeth ravaging her frail old body. The half-burned creatures tore away her clothes, exposing her tough but soft flesh. They attacked her with a ferocity rarely witnessed outside of the animal kingdom. Ravenous in their hunger, some carriers bit away chunks of other carriers in a desperate bid for a turn at the spoils. Grace's struggling eventually slowed as she was crushed under the weight of so many undead.

"Everyone, back to the far wall!" Broderick shouted over the screams of the dying, the moans of the undead, and the crackling of a now raging inferno.

Broderick herded a handful of survivors to the back of the church. The smoke had grown too thick. The young soldier strained to see the person beside him. They were trapped, and he knew it. Broderick and another woman with a rifle shielded the few remaining people against the wall.

He touched the woman on the shoulder. "Make these shots count."

The woman nodded her reply before making the sign of the cross.

The duo fired aimlessly into the blackness. Broderick and the few left alive in the church were swallowed up in a black cloud of blinding smoke, clawing hands, and gnashing teeth.

Fire burst from every window and door of the church. The roof hissed and buckled as a cold rain poured down. Thunder rolled in the distance, nearly loud enough to drown out the screams from inside.

4:22 am - Police Station

Marisol, Soraya, and the two remaining members of their group ran for the back door of the police station. Hundreds of undead were in pursuit.

"Stay close, everyone. We're almost there!" Marisol yelled to the others as she pulled a short-range radio from her belt. "Marisol to Corey. Come in. Corey, do you hear me?"

"Right here, ma'am."

"It's way worse than we thought. We lost almost everyone. Unlock the back door. We're on our way. I can see you from here."

"Already there, ma'am." Corey slammed the door opened as Marisol barged past and into the relative safety of the police station.

"They're right behind us. Grab everything you can and get to the trucks!" the sheriff shouted at the three remaining police officers who were watching the building.

Soraya, Seth, and two more police took up positions at the back of the police station, firing on the approaching throngs of undead. Many fell, but most got back up. Still, scores more descended upon the small building.

In the armory, Marisol reloaded her shotgun, then packed up a duffel bag with guns and ammunition. "Here, put this in your truck. I'm going back for the others." Marisol handed the duffel off to Isaac.

Isaac scurried through the small building and out the front door and made his way to the police SUVs parked in front of the station. Corey was right behind him. Isaac tossed the duffel in the back of one of the vehicles and started the engine. "Corey, get in here and keep this piece of shit running. I'll start the other truck. We have to go. Just keep your eyes open for any of those things. The others will be out in a minute." Isaac ran over to the other truck and quickly turned over the engine.

Back inside, Marisol finished stuffing another small satchel with ammunition, then ran to the rear doorway where the others were still firing upon the oncoming mass. "Let's go! The trucks are loaded and ready. We have to leave now!" Marisol waved them back into the police station.

Soraya was the last one in the building, firing off a few more rounds as she entered. Two more carriers fell. A few more tripped over them and were momentarily disabled, though scores more moved past the fallen as they encroached upon the small building.

Marisol slammed the door shut and locked it before tipping over a heavy file cabinet in front of it as well. "Every little bit, right?"

"Yes. Now we go!" Soraya picked up a gas can as the two women hustled for the exit.

Out front in the courtyard, the others split up into the two trucks and awaited the rest of the group.

Marisol advanced toward the SUVs but stopped short. "You have got to be fucking kidding me." She hesitated for a moment, then handed Soraya her rifle as she ran past the awaiting group and across the courtyard in the direction of Town Hall.

W.J. Hegarty

CHAPTER NINETEEN

Desperation

A flame's reflection danced around Mayor Lancaster's eyes while he leaned against the warm bricks framing the fireplace. A glass of Brandy held tightly to his chest distorted the flames' light into an exaggerated image, illuminating the brown liquid. The swirling liquor and flame exposed decades of lines across the mayor's worn face. Behind him, the large expanse of Town Hall glowed in the eerie, dancing light. His wife, Catherine, sat on a couch a little farther back, away from the fire but close enough to still feel its warmth on her skin. Their thirty-year-old doting son, Bobby, stood behind her, rubbing his mother's shoulders.

Bobby cared little for town politics, though he was quick to make his lineage known. He would never follow in his father's footsteps but would certainly use Donald Lancaster's notoriety and influence to raise capital for personal projects. His most recent work was a shelter for the needy, set up in a Philadelphia borough. It was rewarding work, and he truly cared for those under his charge, but not enough to stay when the city's violence escalated in response to the growing crisis. Bobby knew his father's decision to stay the night in Town Hall with only Joshua, Phillip, and their families worried his mother. Sure, the police station was right across the courtyard, but their hands would be full for the duration of the evening. For all intents and purposes, the Lancasters and their friends were on their own. Bobby kept his attention on his mother. A good shoulder rub usually eased her tension, or so he thought. What better time than now to test the theory?

Mayor Lancaster's two closest confidants pleaded for the lot of them to hole up with the rest of Pepperbush's residents in the north. At least up there, shunned or not, there would be a few soldiers and a hell of a lot more guns, but the mayor would have no part of it. It was a fool's errand, a waste of time and resources. Nothing would happen tonight to jeopardize their safety. Lancaster was sure of it; he guaranteed it, even. Takashi and his men were bringing undue stress into the lives of everyone in town. Mayor Lancaster would prove it by emerging safely from Town Hall in the morning. With one swift move and a heartfelt speech, he would reclaim the people's confidence and with a bit of luck expel these usurpers from his town once and for all.

Joshua and Phillip conversed quietly in a far corner. Their wives and young children sat quietly in uncomfortable wooden chairs away from the men. The two women and to an extent Catherine herself learned long ago the consequences of gossiping against their husbands' goings-on. What the men decided was always for the best, for all of them. Whether the women actually believed that or not was irrelevant; they lived it with little question.

Franklin, Phillip's oldest, pushed away the wooden toy blocks in front of him. "Are the monsters coming here, Mommy?"

Phillip's wife looked nervously toward the mayor, then back around to her husband before answering the child. "No, sweetheart," she said. "There's no such thing as monsters, and even if there were, they can't find us here. Your daddy will keep us safe." She quickly dabbed her red eyes and motioned for Franklin to go back to his toys. She sniffled quietly, trying to stay strong for the boy as Joshua's wife put her arm around her. If the attempt at consoling worked, Phillip's wife had no time to reciprocate as Mayor Lancaster, obviously eavesdropping, interrupted their moment.

"Come now, ladies." Mayor Lancaster turned from the fireplace, a smug grin firmly etched upon his face. "We have absolutely nothing to fear. Come sunrise, when Pepperbush is just as calm as it is now, these soldiers and rabble-rousers with their grandiose plans will certainly look quite the fool." Mayor Lancaster poured himself another drink. "Brandy, anyone?"

A window shattered. Its crashing glass echoed from somewhere down the hall toward the kitchen. The continued banging of wood against wood broke the relative silence of the dining hall.

Mayor Lancaster took another long pull from his glass. "Catherine, would you be a dear and go close that shutter for us? In his haste, old

Benjamin must have overlooked it. Bobby, would you please go help your mother? I swear sometimes that handyman of ours is just plain useless."

Phillip and Joshua exchanged troubled looks.

Catherine and Bobby rounded the corner to the cafeteria. The far door leading outside was wide open, blowing in the wind and banging furiously against the side of the building.

"I'll get it, Mom. No use in both of us getting soaked. Didn't Dad check these doors earlier?" Bobby inquired, turning his head back to his mother's attention as he neared the door.

"Your father was most likely distracted by his one true love, son—that bottle of Brandy of his," Catherine offered with a heavy eye roll while reaching above, deep inside a cabinet, searching for a bottle of her own.

"Well that figures." Bobby glanced back with a chuckle, eager to join his mother in some friendly ribbing of his father. As he reached awkwardly for the door, trying to keep dry, an infected lunged from the darkness, clamping its teeth down tightly on Bobby's arm. The man screamed in agony as a mouthful of meat was torn from his forearm. Another wretched claw reached from the darkness, pulling Bobby's head back, exposing the soft flesh of his neck as a third undead creature took advantage, biting down hard. Blood sprayed from the man's punctured jugular, soaking the nearby wall in crimson.

Catherine screamed. "Bobby!" She closed the distance between her and her son in a matter of seconds, punching and pulling at the carriers upon arrival. Four more infected took notice and rushed in for their turn. The added weight knocked the entire group of bodies to the floor just inside the doorway.

Mayor Lancaster's glass of Brandy shattered on the hardwood floor. Tiny shards of glass danced around his feet. Dark Brandy stained his white leather shoes. He stood frozen, eyes gone as wide as saucers.

"Donald, that was your wife. Snap out of it, man!" Joshua shook the mayor furiously, but the man offered no response.

"Phillip, with me. Everyone else, stay here!" Joshua waved for the women and children to return to their seats. He turned to the mantle above the fireplace and took down two large hunting rifles. He tossed one to Phillip, who was already fumbling for shells in a cabinet below.

Weapons drawn, the men crept toward the cafeteria. Beyond them, just inside the opposite doorway, eight or more infected knelt down around the corpses of Bobby and Catherine, fighting over pieces of the bodies. A female carrier held Bobby's arm close to its chest, chewing on the bloody stump as a second tried desperately to pry it from her grasp. Three more infected tore ravenously at Catherine's intestines, spreading them out across the floor like giant links of sausage. A third carrier had its head buried deep in the woman's exposed chest cavity. Bobby's neck had been chewed all the way through to the spine. His head flopped back and forth as it was kneed and kick by the starving creatures.

Phillip threw up. It ran down his chest and onto his feet. He dropped to his knees and cupped his mouth, attempting to hold back the vomit. Vile fluid spewed from the gaps between his fingers, splashing his companion's legs.

Joshua opened fire. Bullets tore holes in the floor, walls, and ceiling, rarely hitting his targets, much less putting any of them down. Gunfire caught a few of the carriers' attention, as if awoken from a trance, or maybe it was the prospect of slightly fresher meat. The carriers zeroed in on the men and lunged. The first three creatures slipped on the bloody remains of Mayor Lancaster's family. Others climbed over the fallen carriers, using their bodies for traction.

Phillip was off his knees and beginning a sprint. He couldn't take his eyes off the carriers and crashed into Joshua, sending both men to the floor, each clawing at the slick vomit-soaked wood and trying to get to their feet. Joshua overcame the slippery puke and rose in time to be slammed hard into the adjacent wall, dazing him. Eight or so infected were on top of the men in seconds. A carrier bit down on the back of Joshua's neck. Warm blood oozed downward around the man's face, collecting at and then dripping from his lips and nose. The red only served to drive the creatures wild as they dug deeper into the man's flesh.

Phillip never rose. Unable to regain his footing, panic set in, followed by shock, before he fainted. The overwhelming number of infected pouring into the blood- and gore-soaked room broke the man mentally. As Joshua struggled to free himself, he couldn't help but notice his friend's state, but as fast as the thought entered the man's mind, it was gone. Pain was all he knew. Joshua found himself wishing he could trade places with Phillip and sleep through his demise. Eight and then eleven or more infected piled on top of the helpless men, tearing them to pieces. Behind them, a stream of dozens more sauntered around the four bodies, some fighting for their share of the spoils, more still wandering deeper into Town Hall.

Gunfire and harrowing screams yanked Mayor Lancaster from his daze. He righted himself against the familiar warm bricks of the fireplace, finally daring an eyeshot at his friends' families. Phillip's wife held her two young boys close, covering their ears from the sounds of their father's cries. Beside her, Joshua's wife cradled their infant son, rocking back and forth while quietly singing a lullaby in a desperate attempt to ease the child's fear. Phillip's wife looked at Mayor Lancaster, tears streaming down her face as she whispered, pleading for help.

Mayor Lancaster aimed his Walther P38 at her and her child as he backed away slowly, making his way for the front door. Not once did he break eye contact with Phillip's wife, even as she whispered, "Please." His other hand he kept tucked behind his back, searching for an escape. Mayor Lancaster unlocked the door and backed out of the building. Tears streamed down Phillips wife's face, and she finally began to sob. She held her children close. Behind her, Joshua's wife held her infant son and moved fast toward the fireplace. Mayor Lancaster switched the doorknob to its locked position and pulled the large wooden door shut behind him. His final view of the interior through the shrinking gap in the door was dozens of infected filling the room.

Mayor Lancaster secured the door behind him and broke the key off in the lock, temporarily cutting off the carriers' pursuit and condemning those left alive to an undeserved fate. Screams from his friends' wives were clearly audible over the storm. More infected filled the room, drowning the women and children in a sea of rotting flesh. The ones that couldn't reach them made their way to the front of the room, following Mayor Lancaster. They pounded relentlessly against the walls and glass, eventually falling through the broken windows and spilling out into the courtyard.

Mayor Lancaster tossed his broken keys into the bushes while descending Town Hall's steps. He sprinted across the courtyard for the parked police vehicles as Marisol surprised him with a left hook, flooring the man.

"What the fuck have you done?" she yelled as she darted off toward Town Hall.

Marisol was stopped mid-stride by Soraya, who pulled her back.

Soraya held her tight, grabbed the sheriff's chin, and pointed the woman's head toward Town Hall's overflowing windows. "It is too late. Look!" she shouted. Soraya pointed to the eastern wing, then back to the front. The infected were already spilling out from the side of the building and breaking their way out of the front windows. Mayor Lancaster's locked door soon followed. Bursting from its frame, it fell to the ground, carrying a mass of infected with it. "We must go. Hurry!" Soraya insisted while forcing Marisol away from Mayor Lancaster's treachery.

"She's right, Sheriff. We have no time to waste." Mayor Lancaster scurried down the stairs. He touched Marisol on the shoulder while peering into her eyes. "There's nothing we can do for them now, Sheriff. We have to leave this place."

Marisol removed his hand from her shoulder before punching him square in the mouth. The old man fell to the ground. She followed up with a barrage of blows connecting all about the man's face and head. Mayor Lancaster quickly went limp. Marisol wasted no time straddling the man and continued to land blow after blow. Her words were barely comprehensible during the assault. "You left them! Your fucking family, all of them! Fucking piece of shit, I'll kill you!" she screamed as her knuckles tore open amidst her rage.

Soraya watched the beating for a moment while keeping a wary eye on the approaching mass of infected. She knew the man had it coming; the screams emanating from Town Hall as they approached the trucks were clear for anyone paying attention. Under different circumstances, Soraya would have gladly offered Marisol assistance, but time was a luxury not afforded to any that night. "Leave him or beat him later. We must go!" Soraya grabbed Marisol by the arm and again pointed around to the infected spilling into the courtyard from all sides.

Marisol pulled Lancaster up by his disheveled collar. "Get in the fucking truck before I change my mind." She shoved Mayor Lancaster into the back seat of her SUV and slammed the door shut behind him before giving one final glance back at Town Hall and Mayor Lancaster's betrayal.

The two vehicles sped off toward Main Street as the courtyard was enveloped in a mob of carriers. Behind them, a countless number of infected poured out of or came stumbling from around Town Hall, the police station, and the nearby forest.

4:31 am - Northern Perimeter

Away from the conflict, the northernmost section of homes was quiet, save for the tempest. The roads in this stretch of town branched off in all directions, with seven offshoots lined with homes merging with the primary road leading directly to Main Street. More than sixty homes graced this portion of town, and they were spaced enough to afford each lot a fair amount of privacy. On foot, at a brisk pace, one could walk from the farthest property and down to Main Street in twenty minutes, give or take. While planning for the inevitable attack, it was decided the safest course of action would be to house most of the town's residents with those who lived in the north for the duration of the fighting. Every eventuality was considered in regard to keeping the town's people safe, and everyone agreed that there was no chance of the horde attacking from this end of town.

Two Pepperbush residents met at the end of the main avenue for a cigarette, but mostly for a reprieve from crowded houses. Standing beneath thick foliage worked surprisingly well at keeping out most of the rain—until the wind whipped up. Cabin fever had already set in for some; that was manageable for the most part. The issue Dave and Andy agreed upon was their houseguests. Helping out was one thing, but Dave's wife offering up their bedroom to complete strangers was unacceptable. Rather than cause a scene, he felt it best to take a walk, storm be damned. Pouring rain bouncing off their umbrellas and the leaves above only added to the deafening quality of the gale.

"Here, take a pull off of this." Dave handed Andy a pint of whiskey.

"Now that's what I'm talking about, man." Andy greedily pawed at the bottle.

"Take it easy for fuck's sake. That's all I've got left." Dave snatched the bottle back.

"Sorry, it's just the old lady won't let me drink at home anymore. She says I need to keep my head straight, just in case. Can you believe that shit?" Andy begrudgingly returned the bottle.

"I hear you. Betty still won't even let me smoke in the garage. Shit, man, even at the end of the world she's a goddamn ballbuster."

The men shared a laugh despite the conditions, trying to keep their damp cigarettes lit under what little protection their umbrellas afforded. The wind whipped up fast again, nearly turning their umbrellas inside out, followed by the crack of thunder. Andy jumped, dropping his cigarette in the mud.

"You hear something?" He squinted hard, trying to focus on the darkened forest beyond them.

"I don't think so. It's hard to tell with all this fucking rain." Dave was peering, too. "I'm sure it's nothing."

Dave shone his flashlight into the trees just off of Andy's property line, illuminating hundreds of shambling infected closing in on the unsuspecting sanctuary. Andy opened fire while Dave abandoned his friend to run away, taking the only flashlight with him.

"What the hell are you doing, Dave?" Andy yelled after his fleeing companion.

Andy fired left and then right in an arc, spraying the darkness. Muzzle flashes momentarily illuminated his targets, which easily numbered in the hundreds. Beside him, a few infected were crawling just out of sight, twisted, ruined legs dragging behind them. It looked as if their legs had been smashed by a falling tree. They must have wiggled themselves loose, leaving their flattened limbs behind. When Andy realized how close they were, he tried to run, but his legs were caught tight in a fast-moving carrier's grip. Andy turned, tripped, and fell on his upright rifle. The gun's barrel pierced his lower jaw and exited the side of his mouth. Blood poured from the wound, lubricating the gun. Andy's jaw slid down the steel barrel, nearly reaching the stock before he righted himself. The pain was unimaginable, and his eyes rolled into the back of his head. As he gripped his weapon, prepared to dislodge it from his face, flashes of pain coursed through his body.

Even through the downpour, what little senses the infected still possessed became hyperactive over the blood in the air. Another pack of the creatures took notice of this and scrambled for their turn. In their excitement, some collapsed to their knees. Others made a mad dash for the warm wet flesh protruding from the side of Andy's face. The pouring rain had little effect in dispersing the scent in the air. The first carrier at the scene tore into the man's exposed pink innards with reckless ferocity. Dirty fingers clawed their way into his broken jaw, pulling apart his face and breaking off large chunks of bone and the accompanying flesh. Andy was covered by infected in seconds, not too dissimilar to ants swarming an injured insect. As more infected tried in vain to break through an impenetrable shell of bodies surrounding their meal, some carriers moved on, prompting others still to follow, pressing ever forward into the unsuspecting row of homes.

Dave tripped over a small knee-high decorative picket fence. He landed on his face in the mud. His rifle bounced away from him, skidding down the sidewalk to disappear behind a large shrub. He jumped to his feet and stumbled to the closest window, banging hard enough to nearly break the panes of glass. "They're here. Get the hell out!" he yelled at the house before continuing on his way down the block toward home. Even in his panic, he had the sense to repeat the process for every home he passed. "They're here. They're fucking here! Everyone, get out now!" Dave continued his warning until startled by Jeremiah grabbing him by the collar and stopping him in his tracks.

"Hey, hey, slow down. What are you going on about?" Jeremiah shook the man to attention.

"Carriers, man! They're everywhere. Right fucking behind me. We gotta go!" Dave pleaded, pointing back to the edge of the darkened street, only five houses down.

Jeremiah released him and let the man continue his mad dash through the neighborhood as the source of Dave's fear was absolutely clear. A few houses down, the homes at the end of the cul-de-sac were surrounded by infected, hundreds of them bursting from the tree line. Across the way, a family was being torn apart inside of a van, blood-covered windows smeared by flailing limbs. Another woman opened her front door only to let in an avalanche of deadly attackers. Whatever was happening at the southern edge of town was something else entirely. Up here, where it was deemed safe, they had been taken unawares by a second phalanx of infected. Takashi's assessment was wrong—Pepperbush was surrounded.

Jeremiah fired three rounds at the oncoming horde. One of them fell but got right back up. People continued to emerge from their homes in response to the gunfire and increased commotion. Confused and scared, some people darted straight for their cars. Others turned and locked themselves in their homes. An elderly man grabbed his chest and fell to the ground. The situation had grown out of control as quickly as it began.

"Everyone, out now. Leave everything. Just go!" Jeremiah shouted.

He fired off three more shots for the benefit of anyone who thought the first burst might have been a fluke. Jeremiah pointed directly at a nervous couple peering out of a window and waved them out of their home. He banged on the side of their van as he made his way down the street.

Jeremiah turned to his radio in an effort to warn Aiko a few blocks off. "Northernmost homes have been compromised. Repeat, we have been overrun. Infected have breached the area. Aiko, do you copy? Over." Jeremiah began a light jog away from the incoming infected.

Cars sped past, sliding on the slick pavement, while other residents ran as fast as they could. The people on foot tried to keep one step ahead of the undead wave while desperately begging for their neighbors to stop for them.

Three-quarters of a mile away at the other end of the street, Aiko picked up Jeremiah's transmission. "Jeremiah, what's happening up there? Where are you?" Aiko shielded her eyes, straining to see through the storm.

Oncoming headlights grew larger until she jumped out of the way, splashing down in a mud puddle. The car's driver never attempted to slow, much less avoid hitting her.

"What the fuck?" she said as more cars barreled down the street past her.

Her radio came alive. "East end of the block, Aiko. All the way down. It's chaos over here. Hundreds of infected appeared out of nowhere!" Jeremiah yelled. This time, gunshots were clear over Aiko's radio.

"Jeremiah, what's happening? Can you hear me? Jeremiah?" Aiko shouted, though Jeremiah offered no response as the radio went silent. Aiko tried the radio again. "Jeremiah, Jeremiah, come in. Can you hear me? Goddammit, talk to me!" she yelled into dead air.

The distance was black. It kept its secrets, save for the occasional gore-splattered vehicle speeding past.

Tobias locked his front door behind him before joining Aiko out in the street. He pulled his coat tightly up to his neck. Tiny droplets of rain bounced from his chattering jaw. He held his umbrella over the young soldier's head in a near-pointless attempt at shielding her from the storm while she continued to fumble with an unresponsive radio. "Aiko, what's happening?" Tobias strained to see through the deluge.

"It's bad, Tobias. Get your family loaded up. We don't have much time. I have to make a call. I'll be right behind you. Don't leave me." Aiko pointed Tobias back toward his home. "Aiko to Takashi. Come in, Colonel. Do you read me? Over."

"Sitrep, Aiko," Takashi promptly responded.

"Sir, Jeremiah radioed in. Said they were under attack a few blocks away. It sounds like a second wave of infected came out of nowhere. I heard gunfire. Then I lost contact with him, sir." Aiko paced, awaiting a response.

"It's worse than we thought, then. Okay, that's it. Get your people out of there, Aiko. Radzinski and Rachel are pulling back as we speak. The southern defenses are a complete loss."

"What about the others, sir?"

"No one else is responding. For now, I have to assume they're KIA. We have too many civilians depending on us to sit on our hands. Gather everyone up and get them the hell out of here. I'm calling the evac now."

"Yes, sir. Aiko out." Aiko looked around at the panicking people quickly filling the street, then back down the road in Jeremiah's direction. She continued to pace while rubbing her belly. She whispered, "Goddammit, Jerry."

4:36 am - Shearburn Residence

Vanessa lowered herself from the slick roof. Coarse shingles scraped against the soft flesh of her exposed skin, tearing dozens of tiny cuts. Her legs kicked and flailed as she tried to get a foothold on the slippery corner post with bare feet. Exhausted from her encounter with Jim, she lost her grip and fell into the mud below. The cold rain was jarring enough to get her back upright. A myriad of gunshots and moans in the distance kept her moving. She hobbled out of her front yard, across the street, and into the adjacent woods. She leaned against a thick oak to catch her breath. Only for a moment, though, as nearby rustling bushes compelled her to flight.

Fighting through the pain of a badly sprained ankle, Vanessa pressed forward, finding the strength to continue running through the darkened woods. Sharp tree limbs crashed against her wet skin, and pouring rain filled her eyes as she burst from the tree line and into the back of a Main Street alley. Each footfall slapped hard against the saturated pavement. Fatigue and the change in terrain buckled her legs. She tumbled into the side of a dumpster, bounced off the unforgiving steel, and cracked her head against the grimy concrete. Vanessa lay in the alley, unconscious.

W.J. Hegarty

CHAPTER TWENTY

The Gate

The storms fury was unrelenting. Worsening weather conditions remained an issue on the roof of Mother Leeds. "No infected yet on my end of Main Street, sir. Wish I could say the same for the rest of the place, though," Garrett said. "From what I can tell, Miller's position has been completely overrun. I'm sorry, sir, but if any of them made it out, I can't be sure from here." Garrett allowed himself a moment's respite from the scope.

At the other end of the radio, Takashi hesitated for a moment before responding. "It's bad all over, Garrett. I want that gate open ASAP."

"Copy that, sir. How bad is it?"

"Real bad. The town will be a complete loss in a matter of minutes. Get on with it, Lieutenant. Keep the exit clear for as long as you can, but make sure to get your people out of there—all of them. Takashi out." He broke off the transmission.

"Shit." Garrett waved over Damon and Ryan, who by then were standing close enough to have picked up the gist of the conversation.

"I caught enough of that shit to know what's up, man. We should just leave. Fuck this place." Damon dropped his gear and made a beeline for the ladder leading to the bar below.

"I don't know, dude. They said we had to watch the gate." Ryan was pacing, a step toward Damon, another back toward Garrett's nest. "I don't know, man," he said again.

"No one is going anywhere. At least *you're* not. Not yet, anyway." Garrett stood. His imposing silhouette froze both young men in place.

"Say what? If anyone's leaving, it's going to be me," Damon replied with a foot on the ladder.

"You *can* leave, but not just yet. I'll need ten, maybe twelve minutes of your time first. After that, you're free to go. I don't have time to argue, so you're just going to have to suck it up." Garrett reloaded his rifle without so much as a second glance at Damon *or* Ryan. "I have to make this brief, so listen up. We're bugging out, all of us, but I need to open that gate first. We can't exactly go anywhere if we're trapped in town, now can we? You won't make it ten steps past that gate on foot." Garrett offered his rifle up to Damon, who was hesitant. A quick assessment of options brought him around.

"Alright, what do you need us to do?" Damon handled the rifle, quickly familiarizing himself with the weapon as best as he could under less than ideal circumstances.

"Fantastic. Look, infected are beginning to pile up outside the gate. It's not too bad yet, but it will be soon, so I need you to cover me while I make for the bus." Garrett pointed out the lone barrier trapping them all on this side of the berm. "Don't worry about the carriers behind me. Aim for the ones where I'm going to be. Any of those things gets close to me, I'll take care of them. Don't even think about shooting anything close to me. Once I'm inside the bus, aim for the ones closest to the front and work your way out from there. As soon as I get that thing started, I'm going to head south. Most of them should follow me, and when that happens, aim for the ones outside of the gate and nearest to the road."

He pulled the rifle away from Damon's eye. The kid was already lining up shots, and for a moment, Garrett second-guessed his choice for covering fire, until he heard a slight sniffle from Ryan's direction only a few feet from the conversation.

"Listen to me, Damon. It is vital that we do not let those fuckers bottleneck, or no one is getting out of here alive. Do you understand what I'm saying?" Garrett shoved the rifle back into Damon's chest.

"Yeah, yeah, I got this. Don't let them pile up." Damon settled into Garrett's nest and began checking over his rifle.

"Remember, just like we've been doing all night. Ryan will bring you a fresh magazine whenever you need it. Don't panic and we *will* get through this. People are counting on you, Damon." Garrett turned to Ryan, whose hands were shaking but already loading another magazine.

"Are we good, son?" Garrett steadied Ryan's hands.

"Yes, yeah, yeah, I... I'm good, sir." Ryan's reply didn't exactly inspire confidence in the old soldier, but shaky as it was, it would have to do. There was no more time to waste. Garrett had to go.

"Okay, gentlemen, I'm off. I'll meet you just outside the gate on your way out. Fifteen minutes tops." Garrett disappeared from sight, down the ladder and into the bar.

Ayn's fresh cup of coffee smashed to the floor as Garrett burst into the bar and rushed past her in a beeline for Markus. Samantha and Ayn were busy rummaging through a closet when he interrupted.

Garrett tipped over a large plastic recycling bin, spilling its filthy contents about the floor. "Gather up everything else you even think looks useful and pile it up by the door. Food, water, and strong alcohol are the priority. None of that fruity shit. Toiletries and any kind of first aid supplies you can find are essential as well. Anything else you come across that looks useful, great. Pick it up, but save it for last. Remember that." Garrett had a few bottles of whiskey by the neck and dropped them into the container before pulling Markus aside, closer to the front door.

"Wait a minute here, man. What's going on?" Markus tensed up. He wasn't green when it came to having plans ripped out from beneath him, but Garrett was supposed to spend the night on the roof. If he was down here already, and rummaging for supplies no less, something had changed and not for the better.

"I don't have time to explain, Markus, other than to say we *are* leaving. The town has been compromised on two fronts. It's bad out there. Real bad." Garrett grabbed an armful of various liquor bottles and placed them on the bar. He turned his attention to the girls. "This is the kind of alcohol I'm talking about. The stuff we can clean wounds and disinfect with. None of that sipping shit. I can't stress that enough."

"It's that bad?" Samantha's hands were shaking as she rummaged for more bottles. Their clinking together gave her away.

Garrett steadied a bottle she was nearly dropping. "Worse," he said. "A second wave came out of nowhere and hit us up north. We had no idea it was going to be like this." Garrett unlocked the front door. He kept a hand on the doorknob while he peeked through the blinds. "I'm going for the gate. Someone needs to get that bus out of the way if any of us are going to make it out of here alive. I'll get the bus out of sight, and with any luck, the attention will pull most of those things along with me. Wait until I radio back. Then go get the car. The keys are in the ignition and it's got a full tank of gas. You're only going to have about five minutes, so work fast," Garrett explained while checking his sidearm. "The second I'm out there, secure this door behind me—and fast. Infected haven't made it to this end of Main Street in any significant numbers yet, but they'll be here any minute now. You'll need to be gone before that happens. Any questions?" Garrett was hoping to get none.

"No, we're good, man. I think I got it. I'll pick you up a quarter mile down the road near the fork by the downed oak. You can't miss it. Be safe out there." Markus shook Garrett's hand.

"Will do, Markus. Okay, people, let's do this." Garrett bolted through the exit and was gone.

Markus slammed the door shut behind him. He leaned against the door, pressed his head against the cool wood, and closed his eyes. The past month raced in his mind, from his and Damon's first encounter with an infected at the abandoned farmhouse to good times with Vanessa and the people of Pepperbush. He finally found a place he could call home, the sins of his past washing away with every good deed or offered smile. He was finally free to start over fresh, but more importantly to choose for himself the man he wanted to be. Now all of that was gone in the blink of an eye. The soldiers from Philadelphia turned out to be nothing more than the vanguard for another wave of violence, a pattern Markus just couldn't seem to escape no matter how badly he craved it. In a handful of minutes, he would have to leave Pepperbush for good. The realization broke his heart. Behind him, Samantha and Ayn emptied cabinets and closets, gathering supplies for an unknown future.

Garrett slogged through the mud as he approached the gate. Thousands of tiny projectiles bounced off the hollow bus, echoing down Main Street. Had Markus left the door open back at the bar long enough, surely he could have heard the racket nearly two blocks away. Garrett hoped the noise would mask him entering the bus and getting it started. Three infected meandered around Garrett's side of the blockade. They didn't seem to notice him, and whether that was due to the storm or the noise coming off the oversized vehicle, he didn't care as he dropped them with three well-placed shots from his sidearm. He was committed now; his gunfire was surely noticed by any other infected creeping just out of sight. He was inside the bus, securing the door before the last infected fell. He took the driver's seat and wiped condensation from his closest windows.

"Shit," he said. On the other side of the makeshift gate, out on the road leading away from Pepperbush, a small group of infected wandered about.

Some clawed at the bus. Others merely stood in the road, staring. For a moment, he considered that maybe these things knew what they were doing after all and were actually waiting for anyone who attempted to flee. No time to consider that now. He turned the ignition. Nothing.

"Dammit," he said, louder than he meant to. *They definitely heard that,* he thought as he tried the engine again and again.

By then, enough infected had gathered around the opposite side of the bus that they threatened to turn the thing over. As if the horde's incessant rocking woke the thing up, the bus at last roared to life.

Before the soldier's arrival and nearly every day since it was put in place, the bus was started up and allowed to run for a few minutes to keep the battery charged for just such an occasion. Even through the storm, the roar of the bus's engine was unmistakable. Thick black smoke belched from the exhaust as the old beast came to life. Nearby infected, now stirred into a frenzy, were scrambling to investigate the shadowy figure inside, illuminated only by a few dashboard lights. Garrett disengaged the emergency brake. It came loose with a loud *thud*, and the behemoth inched forward.

"That's right, baby," he cheered with a triumphant fist pump as if he'd just scored the winning touchdown.

Though Sam's men started the old bus on a regular schedule, not one of them ever thought to move the relic.

Luckily the brakes didn't stick, Garrett thought as he put the bus in drive and flicked on its headlights.

In front of him, another eight or so infected were making their way toward the commotion. In the distance, the new light revealed even more approaching. He accelerated gently. A stall now would likely be fatal and not only for the sniper; the roadblock would trap everyone else inside Pepperbush.

The bus picked up speed as it barreled alongside the berm, leaving the opened gate behind. Red mist from exploding carriers too stubborn to move from its path coated the front of the vehicle and windshield in gore. The infected didn't bother trying to get out of its way. Heads exploded, and limbs were torn from bodies. An obese carrier's chest burst on impact. Entrails flailing wildly were pulled into the bus's massive wheel well as the creature was dragged in with it. The machine slowed briefly while the tires ground up and spit out the trapped carrier in chunks no larger than a lunch box. Garrett pulled the wheel hard to the right in a desperate bid to avoid a stump. The bus skidded a little before its passenger-side mirror slammed into an infected, sending the creature soaring into another group of oncoming dead.

Even through the maelstrom, Garrett couldn't mistake the distinctive crack from his rifle cutting through the torrent.

"That's the way. Don't let up, kid." He smiled at the thought of Markus and Damon holding their ground.

Another carrier approached the front of the bus. Its shoulder blew apart upon impact. The severed limb tumbled through the air and out into the night. Garrett stood on the brake, sliding through the mud. The heavy bus took far longer than he anticipated to come to a stop. Garrett ran to the back, unlatched the rooftop emergency exit, and climbed halfway out. The rain was relentless in its pounding. He shielded his eyes with his free hand and took aim with the flare gun. The projectile cut through low-hanging branches to find its mark in a small opening near the treetops. It exploded brilliantly despite the downpour. The flare's radiance could be seen miles away. His unit would have no trouble making it out, even under these conditions.

Garrett picked up his radio. "That should do it."

"What was that?" Damon answered back.

"That's a flare, son. It was for everyone else. Takashi and the others will know the gate's open. I'm continuing on now. You did good, but I need you to keep your eyes on the gate for a few more minutes. Keep an eye out for any of those things that don't follow me. Remember to conserve your ammo, though. If those fuckers want to head north and not enter town, let them, but if they even look at that gate, you put them down, understood?"

"Make it quick. I'm not going to stay up here much longer."

"Affirmative. We'll rendezvous shortly. Markus knows the plan, but if it gets too thick with these bastards, bug out. Are we clear?"

"Yeah, I hear you. Let's do this already."

"On my way. Garrett out." Garrett threw the oversized vehicle into drive. He pulled the bus away slowly, making sure to gain the attention of as many infected as possible by flashing the headlights and using the horn. Some infected were crushed under the bus's tires. Others still fell to sniper fire as Damon put down the few that seemed confused about whether to follow the bus or enter the newly exposed town. Garrett drove south along the outer perimeter of the berm, dozens of infected in tow as the bus disappeared into the storm. Pepperbush was wide open.

Inside Mother Leeds, Markus and the others listened to the exchange.

"There he goes. We're on our own now." Samantha paced the front of the bar, picking up supplies and putting them right back down.

"Don't sweat it. Garrett knows what he's doing. He'll radio back soon. Then we're getting out of here." Markus tried to hide his trepidation as he peered through a window into the storm. A few blocks away, the gate remained relatively clear of infected.

Garrett continued down a barely-there fire road, gaining the attention of most of the infected that were otherwise headed for the gate. Not designed for off-road travel, the bus bounced violently on the rocks and bumps. Garrett momentarily lost control, slamming the back end of the bus into a tree. The impact shattered some windows and bent an axle. The determined soldier pressed on. Infected bounced off the bus. Several of their heads exploded in showers of gore. Others flew dozens of feet into the air only to come crashing down in twisted, broken heaps.

A large rock obscured by a bush sent the bus careening up the side of the berm. Garrett desperately tried to regain control of the vehicle, but it was moving too fast. The bus almost reached the top of the berm before falling on its side and rolling down the hill into a tree, tossing Garrett around the inside like a rag doll. His right leg and arm snapped from the impact. Most of the windows had broken out and his weapon was thrown to the back of the bus. His broken leg was twisted and trapped under the driver's seat. Garrett couldn't move. The disabled bus was quickly surrounded by infected shambling about outside the broken vehicle, moments from finding their way in.

Garrett rifled through the wreckage for his radio. "Garrett to Markus. You hear me, son? Come in."

"I'm here, Garrett. Hey, I think it worked. We lost sight of the bus, but most of those things seemed like they *were* following you. How long until you get back to the road?"

"No time for that now. Listen to me, Markus. The gate's opened, but there's a ton more of those dead fuckers out here than I anticipated. You'll have to go on without me. I'll find another ride out of here. Don't worry about me. Get going."

"No fucking way! We're coming for you, Garrett. We've got the time."

"There *is* no time, Markus. Pack it up and go."

"This doesn't make sense. It'll only take a second to come get you. What are you not telling me?"

"Moving this bus was always a one-way trip. Listen to me, son. A second is all it takes out here. One life or five. You said you could handle this, and you have so far, but prove it to me one more time. Get those people out of here, please." Garrett sighed, praying for the correct response from the brash young man.

Markus bit his lip. He looked around the room at the expectant faces of Samantha and Ayn. Since his arrival in town weeks ago, the outpouring of kindness from its citizens instilled a sense of betterment in the man. He appreciated everything Pepperbush offered; they helped him and he helped them when he could. In that moment, he realized this was his chance to make a difference. He would do everything in his power to get these people to safety, even if it meant condemning Garrett to an uncertain fate.

"You *can* count on me, sir. Goodbye, Garrett."

"Goodbye, Markus, and good luck." Garrett gently sat his radio down on the seat beside him, his thumb firmly affixed to the open call button. He laid his head back on what remained of an armrest, stretching his neck just enough for cold rain to wash down his face. It was almost peaceful, he thought, for the briefest of moments as the cold fluid cooled his adrenaline-warmed skin. Heavy breathing slowed from a near pant to a calm rhythm. Garrett closed his eyes.

On Markus's end of the radio, sounds of breaking glass and struggle were unmistakable before Garrett's signal was lost.

"Markus, what did Garrett say? Is he on his way back yet?" Samantha grabbed Markus's arm, her eyes wide with anticipation.

"Garrett's gone, Samantha, and so are we. I'm pulling the car up now. Someone go get Damon. We're out of here." Markus would rather avoid the conversation altogether, but more than that, he didn't want Samantha to take notice of his reddening eyes.

Earlier that evening, and in anticipation of a quick getaway, Garrett parked a sedan in front of the adjacent building, leaving the rooftop shooter a clear view of their escape vehicle. Directly in front of the bar and across the street, Markus approached the vehicle. The storm showed no sign of letting up. Pouring rain and high winds were making it difficult to see.

Markus was careful with his footing as the rain blowing sideways down Main Street threatened to tip him over. He held his arm up, attempting to impede the tiny droplets' assault on his eyes. He was nearly there when he heard a crack. He looked up to see a carrier fall beside the gate. Three more were taking its place. He could barely see or hear through the gale but was certain their escape route was getting crowded. Time was a luxury they didn't have.

Inside, the car was dry but nearly as loud as out in the street with the storm's relentless pounding echoing throughout. The sedan turned over. Markus threw it in reverse. He stepped on the accelerator and strained to see his destination until he slammed into the front of the building, shattering the car's rear window and tearing the bar's door from its frame.

"Climb in. Let's go. Hurry up!" Markus shouted while waving the others toward the broken window.

Samantha was the first to climb in, quickly followed by Ayn. Damon and Ryan soon followed. They handed the women the weapons, ammunition, and boxes of supplies before climbing in themselves.

"That's it, man. Get the fuck out of here!" Damon shouted as he dove in through the back window.

Markus slammed it in drive and again stepped on the accelerator. The tires spun, fighting for traction until finally they caught the sidewalk. With a few bumps, the car and its occupants were jostled back onto Main Street. Markus sped through debris-ridden streets, dodging wrecked vehicles and running down the random carrier until Samantha began hitting him in the shoulder and pointing up ahead of them.

"Wait, wait, look!" Samantha pointed across the street to an adjacent alley and a dark figure shuffling in their direction.

Vanessa stumbled from the alley, limping as fast as she could onto Main Street. She clenched her side with one hand, and with the other she desperately waved for Markus to stop. Even through the downpour, the occupants of the vehicle could see she was covered in blood, barefoot, and her shirt ripped to shreds. The girl was a mess and by all outward appearances didn't look much better than the infected they were fleeing.

"Shit, keep going, man. She's one of them!" Damon yelled as he reached around the vehicle, making sure the doors were locked.

"No fucking way am I leaving her!" Markus pulled the sedan up to about fifteen feet from Vanessa and flooded her with the high beams. He leaped from the car and out into the rain, ran to within a few feet of his friend, pulled his gun from his waist, and aimed it directly at Vanessa's head. "Goddammit, Vanessa, say something! Is that you? If you're still you, you got to let me know, girl! I can't leave you like this. Please."

"Fuck her, man. Get back in the goddamn car," Damon yelled.

"Shut your fucking mouth, Damon!" Markus barked, never breaking eye contact with Vanessa.

Vanessa stumbled closer. Markus backed off a little, keeping in step with her. He chambered a round. His hands trembled. Vanessa's mouth moved open and shut, though no sound escaped her lips. Markus's finger edged closer to the trigger. Tears slid down his cheek, mingling with the rain.

"Please, Van, don't make me do this," he whispered as he fingered the trigger.

"Help me, Markus," Vanessa finally managed before collapsing.

"Oh, thank God." Markus was quick to catch her before she hit the ground. "Jesus Christ, you scared me, girl. Come on, let's get you out of here." He smiled from ear to ear as he raced his friend back to the car.

Her head bobbed up and down as they ran. Her left arm dangled uselessly at her side. She struggled to keep her eyes open, fighting for consciousness all the way to the car.

Ayn opened the back door, welcoming the survivor to the relative safety of the small sedan. Vanessa squeezed into the already crowded back seat.

"Look at all this blood. Where are you hurt, honey?" Ayn asked. "Ryan, hand me a towel and some water."

"I'm not," said Vanessa.

"You're not what, sweetheart?" Samantha used a damp rag, attempting to remove bloody matted clumps of hair from Vanessa's face.

"Hurt. I'm not hurt. It's not my blood," Vanessa muttered.

"What happened to you, Vanessa?" Markus asked.

She whispered, "I'm alive." Vanessa turned her head away from the others to peer into the rainy darkness. Mother Leeds quickly grew smaller as they raced away. The car sped out of town as dozens of infected finally began pouring out of the alleyways and onto the east end of Main Street.

4:39 am - Security Headquarters

Sam's command center was relatively quiet, save for the storm's relentless pounding. Glen had arrived moments earlier after abandoning the north, his family in tow. At the radio, Takashi was attempting a channel-wide broadcast.

"Repeat, for everyone in broadcast range, this is Colonel Takashi. A second group of infected has breached the western wall and is currently overrunning the northern homes. I've been informed the church is a complete loss. The southern perimeter has fallen as well. Fall back. Repeat, fall back. We will soon find ourselves surrounded. To anyone still out there, I am officially calling the evac. Everyone, collect your people and bug out now. Rendezvous at previously determined coordinates. Takashi out." Takashi slammed his radio against the desk, scattering maps and spilling coffee and bullets. The colonel's developing frustration affirmed that Sam's growing concern was well-founded. "Garrett said the church is in flames. Now *he* won't respond. The safehouses up north are being torn apart as we speak. Half my unit is unaccounted for, and the other half is getting its ass kicked. For all I know, no one is even hearing the evac order. Shit, this whole operation has turned into a goddamned clusterfuck!"

"It's bad out there, no doubt about it, sir. I sent Ron to get his family five minutes ago. You and your men did all you could, Colonel. It's time to go."

"Garrett should have the gate opened by now. Go on ahead, Sam. I'm sorry, but in a few minutes, there won't be anything left of your town."

"Come with me, sir. We can regroup at the highway, figure out our next move from there."

"I can't leave yet. Not until I'm sure my men aren't coming." Takashi returned his gaze to the storm.

"That's suicide, man! What good are you to the ones who *do* make it if you're dead, too?"

"You're wasting time arguing with me, Sam." Takashi wouldn't budge.

"What is this, some sort of honor thing? The captain goes down with the ship type bullshit?"

Glen interrupted. "He's right, Sam. It's time for you to go. What you said to Takashi applies to you, too. The folks that make it out of here will need someone they trust to help organize. They all love you, Sam. They'll need you. Besides, Takashi can ride with me. Bonnie's out front with my boy, so you know I'm not staying. Five minutes and I'm dragging him out of here either way. Trust me, we won't be far behind you. Now go."

"Goddammit, fine. But I'm circling around the block for any survivors first. Five minutes. Don't make me regret this, Glen." Sam's face had gone red. His long mustache began to tremble through the man's ire. A sight neither Glen nor anyone else in town for that matter had seen in many years.

"I won't. Now get out of here." Glen nudged him toward the door. "Go."

Sam stood in front of the building in the pouring rain, surveying Main Street for threats. Sporadic gunfire echoed over the storm, screaming and moans seemingly coming from every direction. To his east, Garrett's flare was finally disappearing below the tree line. Far off to the west, despite the downpour, the church burned bright, an ominous sight for all who still drew breath.

Sam beat his fists against the steering wheel as he pressed on through darkened, rain-swept streets. His pickup truck's headlights and windshield wipers did little to help him navigate.

"This is Sam on channel three. If anyone's out there, please respond." Sam drove away from the gate, farther into town. "If anyone can hear me, drop everything and leave now. We've lost the town. I'll make as many passes through Main Street as I can, but we have to go. Can anyone hear me? Please!" Sam desperately shouted into his radio as he pressed on deeper into the darkened heart of Pepperbush.

191

W.J. Hegarty

CHAPTER TWENTY-ONE

Flight

Frantic residents fled in all directions, a few not even bothering with their vehicles, desperate to escape the oncoming horde by any means necessary. Some sat in their cars, paralyzed. Others drove straight on into the masses. Dozens of people merely on foot fled through the forest. Carriers surrounded one couple too slow to escape; the man shot his wife, then himself. A young woman sat in the middle of the street, talking to herself, mind gone. A speeding car ran her down and promptly crashed into a nearby house, exploding on impact with an external propane supply tank.

Jeremiah stood in the center of the street, slowly spinning from side to side, bearing lone witness to so many succumbing to their fear. "Madness," he whispered as his legs buckled, nearly sending him to the ground.

A red pickup truck screeched to a halt next to the stunned man.

Bernie yelled, "Come on, Jerry. Get in. There's no time to waste!" Bernie waved at the distant soldier. "I got a wounded lady up here. We gotta go, man. Snap out of it!"

The stunned soldier looked around in disbelief, tears streaming down his face. "Hell on Earth," Jeremiah whispered. "It's following us everywhere we go. First Philadelphia, now even here in the most unassuming of places."

"What are you going on about, man?" Bernie leaped from his truck and rushed Jeremiah, grabbing him by the collar.

"You don't get it, do you?" Jeremiah returned to his feet. "This is God's wrath for all our wicked ways." Jeremiah almost laughed.

"I don't know about any of that, but you got a death wish or something. What are you doing? For Christ's sake, get in the back, now!" Bernie insisted, forcing Jeremiah into the bed of his truck.

Two more people jumped in beside the unmoving medic. Bernie floored it in the opposite direction of the mass of infected. He glanced in the rearview mirror. A shocked Jeremiah was in silhouette against a backdrop of hundreds—possibly thousands—of undead pursuers.

Aiko shouted through a megaphone. "That's it. Takashi called the evac, people. Let's go. We've got a mess of shit coming our way and I don't intend on still being here when it shows up. Pepperbush is compromised. Get to your vehicles and go. Drop what you are doing and leave the area immediately." Aiko crossed the street again, back toward the Burkes' house.

Inside, Tobias barked orders to his family, desperate to escape the fast-approaching horde. "Tommy, get Dusty in the car. We have to go now. Lillian, help your mother with those bags. We're on the road in sixty seconds." Tobias rushed outside with a handful of supplies.

Bernie's pickup truck came roaring down the street, cutting through the storm and coming to a screeching halt in front of Tobias's home. "They're coming, Toby! Get your ass out of there right now!"

Tobias nodded. Behind him, in their own vehicle, Isabelle buckled young Tommy into his seat.

Jeremiah leaped from the back of Bernie's pickup. The sound of Aiko's voice calmly directing the locals seemed to break whatever spell the disarray held over him. He ran up to meet her in Tobias's driveway and pulled her close. "Aiko, time to go. We are leaving *now*," he insisted. The medic reached out and took her by the arm.

"Jesus Christ, thank God you're alive." Aiko wiped rain from his eyes, ineffectively. He was trembling. "What happened down there, Jerry? Are you okay?"

"I'm fine now. Trust me. But it's a disaster down there and it's headed this way fast. It's all gone. All of it." Jeremiah momentarily looked back to the destruction. "Look, you'll have to ride with the Burkes. I have to go with Bernie. We've got wounded and a pregnant woman with us."

"Do what you have to do. I'll be right behind you." Aiko kissed his cheek. "Thirty seconds!"

"I'll meet you outside of town." Jeremiah slowly pulled his hands from hers. "Thirty seconds, no more," he reiterated while re-boarding Bernie's truck.

"How close are they, Bernie?" Tobias strained to make out any details from the darkened street beyond. The storm made it impossible to see more than a few houses down the block.

"Fourteen, sixteen houses down? They came out of nowhere. Everybody down there's dead or scattered. We gotta go now, man."

"All right, get out of here. We'll be right behind you." Tobias slapped the roof of Bernie's truck and ran back to his SUV as Bernie sped away.

Aiko hopped into the back seat, squeezing in beside Lillian and Tommy. "Let's go!" She slammed the door shut behind her. "Go, go, go, go, go! They're here. Go!"

Swarms of infected closed in as they departed. While Tobias pulled away from the driveway, the closest carriers thumped maddeningly at the rear window of the truck. Rotten flesh and blood caked the windows on impact. Agonizing screams from those too slow to escape pierced the survivors' ears. Tommy held onto Dusty, his eyes shut tight.

Racing through the narrow streets of Pepperbush, several cars led the way as Tobias tried desperately to escape the overrun town. The darkened streets were quickly filling with infected, turning the roadways and the dash for freedom into a deadly obstacle course. Twenty feet in front of Tobias, a blue minivan swerved, trying not to hit a group of infected. The driver lost control of his vehicle, sending it sliding sideways into a curb. The impact flipped the vehicle, sending it and its passengers tumbling into the ditch below. A young woman was ejected from the violent wreck, thrown forty feet into the air and then down again, smashing against a nearby tree. Her wrecked body fell to the ground, arms and legs twisted and bent. Compound fractures wracked her body. The young woman's broken remains were near immediately surrounded by carriers, a half dozen of them chewing the soft moist flesh from her broken bones. The mangled sedan came to a rest at the bottom of the ditch. Rotten bodies caught in its path smashed beneath its twisted metal wreckage.

"Oh my God, Dad! That's the Petersons. You have to stop!" Lillian pawed at the steering wheel in a desperate bid to force her father to pull over.

Aiko reached forward, pulling her away from Tobias. She slammed the scared young woman back into her seat. "Do not slow this vehicle. Do you hear me? If you stop, we all die!"

Lillian hid her head in her lap and began sobbing. "Dad, that was Cindy," she whimpered.

"I know, baby. I know." Tobias barely held it together, on the verge of tears himself. "Please don't look at it, honey."

4:57 am - Main Street

Undead invaders reached every corner of town. Carriers were packed in shoulder to shoulder in places as the mass of rotting attackers filled the streets and alleyways. A group of infected would enter a home or business as another was leaving; they had overtaken the town. Burning dead left fire in their wake. Pepperbush was lost.

Rachel stood her ground, careful to make each shot count, though there were far too many infected converging on them to make a difference. Behind her, Radzinski and another survivor of the overrun southern line were trying in vain to hot-wire a car.

"Let's go!" Rachel shouted. "Either you can do it or you can't, but we *cannot* stay here!"

"All right, all right. Sixty seconds, Red." Radzinski was fumbling with wires he couldn't make heads or tails of.

"We don't have sixty seconds, goddammit!" Rachel snapped through the crack of her rifle.

"You have any idea what I'm doing wrong here?" Radzinski asked the other man.

"How the hell should I know? Six weeks ago I was a taxidermist for Christ's sake." The man checked his empty rifle again, the third time in as many minutes. Still no bullets.

"Jesus Christ!" Radzinski slammed the roof of the vehicle and kicked its door shut. He tapped Rachel on the shoulder and pointed out a nearby cluster of homes that looked relatively clear. "We can try to hold out there for a while." He was cut short as an old beater of a pickup truck came plowing through the nearest portion of the horde. Heads were crushed under its wheels, bodies thrown dozens of feet into the air only to come crashing down again and skid off over the pavement. The truck came barreling in with a power slide, stopping only a few feet from Rachel. The driver leaned out of the window and yelled for the small group. It was Sam. "Let's go, goddammit!" He banged his hand furiously on the side of his door.

A tall woman burst from the passenger side door, long black curls matted to her face in the rain. She frantically waved Rachel and the others over. "Get in. Hurry up!" Nisha yelled.

"Where the hell did you come from?" Rachel's eyes went wide.

"Who cares? Just get us the fuck out of here!" Radzinski shouted as they boarded the old pickup.

"Thank God you came back, Sam! I don't think that car was going anywhere." Rachel laid her head back in the seat. Her chest heaved under a massive sigh of relief.

Sam sped away, seconds before the car Rachel and the others were working on was swarmed with infected.

"Thought I'd make one more pass down Main Street before I left," said Sam. "I saw Nisha there stuck on a curb down the block with a flat, so I stopped. That's when I heard your gunfire. We gotta hustle. They're saying over the radio these dead bastards are piling up at the gate. If we want out, we have to go now." Sam floored it. His beat-up old truck plowed into the storm.

5:10 am - Main Street

Tobias smashed another small group of infected under his wheels. "Everybody, hold on. We're almost at the gate!"

Ahead of the truck, a lone soldier ran down Main Street in the direction of the exit. Carriers dotted the landscape ahead of him.

"Shit, is that Miller up there?" Tobias strained to identify the lone figure.

"He's alive!" Aiko forced her way as far as she was able into the front seats. "Pull up next to him and slow down a little, but don't stop. He'll catch up."

Tobias flicked his high beams a few times to get the man's attention. Miller nodded in recognition. Tobias pulled up at a jogger's pace beside him.

Miller ran alongside the truck, still firing his rifle into the oncoming infected and helping to clear a path. He grabbed the rear door frame of the SUV to steady himself and handed his rifle through the window to Lillian. "Take it!"

"Come on, Miller. Give me your hand!" Aiko shouted as she reached out, taking hold of his other hand. "Go, Tobias. Go!"

Tobias picked up speed as Miller leaped into the window and grabbed a loose seat belt. His feet dragged against the ground, inches from being sucked under a rear wheel. As Aiko and Lillian pulled him inside, an infected latched onto his leg and bit down hard.

Miller squirmed and kicked, trying to dislodge the monster. "Shoot it, Aiko! Shoot it!"

Aiko fumbled with Miller's rifle for a second before shooting the thing twice in the head.

The creature ceased clawing at the soldier and was dragged under the crushing wheels of the truck. Tobias ran over the carrier's chest. The obstacle shot the truck into the air, sending the passengers bouncing around its interior.

Miller came to rest mostly on the floor at the feet of Aiko and Lillian. "Thanks, Aiko." Miller breathed heavily while rubbing his leg as he rose from the floor.

"Miller, your leg?" Aiko kept her rifle at the ready. She maintained trigger discipline but was ready to act if the need arose, her gun trained inches from Miller's head.

Expecting the worst, Miller pulled up his pant leg. Everyone was relieved to only see a bruise where the carrier's mouth had been.

"Not sure if that thing had teeth or not, but it didn't get through my BDUs." Miller closed his eyes and nearly smiled. "Still hurt like hell, though." He laid his head down on the seat and promptly exhaled a long, loud sigh. It was the first taste of rest he had in what felt like ages.

"Thank God." Aiko breathed as she raised her rifle away from her commanding officer's face.

"I've been out of contact for the better part of an hour. Lost my radio when we were overrun. What's everyone else's status? Does anyone even know?"

"Well, sir, we don't know much" Aiko began. "Jeremiah's in the truck ahead of us with a few survivors from the northern sector. We got hit hard up there. No one saw it coming. Garrett said infected were piling up outside the gate, but he should have it cleared by now. Takashi told him to open it, but that was more than ten minutes ago, so it's anyone's guess how it looks now. I haven't heard from either one of them since. Everyone else is MIA as far as I know." Aiko peered out of a gore-soaked window, the last few weeks replaying over in her mind. "You might want to prepare yourself for taking command, sir," she suggested. "We may be all that's left."

"Shit. Step on it, Tobias. Priority is getting as many survivors as we can to safety," Miller insisted. "One disaster at a time, Aiko."

They raced through Main Street, past Mother Leeds. Salvation was in sight. Ahead of them, more than a dozen infected began to clog the gate, threatening to block their escape.

"Bernie can't be more than a minute ahead of us. How is the gate filling back up so fast?" Tobias asked.

Miller pointed at the distance beyond the gate. "Not now, Tobias. Step on it! Don't even slow down!"

Tobias barreled through the pile of infected. Dozens of the mindless creatures bounced off his truck. Others were crushed under its weight. The bloody vehicle successfully plowed its way through. Free from Pepperbush, Tobias drove toward the highway.

5:18 am - Main Street

Marisol's SUV cut through Main Street, followed closely by Corey. The crowded gate was within sight. Infected were spilling out into the streets, emerging from every alleyway that separated Main Street's many buildings. As the road grew narrower with infected, their increased numbers began bouncing off the vehicles, slowing progress.

"Hold on, everyone!" Marisol floored it.

The SUV plowed at full speed into the crowd, sending bodies flying through the air and bouncing off the truck. The windows darkened with gore and pus as some infected came apart on impact. Those that remained standing thumped on the windows and doors, desperate to reach anyone inside.

The force of the impact sent one of the creatures headfirst into a side passenger window, shattering the already damaged surface. The creature's neck was caught up on the window frame, though it continued flailing its bony arms at the occupants. The trapped carrier was dragged along for the ride. All the while, the thing scraped at the truck, trying to gain entrance. The carrier desperately clawed at the passengers, its rotten hands leaving black and red smears all over the upholstery.

"Out of the way!" Soraya yelled. She leaned back against the men for leverage and sent a boot into the ghoul's face, dislodging it from the vehicle. The creature tumbled from the truck and fell to the road, where it broke against a concrete flower planter.

A car length behind, Corey watched the carrier fly from the sheriff's vehicle as they approached the now semi-cleared gate. He sped up for the opening as a sudden, violent collision flipped his truck onto its side. Corey and his passengers were flung around the inside of the vehicle, heads and limbs splitting and breaking against the car's unforgiving surfaces. An out-of-control car careened into Corey's SUV, pushing the transport up onto the sidewalk. Both vehicles continued to skid across the pavement, eventually crashing through a storefront.

199

W.J. Hegarty

Seth shouted, "Holy shit! That was Ron. He just T-boned Corey!"

Mayor Lancaster pushed forward on Marisol's shoulders. "Forget about them. Get us out of here!"

"What the fuck are you doing, goddammit?" Marisol elbowed Lancaster in the throat, sending him back into Soraya's arms.

Soraya followed suit, she elbowed Mayor Lancaster in the mouth, splitting his lip and cracking a tooth. "You shut up now!" The man went silent, searching for composure.

"We have to go back for them!" Isaac pleaded.

Marisol locked the brakes. The truck came to an abrupt halt just outside of town limits. A growing horde of infected stood between them and the gate, the distraction momentarily ceasing the monsters' march on Pepperbush. Some infected peered around, confused and wandering aimlessly. The majority, though, picked a direction and continued onward with the rest, straight into town.

"We can't go back for them. Look!" Marisol grabbed Isaac by the collar and forced him to look behind them through the gore-encrusted back window of the truck.

Dozens of undead already converged on the disabled vehicles. Some infected were already crawling their way inside through the wreckage, having their way with the unconscious passengers. Within seconds, hundreds more surrounded the remains until both vehicles finally disappeared in a sea of rotting flesh and flailing arms.

"Do you see that, Isaac? Do *you* see it?" She shook him hard, though he refused prolonged eye contact with the scene. "What about the rest of you? Do you see him? Can you see Corey?" Marisol yelled, forcing each occupant to look back on what they left behind.

Isaac quickly lowered his eyes. Even Mayor Lancaster did the same.

"If we go back for Corey and the others, we *will* die." Marisol pushed Isaac aside as she put the truck back into drive. "Now keep your fucking mouths shut unless you've got something constructive to add."

5:27 am - Mainstreet

Glen's car burst from a narrow alleyway and onto the already crowded Main Street. The road was nearly filled with infected. Bodies bounced off the vehicle as they approached the congested gate. Ahead of them, the bottleneck was filled with infected. Hundreds of carriers were crammed in shoulder to shoulder, half of the mob trying to get into town, the other half

200

clawing its way out. Glen was cautious with the accelerator. A wall of bodies stood between them and escape.

The gate was packed edge to edge with walking corpses. As far as Takashi could surmise, the mass was twenty yards thick, easy. He pointed forward and pushed on the man's leg, driving the pedal into the floor. "Don't stop, man! Go!" Takashi yelled at the overwhelmed driver.

Glen floored it into the mob. Bodies bounced over the top and to the sides of the car as he muscled his way through the horde of undead.

"Oh my God, they're everywhere!" Bonnie began to panic. As a reflex, she pounded on the windows at the infected on the other side of the glass, as if she could somehow shoo them away. A block later, she gave up the endeavor and turned her attention to their son, grabbing him up and squeezing him far too tightly.

"Mom, please," the boy begged, prying her hands from his abdomen.

Glen dared a peek into the rearview. "Keep it down. I can't think straight!"

They hit the mass at full speed. The impact shot the front end of the car up into the air, dragging multiple carriers into its wheel wells and chewing them up like a garbage disposal. Pieces were spit out all over, covering the windshield as well as the crowd itself with blood and gore.

"Can't see a damn thing!" Glen shouted. The gore-soaked road beneath his wheels had become as slick as ice. "Shit, we're not going anywhere!" Glen yanked it in reverse, searching for the smallest trace of dry pavement. The wheels spun and smoked, screaming against what little purchase Glen could find. A pile of corpses under the front of the car threw off its balance. Spinning wheels could not catch the pavement. The distressed car spun sideways into the main mass of infected, smashing even more of them under the car's weight. "Shit, shit, shit!" Glen spun the wheel, trying to right the car.

"Punch it!" Takashi shouted. "Go, man. Go!"

There was no dry pavement to be found—nothing more than ground-up body parts for a surface. The wheel wells were clogged with meat and bone to the point that the old gore was slowly pushed from the top of the cavity as more churned-up bodies squeezed their way in from below. The rear end of the car finally stopped sliding back and forth, though the tires continued churning up meat. Smoke from countless pounds of burning flesh billowed from beneath the undercarriage. Glen's forward progress was halted for good. After a few more brief tests on the accelerator, he succumbed. They were going nowhere. Roughly thirty feet from the gate was as far as they made it. Within seconds of stopping, Glen's car was surrounded by walls of rotting flesh and pounding arms.

From Takashi's vantage point, there was a sea of black outside his window. Even the car's headlights couldn't pierce the mass of bodies surrounding them. "That's it, then," Takashi whispered.

"We almost made it." Glen stared at the clogged gate. He released the wheel and leaned back in his seat. Glen focused on a small imperfection on the upholstery next to the light above his head. Had someone done that in a factory hundreds of miles away? Machine error, perhaps? Did it form over time slowly or was it a quality-control mistake? He imagined the inspector at the factory signing off on the car with a smirk, pleased with himself for having left an indelible mark upon this car for the vehicle's life. Somewhere out there in the world, someone would see this invisible man's work, never realizing that they were actually viewing a signature on a one-of-a-kind piece of art. Glen closed his eyes again, and the blemish faded from thought, a pointless entry in a lifetime of meaningless musings he passed the time with. Quiet moments alone in his head like that kept him sane through the years, clearing the clutter of the day and allowing him to start again with a blank slate, priorities in order. He reached behind his seat, searching for his wife's leg. If he could hold her one last time in these final moments, it would make the struggle worth it. *I tried, baby*, he thought, gripping her calf tight. Bonnie leaned forward. She caressed his hand and caught his gaze in the rearview. They locked eyes as quiet tears began to fall.

Takashi's radio shattered the silence. Bonnie jumped, as if one of those creatures had just reached from beneath her seat. "Sir, can you hear me?" It was Miller from almost a half a mile down the road but with a clear line of sight to Takashi's predicament. "Colonel, stay put. We're coming for you. What is your ammo situation and how many survivors are with you? Over." Miller's voice betrayed his sense of complete uncertainty.

Miller's concern wasn't lost on Takashi *or* Glen and his family. His tone was unmistakable. The hopelessness in his voice finally caused Glen's son to begin sobbing. His mother tried to console him as tears of her own mixed with his upon the child's soft cheeks.

On the other side of the gate just out of town, Tobias had pulled over. Miller stood at the side of the road, peering through a rifle's scope. At nearly half a mile away, Miller could clearly make out the clogged bottleneck, the hint of Glen's roof periodically showing through the mass. The carriers were packed in shoulder to shoulder as they squeezed through the narrow entranceway on their trek into town. A few of the creatures managed to get themselves pushed to the sides of the mass only to be pinned against the walls of the gate. By sheer numbers of weight and force, the ones unlucky enough to find themselves pinned were crushed and pulled apart as the horde lumbered ever forward. Miller lost Glen's car again. This time it remained buried.

Aiko's finger bounced around her rifle's trigger guard. She periodically turned her attention to Miller while guarding the perimeter. Leaving Takashi behind was unthinkable, and under normal circumstances, she would have been right behind Miller in an attempt at rescue. This was different, though. Superior firepower didn't scare these things away. *How in the hell could two beat-up soldiers and a terrified family possibly make a difference here?* she wondered. "What are we doing, Miller?" she asked anxiously, rifle still trained on nothing.

"Quiet!" he replied. "Hold your ground." Miller tried the radio again, not sure if he would even get a response. The idea of being thrust into command if the worse were to happen began to stir. "Sir, please, if you can hear me, we are coming for you. Hold your position," Miller pleaded. He checked his scope again. Carriers came in and out of view as his body swayed. Targets down the line that were normally easy kills became uncertain. He felt a hand on his shoulder.

"Let him go, sir," Aiko said solemnly.

Aiko loved Takashi, probably more than Miller could ever understand, but things were different for the captain. Miller came to miss his father in all of this, and Takashi became a surrogate of sorts. That wasn't something easily discarded.

Takashi finally answered. "That's a negative, Miller. Repeat, negative. Do not attempt rescue. Do you copy?"

The radio went silent again, but for a brief moment, Miller could make out the distinct sounds of a child sobbing and what was unmistakably the voice of a heartbroken mother lying to her son.

"Sir?" Miller ran his free hand through his filthy hair. He turned back toward Tobias's SUV and the awaiting eyes inside, then over to Aiko, who he refused to make eye contact with, and finally back to the flooded gate. He paced relentlessly, trekking farther away from the relative safety of the vehicle.

Aiko tracked Miller's movements. She followed his position, slowly inching her way back toward her commanding officer. Aiko had accepted that Takashi was a lost cause; she wasn't about to let anything happen to Miller as well.

Takashi spoke again. "You get those people as far away from here as you can, Captain. That's an order," Takashi said without so much as a hint of uncertainty.

"Sir, I—" Miller began.

"Leave it, son," Takashi replied. "Save who you can. Forget about the rest and put your back to the sea. Takashi out."

The radio returned to static. Miller peered through his scope a final time. The scene hadn't changed, and why would it? Again, he felt a hand on his shoulder.

"It's time to go, Miller." Aiko was gentle. Her touch barely registered, but it was enough.

Takashi yanked the battery pack from his radio before securing both in the glove box. No one still listening needed to hear what was coming, morale and all. He would have preferred to give the remainder of his unit a proper send-off and a few words of encouragement, but time was a luxury he simply did not possess.

Glen's son had fallen asleep—or at least that was what Takashi would have suggested had it come up. Passed out from shock was more like it. Bonnie caressed the boy's tiny head as Glen looked on at his family. She caught his gaze, and if pure love had been enough to change their lot, every carrier in town would have returned to whatever hell bore them. Instead, the interior of the modest sedan went dark. The sheer number of infected covering Glen's car blocked out what little light the distant fires and the earliest signs of dawn provided.

An abnormally large carrier made its way onto the hood of the car. Its slippery surface sent the ghoul crashing into the windshield. The beast's chin shattered and flattened against the glass. Undaunted, the creature continued up and over the roof, slipping down the other side only to right itself and start the process over again. The damage was done. A spiderweb of tiny cracks spread out from the place of impact, growing into fingers stretching the length and width of the glass. The relentless pounding continued as tiny explosions of dust and shards of safety glass finally began to rain down on the dashboard.

Out of Bonnie's sight, Takashi held his pistol at his side. Near empty as it was, he was confident there was one, possibly two, bullets left. He gently tapped the trigger. Glen nodded in approval, leaned back in his seat, and closed his eyes. Takashi turned to Bonnie and the child with a warm, heavy smile.

"Miller?" Tobias attempted, searching for words.

"Just keep driving, Tobias." Miller fumbled with his radio for a moment before tossing it at his feet and kicking the floorboard.

Nothing more needed to be spoken on the decision to abandon Pepperbush as Tobias sped off toward the highway. A few miles down the road, as they drove into the sunrise, the rain had finally broken as Tobias caught up with a ragtag caravan of survivors. Ahead, four more beat-up, gore-soaked vehicles trudged along toward the interstate. Behind the procession, fading in the distance, Pepperbush burned.

The Roaming
The Toll

Book II
Coming
October 2019

For updates on The Roaming, social media links and exclusive content
visit wjhegarty.com

Made in the USA
Columbia, SC
17 December 2019